A ROUGH RIDE

A ROUGH RIDE

An Insight into Pro Cycling

Paul Kimmage

STANLEY PAUL

LONDON • SYDNEY • AUCKLAND • JOHANNESBURG

Stanley Paul & Co. Ltd
An imprint of the Random Century Group
Random Century House, 20 Vauxhall Bridge Road, London SW1V 2SA

Random Century Australia (Pty) Ltd
20 Alfred Street, Milsons Point, Sydney, NSW 2061

Random Century New Zealand Limited
191 Archers Road, PO Box 40–086, Auckland 10

Century Hutchinson South Africa (Pty) Ltd
PO Box 337, Bergvlei 2012, South Africa

First published 1990
Reprinted 1990
Reissued in paperback 1991
Reprinted 1991

Set in 10pt Linotron Plantin by Speedset Ltd, Ellesmere Port
Printed and bound in Great Britain by
Mackays of Chatham PLC, Chatham, Kent

British Library Cataloguing in Publication Data
Kimmage, Paul
    A rough ride : an insight into professional cycling.
    1. Bicycles, racing
    I. Title
    796.62

ISBN 0 09 174926 3

CONTENTS

FOR

Christy and Raphael

and other

'National Suckers'

ACKNOWLEDGEMENTS

Thanks to David Walsh for keeping me off the barstool, and to Roche, Kelly and Earley for those times when we were 'the fab four'. To Gerard and Muriel Torres, Jean and Ginette Beaufils, Marc and Pascal Mineat, for being more than friends. To Angela for sending me to school; Ann for being there; and finally to Vincent Browne for giving me a job.

Photographic Acknowledgments

For permission to reproduce copyright photographs, the author and publishers would like to thank the following: AllSport/Vandystadt; Paul Daly; J.P. Filatriau/La Voix du Nord; Inpho; Irish Press: L'Equipe; James Meehan; Photosport International; Presse-Sports; Billy Stickland; Muriel Vibert

PROLOGUE:
IT WASN'T SUPPOSED TO END LIKE THIS

Toulouse, July 13: the thirteenth stage of the Tour de France. I knew it would be hard this morning. You see, in a race that lasts three weeks there are good days and bad days. It's all about morale. With weak legs and a good head, you can go a long way. With good legs and a weak head you go nowhere. I rode out of Toulouse with a weak head.

If the start had been a little easier it could have made all the difference. Maybe today I would still be a 'coureur cycliste'. But we raced out of Toulouse like there was no tomorrow and I was struggling from the start. The Danish rider Jesper Worre attacked and I cursed him. Cursing him was easier than following him. I quickly realised that my legs were not responding to the demands being made of them. I was dropped. To be left behind at such an early stage was demoralising but I fought back and managed to regain contact with the peloton.

I made my way forward through the bunch but as I did there was a fresh acceleration and I started slipping back again. The bunch strung out into a long line and I realised with despair that I could not match the pace and would soon be dropped again. I pulled over, not wanting to obstruct the riders behind me. And then I heard it. The laughing.

Hateful laughter coming from the mouth of the Belgian rider Dirk de Wolf. I had had a run in with him two days earlier. Was he laughing at me? No, he couldn't be. Yes, yes he is, he's laughing at me. The bastard is laughing at me. And on a good day I would probably have gone to him and spat in his face. But this was a bad day and I was feeling sorry for myself. Something snapped inside me. My spirit.

It had always been my greatest asset. Others had reached the top with talent or class mixed with spirit. I only ever had spirit. Fighting spirit. Never say die, spit in your eye. Courage. Spirit. It was spirit that brought me from a dreaming childhood in Dublin to the Tour de France. Oh, it had cracked before, many times, but I had always managed to repair it. Today was different.

I started thinking. I don't need this shit. I can go home and be a journalist and live happily ever after. I don't need this Belgian laughing at me. Fuck him, fuck the whole lot of them. And then I stopped pedalling.

My mind was confused; it wasn't supposed to end like this. I was supposed to finish the Tour and be handed a medal (everyone finishing the Tour gets a medal). Then I would continue racing till the end of the season and end my career in O'Connell Street in Dublin in the Nissan Classic. I wouldn't win the stage, or anything like that. No, that would be dreaming. I never dreamt as a pro – which was probably part of my downfall. But as a mark of respect the organisers would give me flowers, and my home town would give me a big cheer and I'd wave them goodbye. Then I'd slip happily into oblivion. The following day I would return there to look for a job, any job.

But as the official cars passed me as I freewheeled down the road, 55 kilometres out of Toulouse on the 13th stage of the Tour de France, Dublin was not on my mind. It was the laughing, that horrible moronic laughing. No, I don't need this shit.

The bike eventually stopped and I got off. I was surrounded by photographers; they were probably fed up with taking pictures of LeMond and Fignon – a good sobbing 'domestique' as he abandons the Tour would be a good shot for the evening paper. They like this sort of thing. The best bit was yet to come and they knew it.

On abandoning the Tour one is not allowed simply to slip discreetly into a car. No, you must wait for the broom wagon to come along. I saw him coming and knew what would happen. I spread my legs and placed my two arms on the door and stood to the sound of clicking cameras as the commissar removed the two numbers pinned to my jersey. This is the official court-martialling, the stripping of the stripes. When he finished, I jumped into the back of the bus and buried my head in my hands. I felt like the worst scum on earth. I pulled at the roots of my hair and cried.

'It wasn't supposed to end like this.'

1 MOVING OFF THE BAR STOOL

The rider who abandons the Tour de France is like a wounded animal. He feels shame and emptiness. He needs privacy, to lick his wounds, to heal the mental sores that affect his body. I just had to get out of Montpellier that night. I could not face the company of my team mates or put up with the frowning brow of my 'directeur sportif' for five minutes longer than necessary.

My friend Gerard Torres drove my wife Ann down from Grenoble to bring me home. I was so grateful to him for relieving me of my torture. Gerard is a friend, a *real* friend – I kissed him on both cheeks when he arrived. The drive home is long, but I don't mind. My head is filled with so many emotions, so many questions all tangled and jamming the switchboard in my brain. Gerard talks of my future, of the World Championships at Chambéry in August, of the Tour of Ireland in October: 'Do you remember how well you rode in the last stage in Dublin?' I nod, trying not to offend his enthusiasm. The flattery is not soothing. I cannot face the future. I know I will never race again. My spirit has snapped and it's an unmendable break. My thoughts are not on the future, they are a prisoner of the past. Ann sits in the back of the Renault 21, her arm reaches over to me in the front seat and she squeezes my hand tightly. She understands.

Now, three months later, I feel a genuine relief that it's all over. I have not raced since the thirteenth stage of the Tour de France, my last race as a professional cyclist. The sport is not leaving me: I am leaving it, and there is a great satisfaction in being able to leave on my own terms. The *Sunday Tribune* newspaper in Dublin has offered me a job as a sports journalist, I can slip comfortably into normal living. Without this assurance I would probably have ended my career like a lot of other 'domestiques'. My sponsor would inform me, ever so politely of course, that he no longer wished to avail himself of my services.

3

I'd go banging on the doors of the other teams only to endure the humiliation of getting a No Vacancy sign stuck in my face each time. With all options to continue closed, I would announce my retirement – perhaps it would get two lines in the sports daily *L'Equipe*. Then, if I was lucky, a sympathetic factory owner might employ me for the rest of my life on £500 a month. The *Tribune* has saved me from this, although perhaps this is false. My real saviour was my mother – thank God she made me work hard at school before I threw my leg over a bike. Thanks, Ma.

'Journalist': it has a respectable ring to it. I am one of the lucky ones. I can retire with dignity and in good health. I can return to the Tour de France as a journalist and hold my head high among directeurs sportifs. I didn't give them the pleasure of seeing me crawl; indeed, we can be good mates now. I can slap them on the back and we can slip on to a bar stool talking about the good old days – journalistic cunning contributing to my falseness and obliterating the fact that a year earlier I hated them. They were bastards in a cruel bastards' sport, but I still despised them for their cruelty.

It's easy to forgive and forget when one is reasonably set up for life. It is more difficult to betray oneself. If I slipped on to the bar stool I would be betraying myself. I would be betraying the hundreds of other unknown domestiques who have endured what I have endured. This is the story of Paul Kimmage, but it's also their story. It is dedication to them that welds me to the typewriter and keeps me from the bar stool. I hope I can do them justice.

2 THE FIRST IRISH POPE

Beasy McArdle, the portly staff nurse at the Rotunda maternity hospital in Dublin, loved babies. She used to walk up and down the wards of screaming new-born, pluck them from their cradles and hug and kiss them as if they were her own. Embracing them with tenderness, she caressed them with her soft west of Ireland accent: 'Oh I could love you.'

On the evening of May 7, 1962, another brand-new baby joined the assembly line and took its place beside its mother. Beasy took a long, hard look at the child. She noticed his large head and decided it was the head of a leader – a Pope: 'I'm sure he will be the first Irish Pope,' she said to the mother.

My mother smiled. It had been a difficult pregnancy, full of complications, but she was over the worst and was glad her child was healthy. I tipped the scales at nine pounds and two ounces, a hefty lad with a huge head. My mother remembers the head – it nearly killed her. She already had a name for me: Paul. She thought about what Beasy had said: 'Pope Paul' had a nice ring to it. She would mention it to Christy when he came in later.

My father worked on a more conventional assembly line – cars. He welded car bodies at the Volkswagen plant on the Naas road in Dublin. It was monotonous, tiring work and he looked forward each night to clocking off and escaping into the countryside for two hours training on his bicycle.

My Da was born in Dublin, the youngest of the seven children of James and Mary Kimmage. It's an unusual name, from a suburb of Dublin on the south side, but we can't trace our family tree back very far. We don't know where we come from! Da had three brothers and three sisters and it was his elder brothers Jimmy and Kevin who introduced him to cycling. He liked it, and joined the Dublin

Wheeler's touring section in 1954.

One day they went to see a race, the Circuit of Bray. Seamus Elliot, the best Irish rider in the country, broke clear of the field with two English riders Harry Reynolds and Dick Bowes. He soon disposed of them both, to the delight of the huge crowd that lined the seafront. My Da was touched by the atmosphere, the colour, by Shay Elliot. He wanted to race. The bug had bitten.

His first year of competition was in 1956. The new sport was tough, but he had a talent for it and it wasn't long before he was winning. In 1957 he returned to the Circuit of Bray – and won, the first of four wins in that once prestigious classic. In 1958, he was selected to represent Ireland at the World Championships in Rheims, France. On a searing hot day, the field was whittled down to forty riders with just two laps left. Da was there, he wanted to finish, to be one of the top forty in the world.

A friend of his, John Flanagan, was taking care of him from the pits area. With two laps to go he handed up to Christy a feeding bottle with brandy in it. In sheeting rain or arctic cold, a nip of brandy would perhaps have been beneficial, but not on a day when temperatures were in the 90s. Da, dying with the thirst, took a swallow from the bottle. It nearly killed him – he abandoned.

Rheims was the end of a very successful season for him. Back in Ireland another season was just beginning. The 'be social' season. The Wheelers advertised their regular Sunday outings in the shop window of 'The Rutland' bike shop in North Frederick Street. On the third weekend of September the notice read:

Meal 'alfresco' at Roundwood. Tea at Butler's 6 o'clock

Butler's tea rooms, at the Scalp in County Wicklow, was the traditional rendezvous of all of Dublin's cycling clubs when they came south of the Liffey. The hungry pedallers would devour tea, home-made scones and cakes and then settle down to an evening of songs, dancing and plenty of fun. It usually ended about midnight where the thrill of the day was the mad descent to the city in the dark.

On that Sunday in September, my Da spent the day touring the Wicklow hills and then headed to Butler's for tea. There, a pleasant young 'touriste' caught his eye. Her name was Angela. He liked her.

Angela Davis was the youngest daughter of Francis and Mary Davis of Kilfenora Road, Kimmage. They lived in a two-bedroom cor-poration terraced house – not very big for a family of 14 children. Granda worked nights in dispatch at the *Irish Times*. In the modern era his family would undoubtedly have been smaller, but as he says himself with his typical Dublin accent: 'In dem days der was no television.' My Ma, the twelfth arrival, left school at 14 and started work as a trainee tailor at Weartex, near her home. She saved hard and bought her first bicycle on hire purchase and joined the Dublin Wheelers with her sister Pauline. It was on a run with the Wheelers that she met Christy at Butler's. They talked, danced and although Ma claims it was 'love at first sight', the relationship did not take off immediately. The first real date was months later – a visit to the Theatre Royal for a film and a show.

The following year, 1958, my father enjoyed the best form of his career. He won anything worth winning. In June, Billy Morton organised a prestigious track meeting to celebrate the opening of a new cycling and running track at Santry stadium in Dublin. Shay Elliot, now a professional (Ireland's first), was flown in from France along with French star Albert Bouvet and the Italian 'campionissimo', Fausto Coppi. In front of a huge crowd, Elliot beat the continental pros and my father won the amateur event.

A day later he flew to the Isle of Man for the Viking Trophy race on a small plane with Coppi, Bouvet and Elliot. The flight gave him a nice opportunity to talk to Elliot about the possibility of racing in France. Shay suggested he try his luck in Paris with a club called ACBB. He had contacts there and would arrange it if my Da was interested. He was interested. Elliot won the pro race on the island but my Da was denied victory on the line in the Viking race to finish a narrow second. Twenty-three years later my brother Raphael won that same race and brought the Viking Trophy back to our house. My Da wouldn't admit it, but I know it meant a lot to him.

On returning to Dublin after the Viking, Da got himself organised to go to Paris. He gathered his savings and remembers a friend, John Connon, giving him £25 (a lot of money in those days) and a bike bag. Paris was huge, mind-boggling compared with Dublin. On arriving in the city he got hopelessly lost in the underground, the Métro. He was hampered in the crowds with his bike and bag but eventually found his way to his lodgings, a flat in Montparnasse. The club provided him with a new Helyett bike, but in the two weeks he stayed, he never raced. Living out of a suitcase, unable to speak a word of the language, he felt desperately alone. The life of a professional cyclist was not for him. He didn't want it. He returned to Dublin, and to this day does not regret his decision.

Twenty-five years later, Raphael and I arrived in that same city, with that same objective, to that same club. Before we left we had never fully understood why he only stuck it out for two weeks. It didn't take us long to understand.

When he returned to Dublin, he was selected to ride in another world championship, but a week before travelling, a bad crash at an evening race in Baldoyle sent him to hospital instead. He didn't race again for two years. The crash and the disappointment of Paris had turned him off the sport, but there was another reason – marriage. Ma always claims he wasn't so much homesick as lovesick in Paris, because as soon as he came home he popped the question and started saving for a house.

The wedding was in August of 1961 and they honeymooned in Edinburgh before returning to Dublin to begin married life in a Georgian mansion at 70 Eccles Street. Well, to be honest, it had been a while since old George had had anything to do with the place. The run-down Georgian house was divided into eight rooms on two floors and was home to eight families. There was just one toilet in the building and one cold water tap provided the eight families with their only running water. My parent's flat was on the ground floor and had a window looking out on the street. It was old and run-down, but it was home and they didn't complain – housing in Dublin was hard to come by in the early 1960s.

The flat was my first home in the world. When I was seven months old, Santa Claus brought me a three-wheeled bicycle and it wasn't long before I was racing around the room on it. Ma laughs about that little bike. She remembers when she was toilet-training me, I would be bombing around the flat with nothing on. One day I got it wrong and deposited a huge stool on the brightly painted seat of the bike; she can still see it today. She has other not so pleasant memories of the street.

Sometimes, late at night, they would be awakened by the sound of a banging fist on the window pane and a man's voice calling out for 'Joan!' This occurred regularly. The voices changed, but the demands were always the same: 'Joan!' Inquiries informed them that 'Joan' was the previous occupant of the flat. She was a prostitute. The most frightening incident happened three months after they moved in. It was a typical Dublin evening, raining cats and dogs. My mother was pregnant with me, and suffering from a kidney infection. At three in the morning, they were awakened by a fierce banging on the door. Granda Kimmage was very ill at the time and my father feared it was one of his family with some bad news. He jumped up to answer the door, but it wasn't his brother or sister. There was a tall, uniformed Garda standing in the hall. He was soaked to the skin and reeked of alcohol. He demanded to see 'Joan'. My father explained that Joan had moved out months ago but the policeman insisted on entering the flat. He walked into the room, looked at my sick mother, apologised and left.

Da started to race again at the start of 1962 and my arrival half way through the year did not upset his form for, two months after my birth, he became the Irish champion at Markethill in County Armagh. He had come second in 1958 and 1959, so the elusive title victory brought him great pleasure. I was brought regularly to watch my Da racing and I'm told my first words were not so much 'Da Da' as 'Come on Da Da'. My brother Raphael was born two years after me in 1964. Da called him after the famous French professional Raphael Geminiani, much to the disgust of Granny Kimmage who said it was no name to give a child. Kevin, the third son, was born three years later and suddenly Eccles Street was getting a little crowded. We moved to a new complex of flats in Ballymun five miles north of the Liffey.

The flat was bright and clean, had toilets and running water and had a unique central heating system – the floors heated. But my parents didn't like it. On the day we moved in, the lifts broke down and Da had to carry a washing machine up eight flights of stairs on his back. Soon after, he caught Raphael hanging over the balcony and got a terrible fright. Raphael was given the standard punishment; his bum was reddened. I suppose it's what I remember most about my youth – my father's war cry when we misbehaved or were 'bold', as we say in Ireland: it was always: 'I'll redden your arse for you.' He rarely did – the threat was enough to put the fear of God into us.

We stayed in Ballymun for a year and them moved to a new three-bedroom semi-detached house in Coolock, two miles east. My fourth brother, Christopher, 11 years my junior, was brought up here. The family was complete and Kilmore Avenue remains the family home today. My Da stopped racing in 1972: he was 34 years old, and raising sons was very time consuming. He tried to get me interested in every kind of sport but I was only ever interested in doing one thing, racing a bike. When I was ten years old he bought me one.

3 PACKET SOUP AND FRUIT CAKE

Delving into one's past can be discouraging, even disturbing. Questioning my mother on how she met my father was awkward. Questioning my father on my childhood was as bad. It's as if they have a very precious thing they don't want to share – with anyone. Do they see me as the child who shit on the seat of his bicycle, or the man who has now just quit the seat of his bicycle? It's strange. Maybe an answer will come if I have children of my own.

Ma (Dublin kids always call their mother 'Ma' and their father 'Da') says I was a dependable child. To illustrate this she tells the 'pound of sugar' story. She would often come in from the shops having forgotten a pound of sugar. This was a major headache, as it meant putting my clothes on to go out again. Sometimes, she left me in the middle of the floor surrounded by kitchen chairs and sprinted to Geraghty's in Dorset Street for the sugar. And when she came back I would always be there, not having moved an inch. A dependable child.

My St David's Primary School teacher Michael O'Braoinain tells me that as a child I was a fighter of injustice. I would never let him get away with anything unjust even if I risked a clip on the ear for my insubordination. My father says that as a child I was a nightmare – but he's lying, for I know I was good, so boringly good. This is not to say I didn't get my arse tanned on several occasions. But generally I was good. And this is what disturbs me. It's almost a disappointment to discover that I wasn't a tyrant child, unsuccessful at school and on my way to a life in prison only to be saved by athletic prowess. No, I was good, boringly good.

I don't remember the incident of my three-wheeler. I have a few vague memories of Eccles Street. Of the old and very mad woman we frequently met on the road, who terrified me. Of my father leaving me to go to the hospital late one night. Of Mrs Geraghty's sweet shop in Dorset Street and one or two other trivial things.

My memory banks started functioning when I was six years old and we moved to Ballymun. I loved it there. Much of that concrete jungle was still being built and I found the building sites fascinating places of adventure. Ma would leave me in charge of Raphael (I was dependable, remember) and I would drag him around the sites where we would play. Lipton's Supermarket was another favourite haunt. We would hang out at the incinerator delighting in eating the half-burned rotten vegetables that we found lying around. It was good clean fun, but Ballymun did have its dangers. My father made the flats' underground basement a strict 'no go' area. This was after some pervert had interfered with a neighbour's daughter.

Scuttin' was also taboo. This involved swinging out of the back of the delivery lorries to Lipton's and hanging on till the truck slowed down at a set of traffic lights, and then jumping off. Scuttin' was very popular, and I found it hard to obey my father. It took at least two or three arse-reddenings to convince me that it wasn't worth it.

It was in Ballymun that I rode my first two-wheeler. Da bought it and immediately removed the two stabilisers. He sat me on it in the small car park in front of the flats and then pushed me off. I wobbled once or twice, but basically had no trouble and was delighted with myself. I loved cycling; from the time I was born it had always been part of my life. Whenever possible, Da would bring us to the races to watch him. I loved the races. I loved it when Da gave me a crossbar from the finish to the car after the race was over. I felt so proud. I was fascinated by his legs. The way the bulging muscles shone from the oils he spread on them. But most of all I loved it when he won.

We have a photo at home of him winning a race at Ballyboughal in North County Dublin. Raphael and I are both standing on the small school fence overlooking the finish line. Raphael has his two hands raised and it is clear to see the joy on our faces. Needless to say he lost quite a few also. I could never understand him losing and on questioning him his reply was always: 'Sure I have to give the other fellows a chance sometimes.' This infuriated me. I honestly believed him.

I often asked him if he was the best. Here, he never lied. No, he was not the best. He was good but not the best. Peter Doyle was the best. He used to point out Peter Doyle to me, and on occasions when the great man came to our house he would ask: 'Paul, do you know who this is?' And, finger in my mouth, I would shyly reply 'Peter Doyle'. To me, my Da was God, but Peter Doyle was also God.

Being at the races wasn't always a pleasure. I remember an evening race in the Phoenix Park. I stood with my mother as she chatted with the other cycling widows waiting impatiently for the finishing sprint. There was a gasp from the crowd as a rider hit a parked car and went flying over the top and landed on the grass margin at the side. I remember leaving my mother's side and running to the crowd that surrounded the groaning body lying motionless. I was too small to see over them, but I bent down on my knees and looked through the legs, spotting the rider's number. Number 22. I wasn't sure but expected that it was Da. Then I saw the crash hat. The blue leather crash hat that he always wore: 'It's him, that's my Da.' And then sprinting back to Ma, shouting: 'It's him, it's Da!' And for some crazy reason being glad that my Da was the centre of all the attention. The thought that he might be injured never crossed my mind. He was brought to hospital but got off lightly. His crash hat, split up the middle, had saved him from injury. When I was ten, I rode my first race with the same blue crash hat on my head. There were other, classier, hats, but I wanted this one. This was my Da's. Da was God.

I rode my first official race at ten, but the unofficial ones started much earlier. When we moved to Coolock I used to race the neighbours' kids around the block. I always won or nearly always. Davy Casey my next-door neighbour often beat me. This cracked me. I was a desperately bad loser and would burst into tears of rage when I did. School gave me other opportunities to race. I entered Michael O'Braoinain's class when I was nine. Michael took a great shine to me and instilled in me a new confidence in my academic ability. He made me write poetry, and regularly raved about my offerings. He instilled in us an appreciation of Gaelic culture, and was a great man for playing a jig and a reel on the tin whistle. We laugh about that now. I've played squash with him regularly in the past six months – he claims he always knew I'd end up writing for a living.

In an effort to improve our Irish, Michael organised class trips to the Gaeltacht for a month in the summer. We stayed with a family, Mrs O'Donnel's in Carraroe, a small village 26 miles west of Galway. Speaking Irish for an hour a day at school was fine but having to do it non-stop for a month was terribly difficult. Most of us brought our bikes and I loved taking off for an hour to discover the lovely Connemara roads. But riding on my own soon became boring. I wanted a challenge.

Before I left for Connemara, my Da had just come back from the Tour of Britain (the Milk Race), where he had worked with the Irish team as a masseur. His stories of the race fascinated me and I decided to organise a sort of 'Carraroe Milk Race', among my classmates. Because it was a stage race, I decided I needed food. I knew from going through the pockets of my father's racing jerseys that he often brought raisins with him. There was a small grocery shop across the road so I bought a packet of dried raisins there. I had a bit of a job persuading the others to race, but finally they agreed and I easily won the first stage. But it was too easy and I wasn't satisfied.

For the second stage I decided not to speed off at the start but instead to stay with them for the first mile and then fake a crash. I chose the spot for falling off, a patch of gravel on a corner, as I was planning the circuit. The race started and I purposefully skidded on the gravel in front of the others, making sure they saw me and then jumped back on the bike, caught them and beat them. Persuading them to ride a third stage was now a real problem. I offered them a big handicap before setting out in pursuit. But I was too generous. I soon realised I wasn't going to catch them. I couldn't face being beaten so I took a short cut that reduced my deficit. I came out just behind the leader, Pat O'Grady, and I passed him for my third win. But he saw me cheating. There was a big argument, and the fourth stage and the race were cancelled.

I was glad to return home at the end of the month's adventure. I was homesick. A month later my father started working on an old racing frame of his. He bought some new parts for it and started putting it together. I suspected it might be for me, but didn't dare ask. My suspicions were confirmed when he presented me with it a week later. I couldn't believe it, a real racer with gears. He asked me if I wanted to ride in the under-age championships in Phoenix Park that Sunday. I did – so he took me on a training ride.

We left the house and headed for Balgriffin. He instructed me on the rules of a game we were to play. The idea was for me to stay behind him and to count to twenty, then I passed him and he counted to twenty, and so on. The second part was that I was to ride as hard as I could while at the front – not that I needed any encouragement. At Balgriffin we turned right and straight down to the seafront, then left to Portmarnock and back in the Malahide road, about ten miles in all. The ride finished with a finishing sprint and my Da just pipped me for first to the road sign – although I knew he was faking. When we got back to the house I was shattered, absolutely wrecked. Da sat me down in a chair and asked me if I still wanted to race. After getting the bike, I didn't think 'no' was the right answer so I said that I did.

'Well, that's fine but you must remember, Paul, that in cycling you will experience more heartbreak than happiness.'

God, Da, how right you were.

I don't remember much about my first race, which is unusual when you consider how vivid the memory of beating my classmates in Carraroe remains. Most of the lads were much older than me and I think I finished second last.

I started going out on regular Sunday runs that winter. A few clubs would meet outside the GPO and it wasn't unusual for a thirty-strong 'peloton' to ride out of the city. Most of the lads were from a club on the south side, Orwell Wheelers, so I joined them. On riding home in the second or third week I noticed one other lad from the group heading in the same direction. He told me he lived in Glin Drive in Coolock and was in the Obelisk Wheelers. Martin Earley was a month younger than me and had only just started cycling. We met again a week later and soon became best friends.

Although only eleven years old, I started taking cycling very seriously. As soon as I'd come in from school, I'd meet up with Martin and we'd head off for an hour's training. I won two races in my first full year, both times beating Martin in a sprint finish. In the years that followed, the rivalry between us became too great for our friendship and from the age of fifteen until we both turned professional we became bitter rivals.

Looking back on the early years I can't help laughing at the sacrifices I made for my new sport in my quest to reach the top. But this had its advantages. It protected me from that dangerous adolescent period when teenagers are tempted by all sorts of outside influences such as smoking, drinking, drugs and women. Cycling shielded me from all of this. I lived for the bell on Friday nights. Every second weekend, the Orwell organised youth hostelling weekends to hostels in Wicklow, Meath or Louth. As soon as the school bell rang on Fridays, I'd dash home and pack the sleeping-bag, food and spare clothes for the weekend into the carrier of the bike and then speed into town to meet the lads.

It was through youth hostelling with the Orwell that I first met Stephen Roche. One of my best friends in the club, Paul (Smidler) Smith, asked me to go hostelling with him one weekend. I rode across to Paul's house in Dundrum, and when I arrived he decided he would ask his neighbour, 'Rochee', if he wanted to come along. 'Rochee' was totally unprepared when we knocked on his door; but he said he would join us at the hostel, Baltyboys near Blessington in County Wicklow, next morning.

Smidler and I cycled off in the pitch dark of the night to Baltyboys and, sure enough, Rochee turned up at the hostel next morning with all his gear, having left Dundrum at first light. They decided (being youngest, I always followed) that we should go to Aughavannagh, which meant a long haul over two mountains; Glenmalure and Aughavannagh. On the slopes of Glenmalure, in a small dry ditch at the side of the road, we bivouacked. Tinned fruit salad, my Ma's best fruit cake, and a can of Coke. We munched away in the spitting rain, and laughed and joked about how lucky we were. Then it was back on the bikes and the climb to the Shay Elliot memorial monument, where some film makers were shooting a clip for *The Thirty-Nine Steps*. The evening meal at the hostel was real 'gourmet' stuff: packet soup, beans, smash and sausages, tinned rice and fruit cake.

Oh, how I loved those weekends. They were always innocent and wonderful. I'd arrive home, totally knackered, to my Ma's hot apple tart and a mountain of school homework. Stephen and I still talk with great affection of those weekends; planning each time to do it once more for old time's sake; but knowing that something will come up to prevent it happening. Could it ever be the same? Probably not, and maybe it is this that prevents us doing it again. But remembering is a joy in itself. When I think of the professional life with its glamour, its corruption and its suffering and compare it with those times of innocent purity, I scratch my head and wonder why I bothered.

I stayed on at school until my final exams, for the Leaving Certificate. When I left, a friend of my Da's, Peter Brambell, gave me a job binding blocks at a cement block making plant five miles from our house. It was great to be earning a few bob, and I enjoyed the work and the new freedom. But my Ma wasn't having me binding blocks for the rest of my life, and she made me apply for every job that appeared in the newspapers. When I wrote my address on the application forms, she always made sure that I wrote Artane instead of Coolock. Artane was much more fashionable. I had an interview for a plumbing apprenticeship at Dublin Airport and was offered the job. I accepted and started work immediately.

When I entered the airport in September of 1979, I was seventeen and still cycling mad. As a junior, I was perhaps one of the ten best in the country but was a long way off being in the top three. Martin Earley was easily the best junior. This infuriated me, and incited me to train even harder. For the 1980 season, my last as a junior, we

15

formed a club of our own, Tara Road Club. Raphael and Gary Thompson were my team mates, Da was team manager. He surveyed our training and planned team tactics. He was merciless in his approach. In return for his time he demanded full dedication. Bed at 9.30, hard training, tidy appearance and, above all, honesty. He never accepted excuses and he loved attacking, aggressive riding. We were a phenomenal success. From March to July we won every single race we entered. Sometimes myself, sometimes Raphael, sometimes Thompson – but always a Tara man. But the bubble burst at the junior championships in Lurgan. The whole field rode against us – and, to rub salt in the wound, Martin Earley was champion. In our three years as juniors, he was twice champion while I had just one silver for second. The dice seemed always to roll for him and fall off the table for me. I despised him.

4 THE NEARLY MAN

In 1981, I was 19 and raced my first season as a senior rider. At first, adapting to the longer races was difficult, I was often the victim of my own enthusiasm, attacking too early and exploding before the end. But it didn't take long to adapt, and, once I did, I never doubted I would reach the top in Irish cycling. Most of the young guys I had started with had given up, victims of love, alcohol and pop music. I had been in love, tried alcohol and was a great music fan. Love had left me frustrated and unhappy, alcohol happy but unconscious; I liked music. It was the only thing that didn't interfere with cycling, and I was a regular visitor to the record shops. It was the year Stephen Roche made his professional debut with Peugeot in France. Ireland now had two professionals, Kelly and Roche. Their exploits inspired me. I wanted to be a pro. But all that was further down the road. First, I had to prove I was good enough – it took five years.

In June, I represented my country for the first time. It was in the Manx International on the Isle of Man, a 100-mile baptism of fire around the TT course. Pulling on the green jersey should have been a proud moment – it wasn't. The jerseys were faded and torn. They had been used six months previously in the Tour of Ireland and hadn't been properly washed. The washer had forgotten to remove race food from the pockets and I was able to pick rotten Mars bars and other stinking remnants from them. So much for the honour of representing your country.

Martin Earley made his international debut at the same race. We were both in the front group approaching Snaefell mountain for the last time – going really well. But I was stronger on the 7-mile climb and finished tenth, very pleased with myself.

The Irish championships were a week later in Waterford. One of

17

my Da's greatest fears when riding a championship was to miss out on the winning breakaway through tactical error. At Waterford, I decided that whatever happened I wasn't going to miss the boat. I attacked early in a big group and, on the last lap, went clear with two others, Brendan Madden and Mick Nulty. They were both stronger than I was, but neither was a good finisher. In the finishing sprint, slightly uphill, sheer will to win was the difference between us, and I beat them easily. I was Irish champion at 19, the youngest ever to win the title. I was thrilled.

Stephen Roche was in Waterford that day. He was home on a break from the Continent and he turned up in a lovely white Peugeot with his name on both doors. He had made a sensational pro debut, winning the Tour of Corsica and Paris–Nice – an instant star. He brought a girl to Waterford. She was French, blonde, and wore an outrageous mini-skirt – absolutely stunning. Her name was Lydia, and seeing her with Stephen that day made professional cycling seem very enticing.

Winning in Waterford was so very important to me: I was Irish champion and no one could ever take it away from me. I loved that title. In the pubs in the off season I would often bump into someone who would ask if I was into sport.

'Cycling, hmmm that's interesting and have you won anything?'

And I would reply with a false modesty:

'Well, actually, I'm the current national champion.'

The glamour of being champion didn't last. Later that month, I was picked on an Irish team for the Tour of Scotland. There was a Czechoslovakian team riding, and they were huge brutes of men. Milan Jurco was the most impressive, I had never seen so much muscle on one man – or anyone quite as ugly. The Czechs taught me a new game – the art of riding in crosswinds. In Ireland the hedges are so high that crosswinds are rarely a factor in deciding race tactics, so we were inexperienced. The Czechs toyed with us all week and I can remember going to bed one night and dreading having to get up for another hammering the next day. I remember the second last stage in particular. It lashed down with rain all day, and I arrived in a group hours down and totally miserable. At the finish we rode straight to the dressing room. The Englishman, Mark Bell from Liverpool, was getting changed. He had just beaten two Czechs to win the stage, a fine performance. Someone asked if he wanted to turn pro. He laughed and in his best scouse accent replied: 'No way! It looks great on the telly, seeing them pulling faces on the climbs, throwing themselves all over the place, but it's not like that in real life. It's pain. No fuckin' way.'

I knew that Mark Bell was right, but it didn't change my mind. I reckoned I was still young and had still a good margin for improvement. I reckoned I would go much better with another two years under my belt. But he did make me think about it.

Stephen came home for the winter and was in great demand all over the country. He had won four stage races in his first season with the professionals and was already a big name. I phoned him and invited him to our house for a chat and some advice on going to France. He talked of the problems he had faced as an amateur. Of the need to be two-faced with the team managers and the French riders because they were always two-faced with you. He told us it was important to 'get them before they got you'. The message struck a chord. He promised to find Raphael and me a place at ACBB at the end of 1983 when we finished our apprenticeships. After the talk, he cleared the spread of cakes and pastries my mother had laid on – it was nice to see he had lost none of his old habits.

The year of 1982 started well, then flopped, but was most memorable for meeting Ann. I have always thought it a strange coincidence that I met my wife and best friend on the same day, at the same time and in the same place. It was in Phoenix Park in Dublin, at the end of the week-long Ras Tailteann. I had been noticing Ann since the start of the season. She was a sister of one of the guys who raced, Paul Nolan. I knew Paul was riding the Ras and guessed she might be in the Park. I found her in the crowd after the race and we started talking. She had followed the race for the week, taking notes for a journalist from the Irish press, David Walsh. As we talked, we were approached by David and his wife Mary. Ann introduced me – it was a handshake that would change my life. I arranged to meet her later at the post-race dance. We had two more dates during the week and on the following Sunday I won my first race for over two months at Carrick on Suir.

Carrick was one of the rare occasions in 1981 that I beat Raphael. He had a superb year and was heralded by all as the new Kelly. It was hard playing second fiddle to my younger brother; he was the apple of my father's eye, but we were always close and his success did not change this. Meeting Ann was a great consolation. She came into my life at an important time. My poor form frustrated me. The more I tried, the less I succeeded. I was impossible to live with whenever I travelled with an Irish team: moody, grouchy, a real pain. Ann changed me. She lightened me up, brought me out of myself, got me smiling more. It was no coincidence that I started to ride better almost from the first day we met.

The year of 1983 was about two races. The Milk Race, a two-week Tour of Britain sponsored by the Milk Marketing Board, had the reputation of being one of the hardest amateur stage races in the world. I was a bit dubious about going into it, as I had never ridden a stage race of more than a week, but decided it was time to test my mettle.

The first stage was a marathon 120-mile trip to Bristol. With about 20 miles to go I went clear in a chasing group with race leader Malcolm Elliot and Tony Doyle and finished sixteenth. It was a great start and I was determined to hang on to my 16th place for as long as possible. There was great morale in the team. We had been slaughtered by the Irish press before leaving, but the criticism bonded us together and made us try harder. There was no pressure on us, we had nothing to lose and attacked every day. The good start continued when my mate Phillip Cassidy finished second on the third stage to Welwyn Garden City. He stole a bit of my thunder and spurred me to attack. On the sixth stage to Leicester, I got into an important break that moved me up to sixth overall. Sixth in the Milk Race, I couldn't believe it.

I rang home every night: one call to my parents, another to Ann. They were all very excited and said I was getting rave reviews from the papers. On the ninth stage, a 94-mile mountainous stage from Kirkby to Halifax, I hit the jackpot – race leader. A star at last. Getting the lead was one thing, holding on to it was another. Our team was young and very inexperienced and I was convinced there was no way we could defend the yellow jersey. I didn't sleep at all that night and felt a terrible pressure on my shoulders. I had worn a yellow jersey only once before at a Tour of Ulster and had lost it after one day. The Tour of Ulster wasn't a patch on the Milk Race, how could I possibly hope to hang on? I weighed up my options all night. I had a 42-second lead over German rider Ulrich Rottler and 54 seconds on Peugeot professional Sean Yates. The next day was a 100-mile stage to Hull but this was followed by a rest day. Defending the jersey to Hull would ensure that I kept it for three days. It was a good incentive.

The stage to Hull was flat, and it proved an uneventful stage. We had a shaky start and let a dangerous break go clear, but regained control half-way through, and I rode into Hull with the jersey still in my possession. The rest day was great, it was an extra day to savour the glory. Being race leader was fun but it wasn't enough any more. I wanted to win. I couldn't sleep for thinking about it – so much pressure. There were just three more stages to go; if I held out on two of those the race was mine. The first hilly stage across the Yorkshire Moors to Middlesbrough was the real test. On the first climb, all of my team mates were dropped and I was left alone to defend the yellow shirt. On the savagely steep Farndale Moor, I suffered terribly but broke clear with a 16-man group. Rottler, Eaton and Yates were left behind. I was so happy that I never bothered about going for the stage win and was content to roll in at the back of the group. I had defended the lead on my own. I was convinced I was going to win.

There was just the difficult 70-mile stage to Harrogate to master. It started with a steep first-category climb, The Stang, but I was flying and crossed the summit in seventh place. The bunch had split in two, and all of my team mates were behind and I was vulnerable. The Americans noticed and started attacking. One by one I brought them back, enjoying the defiance. When they saw they couldn't get rid of me they stopped and the pace dropped and my team mates got back on. I met my Waterloo after 13 miles. A mile from the bottom of the second climb, The Fleak, I punctured. Eaton noticed my deflating front tyre and ordered his men to attack. My two team mates Eddie Madden and Mick McKenna waited with me and we changed wheels. I never panicked and felt sure we would get back on. But the Americans split the field to shreds on the climb, and neither Madden nor McKenna could stay with me. I picked my way through the stragglers and chased alone down the descent. But I started to take chances and ran off the road at a T-junction and fell off. A puncture and a crash – it was too much, the bad luck just too cruel. I got back on the bike, but lost heart; chasing alone was now a pointless exercise. I waited for a group and finished the stage 13 minutes down. I slid from 1st to 33rd overall – I was shattered. The next morning Matt Eaton pulled on my yellow jersey and we strolled to the race finish in Blackpool. At the race banquet I was presented with a watch as the most unfortunate rider of the race. I gave it to my father, remembering his words: 'In cycling there is more heartbreak than happiness.'

Looking back, I should never have lost that race – not with what I know now. I should have paid money to another team mate to defend the lead. In the modern era riders do not lose stage races because of punctures and crashes. I was unlucky.

I returned to Ireland a hero. Only one other Irishman, Peter Doyle, had ever worn the yellow jersey in the Milk Race. I had equalled God. Not bad.

The Milk Race had made me the top rider in the country, and I confirmed my new status with two good wins on my return home. Two weeks later I rode the Manx International. I broke clear on Snaefell mountain with six others on the last lap. We dashed down the mountain, turned Governors Bridge and entered the finishing straight. Joey McLaughlin opened the sprint and I came round him heading for the line like a bullet. I got that feeling, that wonderful, 'I'm going to win the Manx International' feeling. The line was there, just in front of me, beckoning to seal my joy. But then the Swiss Hans Reiss passed me ten feet from the line, edged me out by a hair's breadth. Second. So near and yet so far. Again. The Press started calling me 'the nearly man'.

The Tour de L'Avenir was the second memory of 1983. The L'Avenir, starting in Lorient and finishing in Marseille, was a 14-day mini Tour de France for pros and amateurs – my first chance to race against Continental pros. It was so different. They rode so much closer together and I can remember leaving Lorient on the first stage with brake levers in both buttocks and feeling most uncomfortable. The style of racing was also alien to us. With the amateurs it was arse-up, head-down, and go from the gun. But in the L'Avenir, there was never a set pattern to the racing, except at the finish, when it was always eyeballs out. From the opening stages, survival was the goal.

Before riding the L'Avenir I thought I knew what mountains were – I didn't. The first mountain stage was after ten days. It was a split, with a morning stage from Bourg de Piège to La Chapelle en Vercors and in the afternoon a return to Bourg over the same climbs. I had been waiting all week for this day, the day of glory, but I was wiped out. It was so hot and the climbs were so long, I couldn't handle it. On the morning stage I was dropped with John Herety and Paul Sherwen, two British pros riding with French teams La Redoute and Coop-Mercier. Both were noted non-climbers and at the time I felt humiliated to be in their company. I had fancied myself as a Lucien Van Impe. I was deeply discouraged, and for the first time being a professional did not seem such a great thing after all. I reached La Chapelle at least half an hour down. My team mate John McQuaid finished with me, but Raphael and Gary Thompson, the only other Irish survivors, were further back again. We quickly changed and ate a pretty miserable lunch in a run-down shack of a hotel. While eating, I recognised Bernard Thevenet, a double Tour de France winner, at another table. Word had it that he was a native of La Chapelle.

We rested between stages in a cold, stone cottage on damp

mattresses. The morale in the team was zero. We just looked at each other with the same thing going through our heads: 'What the hell are we doing here?' I decided that this pro life wasn't for me. I hated it. The afternoon stage was a nightmare. Some Portuguese bastard attacked at the bottom of the first climb and the green jerseys were immediately dropped. Raphael was in a dreadful state and was coughing up blood. Gary Thompson was physically and mentally knackered. They both quickly abandoned. I rode on in a group of five which included a Japanese rider, Takahashi. Now for a Jap to get this far in the Tour de L'Avenir was for them an outstanding exploit. His team manager was leaning out of the car window with a loud hailer in his hand, and screamed encouragement in Japanese every time the road went up, which was regularly. This started getting to me after a while. I was irritated by my poor form and annoyed that I would have to endure the race for another six days. And now, on top of all this, there was this bloody Jap making all this noise for a guy that was half an hour down. Had they no shame? The rage became uncontrollable and I turned to the Japanese team manager and shouted at the top of my voice: 'Shut fuckin' up.'

I will never forget the look on his face. He was terrified, horrified; he sat back in his car and did not say another word for the rest of the day. I felt guilty about it afterwards. I approached him next day and apologised.

Raphael and Thompson both left for home and I envied them. There was only myself and John 'Kippers' McQuaid left. 'Kippers' would have got great pleasure in returning home the only Irish finisher. I would have heard about it for the rest of my life, and I suppose it was this more than anything that made me go on. But I hated it. I dreaded getting up every morning to face another day's racing. And the pros, they irritated me: always in good humour, always laughing and joking. I had started the race as a morning grouch but by the end I was an all-day grouch. Cyril Guimard, the famous professional directeur sportif, had also upset me. I was on the massage couch getting a rub and the hotel door was open. Guimard walked in, much to my surprise and delight. I looked at him in wonder. The great Cyril Guimard in *my* room. He approached the massage table and lifted the towel that covered my privates and said 'Baf!', waving his hand in a dismissive way and then walked out. The bastard, I hated him for it.

'Kippers' was eliminated with two stages to go, leaving me as the sole Irish survivor. Five of those who had abandoned had flown home but there were no more air tickets and so we had to take the boat. I didn't really care, I just wanted to get away from there. It had been a bad end to a great season. I was saturated with cycling and needed a good rest.

I finished my four-year apprenticeship at Dublin Airport shortly after returning. It was the policy of the company, Aer Rianta, to train apprentices and then get rid of them once the apprenticeship was over. I was out of a job. Where next? The plan had always been to complete the apprenticeship and then go to France to try for a pro contract but the Tour de L'Avenir had opened my eyes. For four years Raphael and I had told our friends, family, and most importantly the cycling journalists that we would be going to France in 1984. How could we turn back now? Then there were also the Olympics to consider. Los Angeles was fast approaching and although I was fairly sure of a place, there was no guarantee. France could clinch my selection and offer me the best preparation. So I suppose it was three things, no job, L.A. and the fear of being called 'chicken', that brought us to the ACBB club in Paris in February of 1984. We were following in the footsteps of the greats, Elliot, Roche, Millar and Anderson. We were also following in the not-so-glorious footsteps of our father, who had set out on the same quest 25 years earlier. Where would our path lead?

5 NATIONAL SUCKERS DAY

A big man met us at the airport. He had huge, shovel-like hands, greying hair and tanned skin. We thought it might be Mickey Wiegant, the legendary ACBB manager, or maybe Claude Escalon, the directeur sportif, but we were not sure and had not the courage to ask. We sat in the back of his car like two terrified children and he brought us to the west Parisian suburb of Boulogne Billancourt.

On our arrival at the ACBB sports centre, a not quite middle-aged man in a leather jacket approached, smiling. There was something almost sinister about his smile. I took an immediate dislike to him because of it. He introduced himself as Claude Escalon. He gave us two new Peugeot bikes, just like the pros had, and some track suits, jerseys and shorts. It was great to be given so much free gear but I wasn't happy with the saddle on the bike. Plucking up some courage I tried to explain to him in pidgin English that I wanted to fit my own. He laughed. We had to use the team issue saddles. Bernard Hinault used the same saddle.

'If they are good enough for Bernard, they are good enough for you.'

There was no arguing with that so I agreed to use his saddle.

At four the next morning, we left in a VW van for the South of France. We were not the only foreigners at the club. There was also a New Zealander (Gerry Golder), two Englishmen (Kenny Knight and Christian Yates, a brother of Sean's), a Canadian and 'les frères Kimmage'. After 12 hours of driving we arrived at our base for the opening races, the 'Hotel La Quiétude' at Les Issambres on the Côte d'Azur. Mickey Wiegant was at the hotel when we arrived. He was an odd-looking man, impossible to put an age to, just one of those ol' fellahs who never seems to get any older. He wore a brown leather jacket and drove a huge Rover car. He spoke at 400 miles an hour and we couldn't understand a word he said. He insisted we call him 'Monsieur Wiegant'. We ate when he gave us the order to eat. We spoke when he gave us permission to speak. He made us feel very small.

The team's French riders drove down in their own cars. There was also a Belgian. I remember him because of all the shit he used to take before meals: pills, ampoules – he was a right bloody pharmacist. When he'd catch us staring during his pill-popping, he'd say 'vitamins'. The French formed a clan and were not too friendly towards us. We, the English speakers, formed our own clan. A Norwegian, Dag Otto Lauritzen, arrived a few days later, but he stayed at Wiegant's house and was clearly the old man's favourite. Training started immediately. We set off in a large group and followed the team car driven by Escalon but directed by Wiegant.

They played little games with us. At the top of a hill, Wiegant would hold a racing tyre out of the window – the prize for the first rider to the top. On the first training spin, I won two tyres. I found the first races more difficult.

Monsieur Wiegant instructed us that in his team the individual rider's personal honour did not matter. It was the victory of the team that counted. To emphasise this he bought a huge cream cake and divided it equally among us any time an ACBB rider won. Lauritzen was the star and he won several of the opening races. A fourth place in a race at St Tropez was my best placing of the month-long stay. Raphael was riding better, and was narrowly beaten in a race at St Maxime, but there was no cream cake. With Monsieur Wiegant cream cakes were for winning; second was nowhere.

During the month some of the professional riders would come to the hotel to pay homage to their former mentor and guru, Monsieur Wiegant. Bernard Thevenet, Robert Millar, Raphael Geminiani and Stephen Roche all visited and lunched with the old man. Stephen introduced me to his directeur sportif, Bernard Thevenet. He had a lovely, warm smile that lit up his face. I liked him.

At the end of February, we drove back to Paris to begin the serious races, the amateur classics. Most of the foreigners stayed together in a flat near the team's headquarters but Raphael and I were brought to a small flat on the opposite side of Paris at Vincennes. As we entered the flat, Abel, the giant masseur who had collected us at the airport, led us down to this underground dungeon with a mud floor. I can remember thinking: 'Jesus Christ, how are we going to survive here?' – but he was just showing us the shed for the bikes. The flat was five floors up a narrow wooden staircase.

We had no problems in settling in. I did the cooking and Raphael the cleaning. The flat had an old black and white telly and a telephone for incoming calls only. The toilet was the hole-in-the-ground type. It doubled as a shower by placing a wooden grille over the hole. This was a great inconvenience at first. To compensate, Raphael took the middle out of one of the wooden kitchen chairs and tried sitting on the wooden frame. It didn't work, and in the end we had to squat. We became such good shots that we could shoot between the gaps in the shower grille after a while. The flat was fine. We liked being independent of the other foreigners and enjoyed the privacy. But it was awkward having to ride across Paris the day before a race to change a tyre or get information on what was going on. Wiegant remained at his residence at Les Issambres, coming to Paris for the big races.

Paris–Ezy was the first classic of the season. It started in the darkness of a small foggy village at eight in the morning. I never understood why the classics always started at such a ridiculous hour. An eight o'clock start meant getting up at four in the morning. Nutrition was the biggest problem – we had to eat three hours before the race. At four in the morning I would fry minced steak and boil rice. We had no appetite and had to force-feed ourselves. As soon as breakfast-cum-dinner was over we would leave the flat, pick up the bikes from the basement and wait in the marble hallway to be collected. We must have looked a proper sight, in our racing tights, to other flat residents returning from discothèques and nightclubs. Their expressions said it all. Getting up at that hour for a bike race was totally insane, and I never got used to it.

As we waited to start the race, I was approached by a Frenchman who spoke absolutely perfect Oxford English. It wasn't our first meeting, as we had talked at a time trial in Ireland a few years earlier when he had visited the country as a guest of the Roche family. I asked him then about the professional life and he laughed at me: 'You don't want to be a professional, it's a horrible life.' I was shocked that a Frenchman could be so dismissive of what I felt was the greatest profession in the world and thought the guy was a nutcase. Today I admire him for his vision. We are still great friends with Jean and his wife Ginette and have not forgotten their kindness to us in a miserable year with ACBB.

Paris–Ezy was run in freezing cold wind and rain. On the finishing circuit, Raphael got into the winning move, but the uphill sprint was too hard for him and he finished fifth. We were absolutely thrilled. Fifth in the first classic of the year, what a great start. But Escalon thought otherwise. There were two other ACBB riders in the break with Raphael and neither had won. One of them, the French rider Thierry Pelosso, had gone to Escalon after the race and said he had lost because of Raphael's 'selfish tactics'. We couldn't understand a word of Escalon's raving and asked Jean Beaufils to interpret. Raphael defended himself but Escalon would have none of it, and made him the scapegoat for the defeat. Raphael's joy soon turned to tears. He was never the same after it.

March and April were grim. Living in Paris was really awkward for training. We had to ride for 45 minutes in heavy traffic before finding some decent country roads. So if we wanted to do a 3-hour ride, it meant that we spent an hour and a half choking on exhaust fumes. We rode just one race a week with the club, which wasn't nearly enough to develop any kind of good form. Training was no substitute for racing and we did not ride well. It was easy to get depressed. Some days we didn't bother training at all; these days we labelled 'National Suckers Day'. It usually rained in the mornings on National Suckers Day. After breakfast we'd sit looking at each other and contemplate going out into the Paris traffic on our bikes: 'No, we will wait till it clears up.' To pass the time we'd take the Métro and sit drinking coffee on the Champs Elysées and try to figure out exactly where the Tour finished. After, we'd visit the Eiffel Tower and then eat out for lunch. The afternoon was spent walking around the record shops or at an English-version movie on the 'Champs'. The day would finish with dinner at the flat, accompanied by a bottle of cheap 'Vin de Table' and we'd sit back and laugh about how we had been ripped off in tourist-trap Paris. But inside, we were not laughing; inside, we were screaming. ACBB was not working for us.

In April I left Paris for a week. I was picked on the national team for the Sealink International, starting at Skelmersdale near Liverpool. I felt sorry leaving Raphael behind. His good humour was a real tonic on the bad days at the flat. He was more deserving of a place on the team than I was, but Irish selectors were always reluctant to pick the two of us and so I got the nod. It was great to get out of France. My parents came across from Ireland and followed the race for the week. I struggled for the first few days – too many National Suckers Days had left me short of condition. But I started to ride well towards the end, and I returned to Paris with much better morale and form.

The classic Paris–Rouen, was my first race with the club after my week's 'holiday'. The alarm went off at four in the morning and we wearily climbed out of bed. Steak and rice were consumed with the usual enthusiasm, and we then gathered our kit and descended to the ground floor. It was a damp, miserable morning so we waited inside the apartment front door, sitting on the cold marble floor. Fifteen minutes, half an hour, an hour. Still no sign of them. We put the bikes back in the shed and walked back upstairs and back to bed. We were sick. Sick of these heartless bastards treating us like scum. Surely we deserved at least a phone call? Furious, I phoned Escalon and demanded why no one had picked us up. He gave me a half-baked excuse about trying to contact us, and to calm me asked if we wanted to ride a race on Tuesday in a place called Ostricourt in Northern France.

Ostricourt was a battle between the two strongest teams in the race, ACBB and the powerful outfit that was being formed in the North, Wasquehal. But the French amateur champion was also riding, and I remember being most impressed with Jean François Bernard before team tactics got the better of him and he retired. It was a circuit race with a short climb and a kilometre stretch of cobbles each lap. On the last lap I attacked alone on the climb and time-trialled to the finish for a solo victory. I had almost forgotten how good it felt to win a race. Ostricourt gave me immense satisfaction. Escalon shook my hand with that big smile of his but I remained cool towards him. Sunday was fresh in my mind.

In May, shortly after Ostricourt, I was told of my selection for the Olympic Games at Los Angeles. Raphael, disillusioned and short of form, decided he had had enough. Most of the foreigners who had started the year with us were gone. But there was no shortage of replacements. Australians, Brits, Americans, all were 'warmly' welcomed, tried and then unceremoniously dumped. It was like a factory production line, and it struck me that in discovering a handful of stars, the club had destroyed the dreams of hundreds of amateurs whose memories of the club would be bitter and resentful. Raphael was bitter and resentful when he returned home. He had talent, a great talent, but Escalon in his ruthless ignorance had destroyed it. How many other talents had he destroyed in the same way?

Encouraged by my return to form, I decided to stick it out. On the weekend that Raphael returned to Ireland I rode a 3-day stage race in the north of France. It was my first stage race with the club. This was because of a French Federation rule that limited each club to one

29

foreign rider per team. The ACBB had up to ten foreigners to choose from and I was never considered good enough, but Ostricourt changed that. Fifth on the first stage, third on the second, I became the race leader with just a 7-kilometre time trial and an afternoon stage to go. Escalon pulled out all the strokes for the time trial. I was given a special carbon fibre bike and a one-piece racing suit for the short time trial. I was so nervous starting the test. Roche, Millar, Anderson – all had 'honoured' the ACBB in races like this one. This was my chance to join them. I blew it, and lost the jersey by four seconds. Four lousy seconds. Escalon was not angry but I knew he was thinking: 'This Irish boy hasn't got it.'

I rode some evening races in Paris shortly after. It was while returning home from one of these that I heard the news. My friend David Walsh, who was working as a freelance journalist in the city for a year, told me that Martin Earley would shortly be signing as a professional with the new Spanish team Fagor for 1985. I was stunned: Earley, my arch rival. The bastard had made it as a professional. I was more jealous than at any other time in my life.

Martin had also been picked for the Olympic Games. In July, we rode a preparation race in Colorado, the Coors Classic, and then flew on to L.A. for the Games. I found I no longer viewed Martin as a rival; he was assured of a pro contract, had escaped up the ladder. We became more friendly towards each other. A few days before the Olympic road race I remember training with him in the Hollywood hills. I told him that if I was given the opportunity I would turn professional for nothing. He said I was mad, but I argued that the ACBB had cost me all my savings and in a pro team I wouldn't have to put up with guys like Escalon.

Looking back, I can see just how naive about the professional game I was. Years later, when I was haggling with my directeur sportif Bernard Thevenet over my contract fee, I would often remember that conversation, and smile. And there were directeurs sportifs far more ruthless than Escalon. The Olympics were wonderful. I had always been sceptical about them but I must admit they were one of the highlights of my career. On the big day, I was desperately unlucky – again. I had just bridged a gap to the leading group of 20 riders when a rear wheel spoke snapped and fell out into the gear mechanism and I skidded to a halt. The 20-man group were never seen again. If only . . . if only . . . 'if', that word again, 'the nearly man' once more. I was riding much better than Martin that day and he finished 19th, the highest ever placing by an Irish cyclist at an Olympics. I was 27th.

I returned to Ireland straight after the Games for the Irish championship in Kelly's home town of Carrick on Suir. My performance at L.A. had not gone unnoticed amongst the Irish press, and they made me favourite before the race. I was obsessed with proving that bad luck had robbed me from being top Irishman at L.A. I had to win. I attacked from the start and followed every move. With one lap to go, I got clear with Eddie Madden of the Irish Road Club. Eddie was riding strongly and my efforts were starting to tell, making me a bit wary of an attack from him. But incredibly he said to me: 'Don't attack, we'll sprint it out at the finish.' I was surprised, Eddie was a hopeless sprinter – he could not have been feeling too good after all. Da drove behind the race carrying spare wheels, with my mother and Ann for company. With two miles to go he drove up alongside and reminded me of the rule forbidding the lifting of both hands from the handlebars in a victory salute. I thought: 'He's sure I will win. But what if I mess it up?' I became suddenly nervous. In the finishing sprint we both kicked at the same time and for a second I doubted but then I drew clear and won easily. Champion again.

I returned to Paris for the end-of-season classics and rode a stage race, the Tour of Seine-et-Marne. I was riding quite well, but in the time trial on the second day, Martin beat me by over two minutes and took the race lead. I made a big effort to win the last stage and thought I had it, but I was swallowed up within spitting distance of the line and finished sixth in a downpour of rain. I remember lifting my head and seeing Martin raising his arms as the race winner; I felt ill. I rode the remaining classics with little motivation or conviction and left Paris with a vague promise from Escalon that I could return the following season. I agreed to return but, in reality, wasn't sure that I wanted to.

On returning home, the gravity of my situation hit me. Should I go back for another year? Earley had made it, but had taken two years. Why not try once more? Work was impossible to find in Dublin. Raphael was also out of a job and we both signed on for the dole for a few weeks. Then a friend of ours, Michael Collins, found us two places at the government training centre, ANCO in Finglas. Michael, who was cycling mad, seemed very keen that we try again. There was no way Raphael was going back to ACBB, but I couldn't make up my mind – at least they assured you a pro contract if you performed. It was a phone call from Sean Kelly that decided things.

He was home for the winter and besides keeping himself fit, he spent his time entertaining the numerous journalists and business men who would flock to his door from the Continent in search of a story or a product endorsement. One of them was a man called Guy Mollet, who did PR for a French company, Reydel. Kelly had used Reydel saddles for two seasons and Mollet was over to negotiate a new deal. Mollet was also the president of CC Wasquehal and he wanted the Irish champion for his team for 1985. He had organised the Ostricourt race that I had won in May. At first, I hesitated and told Kelly I would be going back to the ACBB. Kelly said he was coming to Dublin in the afternoon to leave Mollet at the airport, and arranged for us to meet and talk.

Chubby, curly-haired, nine and a half fingers, Guy Mollet was a shark. He said he was great friends with Kelly's directeur sportif Jean de Gribaldy, and assured me a pro contract with him if I produced the goods. He also promised free lodgings, £150 a month to live off and attractive cash bonuses for winning. I did not have to reflect too long. ACBB had cost me £1,000 and I had never received a centime from them in prize money. Mollet was a rogue but he was a likeable rogue. We shook hands, and the deal was done.

6 GLORY DAYS

January 1985 was like January 1984, a difficult month. I noticed the change in Ann a week before leaving. She became moody and less gay, and I would often catch her with a tear in her eye, which she would quickly brush away and refuse to comment on. I knew what was upsetting her: soon I would return to France and the long winter we had passed together would be just a memory to sustain her till God knows when. I felt the pain, too, but tried not to show it. Men are not supposed to cry. Our relationship was three years old and we were totally committed to each other, but my obsession with cycling made it impossible for us to plan anything.

Wasquehal would be my last chance. I decided to stay with the club for as long as my savings would support me. Raphael and I left for France at the end of January with about £500 between us, half of what we had brought to ACBB. This time it was make it or bust. It was a weird twist of fate that turned us once more into the hands of Monsieur Wiegant. He had been overthrown at ACBB by a 'coup d'état'. Escalon was now in full control of the team. Mollet phoned Wiegant and asked him to look after the Wasquehal riders for the month's pre-season training on the Côte d'Azur, and so, for the second year on the trot, we found ourselves at the Hotel La Quiétude under the spell of the old sorcerer. He was a bit of a swine, but I respected him and felt almost sorry for him as he pined over his downfall. My form on the Côte was dismal, and I didn't get one decent placing. Mollet was getting a little impatient with us, but I promised him I would get better once I was back in the north.

We rode our first northern classic, Amiens–Beaurains, a week after returning from the training camp. With 20 kilometres to go I broke away with three others, and in the finishing sprint was narrowly beaten to the line by my Wasquehal team mate Jean François Laffile.

Mollet was delighted and kissed and hugged me in gratitude. I was pleased, he was pleased, I liked him.

The competition up north was not quite as tough as in Paris and we raced regularly, which was the big advantage. I won my first big race, the Tour of Cambresis, by out-sprinting a 7-man group in a fierce downpour. Mollet paid us regularly, and as the club won most of the races, we always had a share of the prize money, so we made enough money to live on. Raphael, too, was riding better. In May he won his first French race in the coastal town of Boulogne – I was second, and the bitter memories of Paris were effaced for us both.

I had good form in May and was probably the club's best rider for the month. Halfway through the month, I was third in a Paris–Roubaix style classic over the worst cobblestones of northern France. The morning after the race I got a phone call from Mollet.

'Bonjour Paul, c'est Guy. You are riding Bordeaux–Paris this weekend.'

(Bordeaux–Paris was 575 kilometres long, and the longest professional race in the world. Because of its savage distance, only a dozen or so professionals started the race. They lined up in Bordeaux before midnight, cycled 250 kilometres to Poitiers, were given 20 minutes for a change of clothes, and then rode the rest of the way with each rider individually paced behind a motorbike.)

'What? You must be joking.'

'No, no, it's no joke. The race organisers contacted Monsieur de Gribaldy and they want one amateur in the race, and I suggested you.'

I was a bit taken aback and wasn't sure how to respond. The race was just five days away. The pros riding would have more than a month's preparation in their legs. I had five days and would be on a hiding to nothing. Mollet and de Gribaldy could hardly criticise me if I refused to ride, but perhaps they would perceive this as a sign of weakness. And this would be a factor against me when I asked them later about a contract. I needed something to throw me into the national limelight; perhaps this was my chance. I agreed.

I trained twice behind a motorbike that week or rather, I had two 4-hour sessions behind Guy Mollet's daughter's scooter. On Friday, I flew to Bordeaux via a change of aircraft at Lyon. While waiting at Lyon, I recognised de Gribaldy and two of his riders, Dominique Garde and Eric Guyot, as they arrived in the departures hall. I was shy and preferred not to introduce myself. I let them board the aircraft before me. Monsieur de Gribaldy sat in a front row but Garde and Guyot sat at the back. There was a place vacant beside them so I sat with them. It was fun studying them from close up. The next day we would be racing back to Paris together but they hadn't a clue who I was. They read motor car magazines and half-way through the flight, Garde opened a packet of chocolate biscuits which they shared. As they munched they peered over the top of the seats towards de Gribaldy's head and giggled like school kids. I found it all very bewildering, but it was at the dinner table later, when I had introduced myself and had been accepted into the group, that I understood. De Gribaldy surveyed everything we ate. Portions of everything were small, and we were given miserable sweets. Monsieur de Gribaldy frowned at my waistline and said I would ride much better if I lost a couple of kilos. This was news to me. I had always worked on the principle that it was okay to stuff your face as long as you trained hard. But de Gribaldy's method was to train hard and starve. He had extraordinary presence, and I didn't dare argue with him.

We went out for a light spin on Saturday morning. After lunch, we were ordered to bed from two in the afternoon until eight in the evening. Lunch had been extremely light, but I had brought a bit of my mother's fruit cake. I made sure the door was locked before I cut it. I shared my room with a pro, Guy Galopin. He couldn't believe I had been told just five days earlier I was riding. He took a great liking to my mother's fruit cake.

We left Bordeaux at midnight, riding as a group through the blackness until we came to a small village just before Poitiers. Here, we changed into fresh gear, ate a little (a bit of chicken), used the toilet and then jumped back on the bikes. During the stop-over Guy took out some pills and offered me one. I looked at him suspiciously. He said they were for 'le froid'. My French had improved and I knew that 'froid', meant 'cold'. But it was really warm outside. Why the hell was he giving tablets for cold when it was 30 degrees? I took the pill and pretended to swallow it, as I did not want to offend him, but I secretly threw it in the bin.

Looking back, I realise that Guy *was* trying to help me. He had not in fact offered me anything for 'le froid', but rather something for 'le foie' (the liver). When you ride a bike race that lasts more than 17 hours, the digestive system gets completely screwed up from eating sweet things. Guy had offered me a tablet to help digestion, but naively, I had thought he was trying to give me a charge. In my suspicious mind all pills were drugs and I would never take drugs.

I was left behind with about 200 kilometres to go to Paris. Mollet followed in the team car, and each time he was sure that the race commissar was out of sight he instructed my pacer to push me. I freaked out when the pacer put his hand on my back. I told Mollet I was either getting to Paris under my own steam or getting off – a question of honour. I was a sorry sight at the finish and had to be lifted from my bike. Three pros had abandoned and I had beaten one finishing ninth out of 13 starters. I had proved my point. This was a test of courage and I passed. But the price was high. That night I had not the strength to walk up the stairs to my bedroom – I crawled on my hands and knees. The mental strain of the week was over, I felt I had made a giant step towards my contract.

In July, a stage of the Tour de France finished near Wasquehal. I went to the stage start the next day with the intention of talking to Kelly and Roche but instead ended up spending all my time with Martin Earley. He was riding in his first Tour and looked splendid in his Fagor jersey. He looked the real pro, quite unlike the scrawny amateur I had grown up with. I envied him as he rode off on the stage to Rheims. It was the first time in my life that I actually admired him for something.

Later in the month, I had my first bad argument with Guy Mollet. I had taken a complete nine day's break from competition but on the tenth day, a Sunday morning, he stormed into the house and demanded that I ride the race later that day. I shouted back at him, replying that the professional contract he had been promising me since Bordeaux–Paris was long overdue. He assured me that he would fulfil his promise, but only on condition that I raced immediately. I raced and he was happy.

At the end of July, I rode the Tour of Poland on the Irish national team. It was probably the hardest amateur stage race I ever rode. Conditions were horrible, the hotel food was tasteless – the bare minimum – and it was impossible to buy supplements. The racing was pretty savage and we took a hiding the first couple of days. On the seventh stage I broke clear at 20 kilometres with a Polish rider. He attacked me with a kilometre to go to the finish and won the stage. I was really disappointed with second place, but I learned a month later that the Pole had tested positive in dope control after the stage, and I was awarded the victory. But it wasn't the same. It was a prestigious addition to my list of victories, but I had been robbed of the pleasure of winning. The Pole had raised his hands to the huge crowd, he had milked their applause and kissed the pretty girl with the flowers. No, it wasn't the same.

From Poland I returned to France and raced the Tour of Normandy again with the national squad. Peter Crinnion was our manager. Peter was an ex-pro and had helped Stephen Roche to go to France. I respected him greatly. Before the race he pulled me aside from the others in our team group and told me I could win the Normandy. I looked at him as if he had two heads, but then asked myself: 'Why not?' It was one of the best weeks of my career. I won a stage and finished second in two others and finished fifth overall. I would undoubtedly have finished higher, but in the race's only time trial I had the incredible misfortune to puncture twice in 10 kilometres. I was flying.

I returned to Wasquehal and rode a small race that Mollet insisted I ride. A 5-man Mafia, a mix of Poles and French who toured France and split all prize money between them, were riding. Near the end of the race I broke clear in a 5-man group with two Mafia men. One of them approached me on the last lap and offered me £50 if I did not sprint. Surprised, I thought about it but told him 'No'. He increased the bid to £100. I had become a bit hungry for money, so I agreed – but it bothered me. So I thought about it: 'Mollet would probably give me a bonus if I won, and another win would do my chances of a contract no harm.' I went back to the Mafia man and told him there was no deal. He spat in disgust, and I immediately felt pressure. If I won, I would justify my argument. If I lost, I'd be £100 poorer and the laughing-stock of the Mafia. The sprint to the line was a desperately close thing, but I managed to edge him out. Mollet was delighted. He announced to the crowd at the prize ceremony that Kimmage would be riding the World Championships for Ireland one week later in Italy. But he also announced that Kimmage would soon be turning professional. I laughed, very pleased with myself, I liked winning. I had no idea that it was the last race I would ever win.

The World Amateur Championships were in Montello, Italy. Even though it was very hot, I managed to pick up a bad head cold two days before the race. We rode the circuit in training: it had a hard hill, and I liked it and felt optimistic about my chances. Poland and Normandy had given me a new confidence. On race day, I was given a great boost when a note scribbled on a piece of paper was handed to me. It said: 'Compared with all you went through in Bordeaux–Paris this will be nothing. Good Luck. Raphael.' The note gave me great heart and I started the race, tense but incredibly determined. I was content to just follow the others for the first half of the race and didn't feel too good.

To please the Irish supporters on the circuit, I attacked on the climb at half-way, but I didn't get very far and instantly regretted my foolishness. The World Championships were a gradual process of elimination. Over 200 had started, but with just one lap to go there were just 26 men in front and I was one of them. Just before we entered the finishing straight I noticed that my rear tyre was deflating ever so slowly. There was no question of changing a wheel so close to the finish, so I carried on. I started the sprint early to avoid being boxed in; the tyre was softening but holding. The Polish rider Lech Piasecki passed me like a bomb but as the line approached, no one else arrived and I thought: 'Christ I'm going to get a medal.' But then a Danish rider, Weltz, passed, then a Belgian, another Dane and an Italian, Maurizio Fondriest. I crossed the line and counted. Six. Sixth in the world. The sixth best amateur in the whole fucking world. I was overjoyed. It was the summit of my career.

I watched the pros ride next day. I visited the pits after the race and received congratulations from Roche, Kelly and Earley. Kelly was the last to leave for his hotel. A man of few words, he turned to me just before getting into the team car, and said, 'De Gribaldy will be talking to you.' This was music to my ears and I returned to Wasquehal a happy man. I met 'de Gri' on the eve of the pro-am classic, the Grand Prix d'Isbergues, at the small hotel where his team were staying. He made me wait for half an hour but then sat down beside me at a table in the bar. He looked at me and said I would have to lose some weight and then asked me some details, including my age. I had expected him to produce a contract for me to sign and had already decided I would not sign for less than £600 a month – de Gri was a notoriously bad payer. But he produced no contract and made no promises. He just said we would meet again after the race which I was riding with the Irish national team. Three-quarters of the way through the race I was following French pro Jacques Bossis down a narrow gravel-lined descent. There was a sharp right-hand bend at the bottom, and I failed to round it and ran off the road. The front wheel dropped into a sharp dip in the ditch, throwing me over the handlebars, and I landed face down at the edge of the road. I don't remember much, just the pain from my back and left wrist and the sensation that someone had kicked my lips in. I spent five days in hospital in Béthune with a fractured vertebra and left wrist. I had expected de Gri to call at the hospital with my contract, but he never came. I left the hospital dejected. Raphael packed my things and we returned to Ireland – to wait.

The phone rang six weeks later. It was Mollet. He was sending me a professional contract with a new French team, RMO. I would be paid

£700 a month and the contract was for two years. I put the phone down and danced a jig of joy. The struggling was over. All the sacrifices had paid off. I had made it.

7 BRAND NEW ANORAK

The first meeting took place at a ski station at Grand Bornand, on the slopes of the Col de Colombier. RMO, a firm specialising in temporary employment, gathered together the eighteen cyclists who would wear their colours in the professional 'peloton' for 1986. It was a mixed bunch of old-timers, established names and new pros. There were four new pros taken on. Two, Jean Louis Peillon and Bruno Huger, were French. Per Pedersen was Danish and I was Irish. It was hard for Pedersen and me to integrate. He spoke no French, and shyness prevented me from using the bit that I knew. I spoke only when I was spoken to and tried to smile as much as possible. I wanted desperately to be accepted. I felt so awkward, so out of place, just like the first day in school.

In the mornings we would do cross-country skiing. I had never skied before and spent the whole week slipping on my arse. This helped my integration, as I was a source of constant amusement to the suave French, who had learned to ski in childhood. I tried to fall as little as possible, not because I was afraid of getting laughed at. No, because it was excruciatingly painful. The vertebra I had broken while riding my last amateur race three months earlier had not quite healed. No one knew I had cracked vertebrae, and I wasn't telling them. I had fought all my life for this pro contract and I feared that the revelation of a back problem might discourage my new sponsor from employing me. So I said nothing and secretly skied with a steel corset strapped to my back for support. In the afternoons we were free to do what we pleased. The French lads invited me for football, but fearing for my back I hired a mountain bike and cycled to the top of the Colombier alone. I had never seen such an enormous climb and was so overawed by the view that I wandered off the road and plunged down a sharp incline and went over the bars, landing on the steel corset. I went numb with pain. Picking myself up, I quickly descended the Col and took refuge in a small tea room in the village.

I was half-way through a 'brioche chaude' when one of the French guys came in. I tried to hide, as I was enjoying my solitude and was in no humour for making small talk; but he saw me and sat at my table. He ordered a cake and coffee and we chatted amiably. He liked the ambience in the team and said the absence of real stars would mean we would get on so much better. He paid for both of us, and as he walked out the door I tried to put a name to his face. It was Chappuis – André Chappuis. I immediately took a shine to him.

The evenings were taken up with team talks. Bernard Thevenet our team manager, or directeur sportif, gathered us round after dinner, and explained the early season programme of racing, ironing out any problems we had. I never had any problems. As far as I was concerned, it was all a game of survival. Two years spent as an amateur in France had taught me to keep my mouth closed and my ears open and to pedal as quickly as I could. I decided to adopt the same tactics as a professional, at least until I understood what it was all about.

After the meetings we were free to do as we pleased. The French played cards among themselves, I chatted with Pedersen and, without realising it, two clans were formed. I returned to Dublin on December 23 with a jersey, a bag and a red anorak, all adorned with my sponsors' logo, RMO. I didn't dare ask them for the travelling expenses of the trip. I was afraid they might change their mind about hiring me – so desperately naive. But I was a pro. The bag, the jersey and the red anorak said so. I wore them whenever the occasion presented itself, it was my way of saying: 'Look at me, I'm a pro, I've made it.'

This was my first mistake.

8 SHATTERED DREAMS

January was spent in Ireland, preparing. The broken wrist and vertebrae had left me immobile for most of the winter and as a result my physical condition suffered. I trained most weekends with my brothers, Raphael and Kevin, and I was a little concerned as both were riding more strongly then me. I trained twice with Martin Earley and Stephen Roche. Stephen had ridden with five of my team mates, Gauthier, Claveyrolat, Le Bigaut, Simon and Vermote, the year before on the La Redoute team. He recommended Jean Louis Gauthier as the most dependable, and praised him as being one of the best 'domestiques' he had ever had. I made a mental note of this; for Stephen, a perfectionist who demanded perfection from everyone around him, did not distribute praise for others easily. This Gauthier must really be good.

We talked of other things, of drugs. I was worried about the job I was going into. I had heard so many stories of professional cyclists taking drugs and was frightened that they might all be true. Now that I was a professional I felt I had the right to ask Stephen to enlighten me on the subject. He talked first of our two 'soigneurs'. The verb 'soigner' means 'to treat' or 'to take care of'. A soigneur takes care of his riders by massaging their legs, listening to their problems, dressing wounds and giving vitamins and minerals. Stephen had worked with Claude Wery and Emile Thiery at La Redoute. He said that Claude was a bit lazy, and that he preferred Emile and told me he would have a word with Emile to take me under his wing. He told me that professional cycling was not like amateur cycling – one had to take care of oneself. The racing was so hard and frequent that it was important to keep up the vitamin and mineral level in the body, and to do this vitamin B_6 and B_{12} injections during the season were a necessity. I said nothing and just nodded my head, but inside I was horrified. In my mind a syringe was drugs, and to have to take injections meant having to take drugs. I returned home and talked to my father about my fears. He told me to just do the best that I could without getting caught up in it, and I put it out of my mind.

On Tuesday February 4 I made my professional debut at the Etoile de Bessèges stage race in the south of France. I arrived late the night before and was handed a new bike and all my equipment on the morning of the race. I was also handed my wages for January, a cheque for £600. I was shitting bricks before the start. The bike was all wrong, but there was no time to change and I raced the 100 kilometres feeling like an alien. It was strange to be riding alongside Fignon and Zootemelk. The previous five years I had been a star, a top amateur, recognised and admired. Now I was just another one in the bunch. Everything I had ever done now meant nothing and I was starting all over again at the bottom of the ladder. My two worries were crashing and bringing a star off and getting dropped, and I managed to avoid both.

Later in the evening I bumped into my team mate Regis Simon while taking a leak in the bathroom. He was bent over the bathroom sink scrubbing the jersey and shorts made filthy by the wet roads earlier in the day. I almost laughed and asked him why he was washing his clothes by hand. 'Why, who else will wash them for me?' was his reply. I had always thought the gear would be washed for us – but no, we had to scrub it and dry it ourselves and I borrowed his washing powder and set to work. It was the hardest part of the day.

Bessèges, being the first stage race of the year, was not too hard, and I managed to finish in the bunch most days. It felt great to be encouraged in the time trial by Thevenet, a double Tour de France winner, whose photograph had adorned my bedroom wall when I was a child. The only real problem was the bitterly cold weather. The team rode well; Per was riding really strongly, and he took the race lead with one day to go. It would have been great publicity for a new team, RMO, to win the first race of the season; but his advance was slim and that night Thevenet was forced to telephone the other directeurs sportifs to try to do a deal. The idea was to offer money to a rival team, who did not have a man well placed overall, in return for help to defend a jersey. If the team accepted, then for the following stage RMO would defend the lead alone until they could no longer control it, and then it was time for the others to earn their money. This was no surprise for me, for as an amateur I had ridden stage races and seen leaders in trouble with no team mates to control things, only for a rival team suddenly to intervene and restore order. I suppose it was just good business sense, for if there was one thing I was learning it was that pro cycling was a business. Before each race we were told how much of a bonus we would receive from the sponsor for winning, and how much of this bonus we could use to negotiate with other riders if we got into a winning position near the end of a race.

All of our rival French teams had men well placed for overall victory and none were interested in doing a deal. The next option was to approach a Belgian or Dutch team, but this was dismissed. The Belgians, and especially the Dutch, were real mercenary bastards. They would do the job, but the price was always very high and for a small race like Bessèges it was not worth it. So the pressure was on us to defend Per's lead alone. I did what I could, but it was bitterly cold and I could not feel my legs at all. My drinking bottle froze solid and I abandoned the race when I was dropped, with 40 kilometres to go. Per lost the lead but wasn't too disappointed, for it was a great debut for a new pro.

The Tour of the Mediterranean was next. This was limited to eight riders per team and I was surprised when Thevenet announced the selection as I did not think I was worth my place on my Bessèges form. I wasn't; it was just the fact that Pedersen was riding so well. He spoke no French and Thevenet little English, so I was brought along as interpreter. It was during the Med that my problems really started. I was four kilos overweight and, as a result, suffering like a dog on the climbs. But I still managed to hang on, only to be left behind on the descents. The memory of my crash at Isbergues was still fresh in my mind and it scared me. I had lost my bottle. I wasn't too bad in the dry, but in the wet I was a complete disaster and I had to endure the insults from other riders as I let huge gaps open up and they were forced to come around me and close them. This depressed me, and my morale was really bad after two stages of being left behind. On the night after the second stage Thevenet came into my room and asked me what my problem was. I explained to him about the crash, expecting to receive a bit of a bollocking. But no, he was kind and understanding. He too had had the same problem during his career, and he told me to relax more and it would sort itself out. He demanded more participation from me in helping the team. 'In professional races, the individual does not matter, it is the team that counts. This is now your job, so each time you race you must try and make some sort of contribution to the team. The best way is to win races but this is not always possible so you must contribute in other ways. It may be only a small thing like fetching a bottle or waiting for a colleague who has punctured; but it's important, for at the end of the day you can get off your bike and say, 'yes I did my work today.' His talk worked wonders on me and from the next day I was riding much better.

It was strange, therefore, to get told off on a day when I felt I had made my biggest contribution. It was on the fourth stage, to Marseilles. I was prominent in two early breakaway attempts and then, as we were caught, another group got away with two of our riders Regis Simon and Pierre Le Bigaut. I sat back in the bunch, delighted to have men in the front and the pressure off but suddenly Thevenet came up in the team car and shouted that he was tired of seeing me at the back and that I was to move to the front to hinder the chasing attempts immediately. Our lads were eventually caught and that night I was given my first official bollocking. I was a bit pissed off, but had to accept it. I became aware of the need not only to be at the front but to be seen to be at the front. It was another lesson learnt.

Two days after the Med we raced a single day-race, Nice–Alassio. I was knackered after the Med, and asked Thevenet for a day off, but he told me to start, and to abandon if I felt too tired. I met Jean de Gribaldy before the start and he told me I was carrying five kilograms of extra weight and explained what a terrible handicap this was. I nodded in acceptance but inwardly was puzzled. As an amateur I had also worked on the principle that you could eat what you wanted as long as you raced and trained hard. But these pros were so skinny and bony and almost sick-looking, and they managed to pedal at unbelievable speeds. I was confused. The race was a disaster for us and the whole team abandoned. Thevenet was angry, but accepted the excuses given to him from the experienced campaigners Gauthier and Le Bigaut that the Med had been especially hard and we were all a little tired. But next day, some smart-arse journalist from *L'Equipe* wrote that not a single rider from the RMO team had made it to Alasio, and that Bernard Thevenet was still out looking for us. This brought an angry response from the team sponsors, who sent a telegram from head office: 'We are not in this business to be laughed at.' Monsieur Braillon, 'Mr RMO', expressed his displeasure at his team's performance to date, and suggested an immediate improvement was imperative and that the next race, the Tour of Haut Var, was a good place to start. This annoyed us greatly, for the opening races were viewed by all as preparation races, and to be criticised by the sponsor after not even three weeks' competition was unfair.

I rode well in the Haut Var, finishing about 25th, but was really tired after it. That night Emile called me for massage, and as I entered he was giving an injection to the Brazilian rider Ribeiro. He said it was just vitamins and suggested I take one to help me recover. I declined, explaining that I never took injections and he seemed surprised but did not insist. The following day we raced the Grand Prix of Cannes and I was totally shagged. I stopped after a hundred kilometres and climbed into the soigneurs' car at the feed. They did not say anything, but had 'I told you so' written all over their faces. I sat in the back and thought about it. My principle was that if the body was tired you gave it rest, not vitamins, and I was sure I'd be fine after a day's rest. That night, the team split up, with the riders allowed home for the first time in a month. I had no fixed address in France, but Guy Mollet had offered to let me use a house in Wasquehal where he was going to lodge the foreign amateurs in his team. I felt quite ill before getting on the plane, and the assistant 'directeur sportif' Jean Claude Vallaeys, who lived in Lille, gave me two Alka-Seltzers. Emile, who was also travelling on the same flight, suggested it was a problem with my liver – that I had not looked after myself and that this was the result. He produced two small pills to help my liver, and I pretended to take them. Half an hour later I told him I was feeling better, which seemed to please him. I did not want to hurt his feelings, for I knew he was only trying to help; but I just didn't trust him and was suspicious of anything he gave me.

After the glory of racing with the team for the month of February, Wasquehal was an unpleasant shock to the system. I entered the house and it was totally empty. There was just a bed. No cups or saucers or anything, just a bed. I instantly regretted having come here. The Brazilian was lodged by the team at Grenoble. I had never been there but was told it was a beautiful city that sat at the foot of the Alps. It appealed to me greatly, but I had finally chosen Wasquehal, whose greyness and Coronation Street decor I was familiar with, having spent a year there as an amateur.

I was not picked to ride in the Paris–Nice, but I did not mind as I knew the pressure for results would be high. Instead I was selected for Het Volk, the one-day Belgian classic. I had hated Belgium as an amateur. Too much wind and rain and cobbles and flat roads. I dreaded the thought of Het Volk. We stayed at a hotel at Moeskron on the eve of the race, and as I was going to bed I noticed it had started to snow. I prayed that night that it would lash down, and my prayers were answered: for the next day the roads were smothered with it and the race was cancelled. I returned to the emptiness of the flat. I had not trained for two days, and it would probably be another two before I got out. As a result my physical condition would drop, and this would make the next race even harder. I realised it would have been better to have raced, and regretted the cancellation. Twenty-four hours earlier I had prayed for snow. It had snowed and I was now sorry. This did not make sense.

The house filled up during the week, when some Kas riders arrived. Kas was de Gribaldy's team, and he had sent three of his riders to Wasquehal to ride in some Belgian races to be held during Paris–Nice. The weather for the first race was dreadful, and I abandoned after being dropped quite early. The second race was a 'kermesse' race, or circuit race, at Ostend. It was cold, sunny and windy. Former cycling 'great' Freddy Maertens was riding and I could not help noticing what a pathetic sight he was as he took his place on the start grid. He had had it all, this man. It was rumoured he had lost everything through poor investment and that he was penniless and forced to get back on the bike after years in retirement. The race started, and we took off like rockets. The fast start surprised me and I was immediately in trouble. Slipping down through the bunch I had almost reached the end of it, going into this corner, when Maertens came up on my inside and nearly lifted me out of it with his elbow. I lost a length, two lengths and was dropped. This was the final straw: to be dropped after six miles was too much to take, and I abandoned and told myself I was finished. I phoned home to my parents' house to talk about my problems. They did not really understand. How could I be disheartened about something I had dreamed all my life of achieving?

The three Kas boys were kind. One of them, Jacques Decrion, offered to take me to his house in Besançon, where I could train with him in the mountains and get my morale back. We rode one more race in Belgium, which I managed to finish and I left for Besançon with the three lads. I stayed with Jacques for five days, and then we all left for a race near Nantes at Mauleon, where I was to pick up my team. On arriving at Mauleon I got out of the car with my suitcase, brief-case and bicycle. On seeing me arrive at the hotel my team mates started laughing at my brief case. 'Ah, Paul, the brief-case, you're a real warrior all right.' I hadn't got a clue what they were talking about. On visiting the riders' rooms that night I noticed that many had briefcases. But whereas mine contained my passport and letters and writing materials, theirs contained pills, syringes and little bottles of liquids of every colour and shape. 'So that's what they were laughing at, they thought my brief-case was full of pills. They thought I was a fucking junkie. Jesus, I am guilty without even a trial.' I was shocked, and decided to leave my brief-case open in my room so that any passers-by would notice it contained papers and pens, and wasn't a medical cabinet. Not all of the riders had brief-cases. André 'Dede' (pronounced 'deaday') Chappuis used to store his gear in an old shoebox he hid in his suitcase.

I asked about the contents and Dede went through the various boxes and pills, explaining what each was for. There were pills for avoiding cramp, for cleaning out the liver, vitamins, caffeine tablets, salts, minerals and small glass tubes of a white liquid he laughed and joked about. He said it was 'du peau' ('skin') a slang word for pervitine. 'Ton ton,' 'tan tan', slang words for tonedron. I hadn't a clue what he was talking about, and my ignorance seemed to make him laugh even harder. 'Amphétamines.' This I did understand. 'But what about the controls?' I asked. 'There are never any controls at Mauleon,' he replied. This point was validated later that evening at the team meeting by Vallaeys, who was looking after us in Thevenet's absence. There were grins all around the room and we left. Vallaeys did not directly encourage us to charge up for the next day, but in reminding us that we were professionals he was giving us the green light. This was worrying.

The peloton was unusually jolly at the start next morning. In the opening kilometres where the atmosphere was relaxed and jovial I noticed a new game being played. Riders were going around and putting their hands in the back pockets of other riders' jerseys. To me it didn't seem all that funny, but they seemed to be finding it hilarious. It was explained to me that the rider who was prepared to inject himself with amphetamines had to do so two to two and a half hours from the finish. A normal bike race lasted six to seven hours so it was necessary to carry the amphetamine for three to four hours before using it. It could be taken in tablet form or through injection. Tablet was handy, as it could be carried and taken discreetly; but because it had to pass through the stomach, the effects were slower and not as good. Injection straight into the muscle gave almost instant reaction and was much stronger, but it was a bit awkward as this meant transporting a syringe for most of the race. For transport, the syringe first had to be doctored. It was cut just above the piston that pushed out the liquid and a plastic cap was placed over the needle. Then it was placed in a metal tube, usually a vitamin tube, and a piece of cotton wool pressed in on top to protect it from vibration. The tube was then placed among the fruit cake and other race food in the rider's jersey pocket until the time for consumption arrived.

As we rode out of Mauleon the game was to see who had the tube and who hadn't. From the sound of the guffaws and ha-ha's it became clear to me that quite a few tubes had been found. This was very disheartening. What chance had I against guys riding on amphetamines? At the time I looked on them as cheaters, and as I had always despised cheating I couldn't understand how they could be happy winning, knowing they had taken a stimulant to do so. Try as I might, I could not catch anyone actually taking the stuff, and was still convinced I could not do anything, so I was content to finish in the bunch.

Because I lived in Wasquehal, 15 kilometres from the border, Thevenet assumed that I liked racing in Belgium. I was, therefore, a natural choice to dispute the one-day classics that were now imminent. The Tour of Flanders was the first. I raced the first 150 kilometres trying my hardest to get out of the bunch before we reached the series of cobbled climbs near the end, where the race would be blown apart. I tried, but to no avail, and I was forced to remain in the bunch until the approach to the first climb. Twenty kilometres before it the pace started hotting up. Thevenet had told us that unless we were at the front going into the first cobbles then we could forget about it. But the only problem was that every rider in the bunch had been told the same thing by their respective directeurs sportifs, and the result was absolute mayhem. There was pushing, shoving and shoulder rubbing at 40 miles an hour on narrow roads full of holes and other hidden traps such as raised shore covers and ridges. I suddenly realised that all it took was for one rider to fall in this speeding packed bunch and he would bring fifty per cent of the others with him. I chickened out of trying to stay in the front, and slipped down to the back, where it was much more sociable. I knew that our team car had had a bad draw, and that Thevenet was seventeen cars behind and so could not possibly see the tail of the field and therefore was unaware of my presence there. I was soon dropped, and I abandoned after just a hundred and fifty kilometres.

Ghent–Wevelgem was next. The difficulties of this are the cross winds which blow in from the sea when the race hugs the coastline between Zeebrugge and De Panne. On a cold Wednesday morning the winds were of gale force, blowing sand all over the road as the bunch split into ten large groups on the seafront. I was in about the seventh group but then slipped back to the eighth, the ninth and the tenth.

Questioning the point of this madness, I lost contact and was passed by the different team cars. Thevenet drove alongside but it was Vallaeys who rolled down the window. 'What's the problem?', he asked. Now, with the bunch in ten groups and bodies literally everywhere, it seemed perfectly obvious to me what the problem was; but just as I was about to answer another gust of wind blew sand across the road and into his face, blinding him. He quickly rolled up the window without waiting any longer for a reply and I laughed to myself: 'I think he got the message.'

Jean Claude Vallaeys was not liked among the riders, which made his job of assistant directeur sportif very difficult. His problem was that he had never raced and so did not command the same respect from us as Thevenet, who had won the Tour de France twice. Vallaeys had been secretary of the La Redoute team and at paper work and organisation he was very efficient, but we didn't think he had a clue about pro cycling. How were we supposed to take orders from a man who chain-smoked, and ate like there was no tomorrow? I didn't like him; I found him false and insincere. He often made fun of my efforts to speak French, which I would have accepted if he spoke English – but he hadn't a word. It was a mystery to me how a guy like Vallaeys could be at the head of a professional cycling team.

Two days after Ghent I abandoned the Grand Prix Pino Cerami in Belgium. It was a vicious circle. I needed a stage race to build up strength for the classics. But as I had not ridden Paris–Nice I was unprepared for these savage one-day events and was unable to ride much further then half-way in most of them. In between races we stayed at a hotel in Moeskron, where they served the most gigantic juicy steaks, and we ate like kings; but we raced like juniors, and the result was that my condition deteriorated instead of improving. There was also the mental side of it. Not finishing races was a bad habit that was becoming addictive. When it snowed or rained or was freezing cold, as it often was for the classics, it was all too easy to abandon the bike for the warmth of the soigneurs' car. Once in the car the remorse would start. The self-analysis that led to deep depression. Finishing races installed confidence and self-respect. Abandoning destroyed both.

Two days after Cerami we drove to Compeigne for Paris–Roubaix. The weather was atrocious, and I wondered if the race would be cancelled as it was snowing heavily as we went to bed. The La Vie Claire team were staying in the same hotel and during the night one of their new professionals, the American Thurlow Rogers, left his room and the hotel without saying a word. The next day the story was that he had cracked mentally and was returning to the States. The hardened Europeans found this very amusing but I understood how he felt and often considered doing the same. On this cold, wet morning it was easy to make such decisions. It was snowing in Compeigne when we rode out of the cobbled square and I knew there was no way I was going to make it to Roubaix. The tactic was simple: try to get the hell out of the bunch before crossing the first 'pave'. I attacked several times in the first hundred kilometres without success and as we approached the first pave, the pace shot up as the big guns moved to the front, while the small fry like myself slipped to the back. I bumped into Kelly. He was on the way up and I on the way down. For him the race was now starting; for me it was over. The enormous gap in our abilities became apparent to me.

There was a huge crash just before the first section, and I fell off without hurting myself. I met Dede at the bottom of the tangled mess and he had lumps out of him so I waited and we chased together. At the exit of the first pave we were seven minutes behind the leaders and we abandoned almost immediately. We climbed into the broom wagon and were brought to the showers, where I washed and changed in time to see 'King Kelly' win his second Paris–Roubaix.

It was obvious to me that drastic action was needed to climb out of the pit into which I had fallen. Thevenet was not pleased with my performances, and after a long discussion I told him I wanted to leave Wasquehal and move to Grenoble. The head office of RMO was based in the Alpine town, and five of the team's cyclists lived in the region. The only problem would be a place to stay. RMO sponsored the Grenoble football team and also a training centre for its apprentices. Thevenet rang the centre and they agreed to lodge me until I could find an apartment. The thought of getting out of Wasquehal worked wonders on me. A week after Paris–Roubaix we rode Liège–Bastogne–Liège. In freezing cold rain, Bruno Huger and I were the only two riders to finish from our team. Only sixty riders finished, and Thevenet praised me for my courage – and it was the first good word he had for me in a month. Not that I blamed him, for I had abandoned seven races on the trot but I felt sure the run was at an end. For finishing 48th I managed to get my name in *L'Equipe*. This may seem a trivial thing, but it was quite important. Monsieur Braillon would buy the sports daily every morning and scrutinise the results to find where his men had finished. By having my name in print, I proved to him that I did in fact exist, which would make it easier for him to sign my pay cheque at the end of each month.

Grenoble was sunny, bright and beautiful. From the first glimpse of the city I knew I had made the right decision. Things would now get better, and I felt the page had turned.

9 GRENOBLE

In life, I like to think that I am a survivor. I've always had good survival instincts. Moving from Lille to Grenoble was not just a matter of a change of scenery: it was essential for survival. The two months spent at Wasquehal had given me time to analyse my situation. Because I lived so close to Belgium, they thought I liked racing there. I hated it. By living so close to Vallaeys, I was under his thumb, one of his boys. I didn't like him; and worse, he knew I disliked him, so it seemed to me he was never going to do me any favours. I had to get out. 'Go south, young man.'

Grenoble was the hub of the team. The firm's headquarters, the team's headquarters, the decision-making, all were here. France is a huge country. The flight time from Lille to Grenoble is the same as between Paris to Dublin. So to Thevenet it was all the same if I lived in Dublin or Lille; either way, I was a foreigner. Now, if I were a foreigner like Stephen Roche or Sean Kelly and could pedal my bike faster than anyone else in the world, then my sponsor and directeur would bend over backwards to please me, no matter where I lived. But being Paul Kimmage was different. I knew that once my two-year contract was terminated they would look at me and say, 'Well, Kimmage is Irish but he's not Roche or Kelly; he's an ordinary solid pro but why bother hiring a foreigner when we can hire a hundred Frenchmen with the same ability?' I knew this would happen, so I had to get close to them. Living in Grenoble would enable me to keep my finger on the pulse of all that was happening in the team. I had to integrate as much as possible, make them forget that I was Irish. I told them I loved France and especially Grenoble and that I was going to remain here long after my career was finished.

This wasn't a complete lie. I did like the region, and as I knew that there would be very few job opportunities in Ireland for a not too famous ex-professional cyclist, there was a good chance that I would stay on. But still, I must admit to playing the role of Uriah Heep quite well. I should have been given an Oscar.

It worked. I had only spent two days in the city when a man from the company invited me for dinner in his house. Marc Mingat worked in the firm's public relations department and was ideally placed to fill me in on Marc Braillon's moods and humours. Mingat would give me the feedback on Braillon's meetings with Thevenet, so that I always knew the temperature of the water before taking a bath. I was invited to assist at the openings of any new company offices in the area. Braillon would be present at these, and I always made sure I was well dressed without being flashy. Braillon didn't like anyone too flashy. It was rumoured that one day Braillon was looking out the window of his office, and saw one of his employees arrive in a huge, flashy car – he fired him. Braillon himself drove a Mercedes 300 but it was a drab mustard colour; it was classy but not extravagant, and he expected his employees to follow suit. There was one golden rule never to be broken: in our interviews with the press we were to talk not so much of the company but of the company chief. We were to talk not of RMO but of Marc Braillon.

I shared a room at the football club with the Brazilian Mauro Ribeiro. Mauro was, like myself, a new professional. He spoke excellent French but with a very heavy Latin American accent. By moving to Grenoble at the start of the year he got to know the other French riders in the area much better than I. But this was a double-sided knife, for they also got to know him. He wasn't liked. I learnt this from Thierry Claveyrolat and Patrick Clerc. Thierry was a former team mate of Stephen Roche's at La Redoute. He lived in the village of Vizille, twelve kilometres outside Grenoble. Patrick had raced with Sean Kelly at Sem; he lived at Brignoud, north of the city. Both had trained regularly and had travelled to races with Ribeiro since the start of the season. They had a nickname for him: 'Sent la Merde' ('Smells of Shit'). This was because one day he had not turned up for a training ride at the appointed hour, so they had cycled to the football centre to find him. When they entered his room he was just getting out of bed and there was a strong, nasty smell in the air. They also complained he was a miser, always the last to put his hand in his pocket when it came to paying for coffee on the way to a race. When I told them I was sharing a room with him they gave me an awful slagging. I refused to criticise Ribeiro in front of them at first. I believed in giving him a fair trial before making my judgment, but I must admit to being influenced by their revelations – so I'm not sure if his trial was all that fair. It's the old story about the boy in school who forgets to change his underpants one day and gets branded by the class 'mouth' as smelly. And for the rest of the year it's not Tony Bryne, but Smelly Bryne; it's not Jimmy Murphy, but Smelly Murphy. And it's totally unfair, but few of his classmates will defend him against the class mouth. And so it was that Ribeiro became 'Sent la Merde'.

I didn't find him smelly but I did not tell 'Clavet' or Patrick so. I was a new kid in town, and I needed desperately to be accepted. It was vital to my survival. If I told them they were wrong about Ribeiro maybe they would stick the name on me, 'Smells of Shit Kimmage'. Jesus, no, not that – so I joined in their criticisms of my room mate. I didn't like him, anyway. When I saw him taking a vitamin injection after the Haut Var race in February, I instantly branded him as a junkie – although this was most unfair. The two lads were right about one thing: he was unbelievably tight with money. Because he never spent much, I presumed he didn't have much. Because I was a better rider than he was, I was sure I earned more than him, and so I was always prepared to put my hand in my pocket first when it came to buying papers, cakes and coffee. But I was wrong.

I learnt this in a conversation with Marc Mingat. Marc informed me that Ribeiro was paid £500 a month more than I was and had two return flights to Brazil paid for by Braillon each year. Braillon had an office in Rio de Janeiro and it was good PR to have a Brazilian on the team, so when Ribeiro came on the market he was snapped up. This revelation turned me completely against Ribeiro, and I told the others the news – which turned them against him also. This was a mistake, and very petty of me, but survival was the name of the game and the revelation would gain me some extra points.

A week after moving to Grenoble we flew to Holland for the Amstel Gold Race. It was a bit like Liége–Bastogne–Liége and I rode really well and finished as the top rider on the team, placed 21st. Two important stage races were approaching, the 'Quatre Jours de Dunkirk' and the 'Tour de Romandie'. I knew I was starting to find good form and I desperately wanted to ride in the Romandie. Dunkirk would be cobbles and cross-winds and I knew I would be much more suited to the hard climbs and more sheltered roads of Switzerland. In stage races, teams were limited in the number of riders they could engage. At Dunkirk it was eight. At Romandie it was six. There were eighteen riders on the team, but places for only fourteen, which meant four would remain at home without racing. Not racing meant having to train each day alone. There was no way of simulating racing, so inevitably the rider's condition would drop, making it hard for him to impress when he raced again. I didn't want to ride in Dunkirk but it was better than being at home. Thevenet explained he was sending all his pure climbers to Switzerland and that I should be grateful to ride in Dunkirk, as four riders would ride in neither race. I wanted to argue that I was a pure climber, for I felt I was, but decided to say nothing. Dunkirk was better than nothing.

I rode poorly all week except for the last day, when we had a hilly circuit race around the town of Cassel. Here, I was given instructions to go up the climb as hard as possible. My team mate Regis Simon was lying second overall to the Belgian Dirk de Wolf and we thought the heavily built Flamand might crack on the steep but short slopes of Cassel. I gave it everything I had and split the bunch to bits, but we could not get rid of De Wolf, and Regis finished second.

A week later we were in Bordeaux for the marathon 585-kilometre Bordeaux–Paris. On the morning of the race we went out for a light spin in the vineyards. Wine didn't mean too much to me at the time, and the team leader Bernard Vallet couldn't believe my lack of enthusiasm as we rode through Margaux and some of the best and most expensive wine châteaux in the world. His excitement about wine amused me. Back in Ireland, wine was what the priest poured into the chalice every Sunday. Guinness, now, that was a real drink. I couldn't understand this Frenchman nearly bursting into tears about us riding around a few fancy houses and fields of grapes. But his passion was obviously real, and in an effort to impress on me the value of the vineyards he said, 'Polo,' (this was my nickname) 'if you owned forty feet of that land you would never have to throw your leg over a bike again.' At lunchtime he ordered a good bottle of red which I found no more than OK, but from that day I started to take an interest and now, four years on I am a wine fanatic. Margaux, Rothschild and Yquem are châteaux cherished, although the outrageous prices mean they are infrequently sipped, in our house, and I now understand Vallet's emotion on that day.

Bernard Vallet had prepared especially for Bordeaux–Paris and at the team meeting two hours before the race, Thevenet insisted that all our efforts were to be directed towards helping him. We raced out of Bordeaux in the black of night, each rider with a set of front and back lamps. Visibility was a problem, and eyes were strained to distance oneself properly from the wheel in front. The crack was good though, some of the lads would turn off their lamps and try to sneak off without being seen. It is a bastard of a race. I started to fall asleep on the bike at around seven next morning when we had ridden 300 kilometres. It seems an exaggeration, but it's not. My eyelids were so desperately heavy and my head would keep falling forward, until I would realise what was happening and wake up. Caffeine tablets would have been the answer but as I was 'pure', and regarded this as doping, it was out of the question. So I fought back the z's and the danger of crashing. An important break developed near the end of the race with just Patrick Clerc from our team present. Thevenet ordered Dede and me to the front to chase it down. We had to ride our eyeballs out to bring it back, but we did; and then a fresh attack developed but this time with Vallet present. Dede and I were dropped 30 kilometres from Paris, and we immediately got into the team cars. As an amateur the objective had been to finish. As a professional it was to win, or help someone else to win. Our work was done and there was nothing to be gained in struggling on to Paris. To say I was tired was an understatement. I had been in the team car two minutes when I fell asleep. I showered and we got a taxi to the airport, where I slept again. I slept on the flight to Grenoble, in the taxi to the football club, and as soon as I arrived I went straight to bed. My fascination with Bordeaux–Paris was now over and it was definitely a case of never again.

The 'Dauphine Libérée' stage race was fast approaching. Nine days long and with stages climbing some of the biggest mountains in the Alps it is the second biggest stage race in the country after the Tour. But because it took place in RMO's back garden, i.e. in the Grenoble region, it was equally important to our beloved sponsor. This was the reason Thevenet gave for leaving me out of the team. He wanted the best nine possible and I was no higher than twelfth on the team ladder. I accepted the decision, and prepared myself to ride the Tour de l'Oise, a short three-day event, taking place at the same time. A week before the Dauphine, Thevenet organised a training run over one of the Alpine stages and invited me along. It was my first opportunity to attempt the really big climbs, and I was excited about discovering what until then had only been photographs on a bedroom wall. Thierry Claveyrolat was the team's best climber, but I managed to stay with him almost to the top on three of the mountains, and he was surprised I was climbing so well. Two days later, one of the selections, the veteran Jean Louis Gauthier, pulled out of the team, leaving a place vacant. Thevenet had heard that I had climbed well in the training run against Claveyrolat and he offered me the berth.

The race started with a prologue time trial on the shores of the beautiful lake at Annecy then moved across to Lyon, St Etienne and then back across to Chambéry, Albertville and Grenoble. On the third stage to St Etienne, Thierry Claveyrolat outsprinted Laurent Fignon for a prestigious stage victory. By winning a stage, Thierry had saved the team's honour on its home ground. The pressure was now off, and we could enjoy things just a little bit more. A plan was drawn up for the following stage to Charavines, where we reckoned our sprinter Francis Castaing had a good chance. Castaing was perfectly led out by Regis Simon, Vincent Barteau and Pierre Le Bigaut and looked set for the win, but then the La Vie Claire sprinter Jean Francois Rault moved up on his shoulder. Sensing Rault's presence, Castaing moved across, pushing the Breton into the barriers, but Rault, quite rightly, refused to be intimidated and stuck his elbow into Castaing to protect himself. Castaing insisted, and they both crashed at 40 miles an hour. Le Bigaut, Simon and Barteau could not avoid the two bodies sprawled across the road and they fell also. That night, Castaing was heavily criticised for his unprofessional behaviour. Le Bigaut and Barteau were knocked out and missed the remainder of the race. In endangering the lives of his team mates Castaing had committed a professional fault.

I was riding very well and was lying 17th after the first mountain stage to Chambery but I cracked badly on the third climb on the following day and slipped to 34th. I cracked completely on the last mountain stage from Grenoble to Puy St Vincent, but no one noticed too much; for Thierry won the stage, and Thevenet waited patiently for the forty minutes it took me to finish. He patted me on the back, and then brought me to the medical caravan – I had been picked for a dope control. The seven hour stage in the hot sun had left me dehydrated, and I found it difficult to piss. But there was beer and water present, and after a fifteen-minute delay I felt the urge. I was given a clear glass flask and told to strip. The prying eyes of the commissar surveyed me as I tried to piss, and at first this irritated me. Then I tried not to think of him, and imagined waterfalls and flushing toilets, and at last the clear yellow urine started flowing. I watched as he split my sample into two small bottles then gave each a code, which I chose, and the bottles were sealed with candle wax, one for analysis, the other to be opened for a second analysis if the first one was positive. I never heard any more of it so I presumed I was negative. Effervescent vitamin tablets and glass tubes of minerals and iron was all I had given myself, but even so I felt afraid – afraid that there would be some mix-up in the samples and I would be found positive. I could see myself protesting my outrage and proclaiming my innocence, and no one listening. For no one ever listened to a 'positive' protesting his innocence. The shame of it! I could see the headlines in the papers back in Dublin. KIMMAGE TAKES DRUGS. Oh, the shame of it! I was thankful that I was pure, and sure I was negative.

The race finished next day. Clavet was leading a competition for the first rider under the 'kilometre to go' flag. Sponsored by Fiat, the winner would receive a car, a Uno. To assure victory he had to make sure he won the last sprint. I had ridden well for him throughout the race, helping him wherever I could. With ten kilometres to go on the last stage he asked me to lead him out for the sprint. Castaing, Barteau, Le Bigaut, Mas and Vallet had all abandoned, leaving us with just four riders on the team still in the race. I was a bit taken aback when he asked me. Bunch sprinting was not my thing, but I agreed without hesitation. My job was to bring him to the front with a kilometre to go and then open the sprint for him. It was hard trying to get to the front and I felt sure I was going to crash as I tried to squeeze my way through the tightly packed bodies but I hit the front at just the right time, and on his prompting of 'Allez!' I opened the sprint. I was so pleased at having done everything right that I nearly jumped out of my skin – to the extent that I forgot that the idea was not for *me* to win, but Claveyrolat. He was following me but having difficulty in passing. Luckily I remembered just in time, and pulled across. Thierry won the prize and was lavish in his praise of my efforts. It had been a hard nine days but I had come through it well. Thevenet was pleased with my contribution, and for the first time I started to think about the possibility of riding the Tour de France.

A week later we rode the Grand Prix de Plumelec in Brittany. Clavet, Dede and I were provided with a team car. We drove a thousand kilometres to Plumelec on Saturday, rode the 200 kilometres race on Sunday and then hopped straight back into the car for the long drive home, arriving at half-past four in the morning. Clavet and I both rode well; he was sixth and I eighth and morale was high on the long return to base. This was the hardest part about being a pro – the travelling. The hours spent in cars and airports. But the Plumelec trip was great fun, for Dede was in great form and he kept us entertained with his never-ending stories of the crashes he has had with his cars. He had written off twenty cars in different accidents but each time he returns to drive as madly as ever. He is fearless, and his philosophy on death is 'The day, the date, it's all written down.'

I was given two weeks off after Plumelec so I merely did some light training and spent my spare time wandering around the shops of Grenoble. The football centre was starting to get me down. There was no privacy and the young footballers were a bunch of ill-mannered, undisciplined louts. Ribeiro seemed to get on quite well with them, which puzzled me and turned me against him even more. It was at this time that we learnt that Patrick Clerc had been sacked.

Patrick had, a few years earlier, been one of the classiest domestiques in the peloton. But a year before joining RMO he had had a poor season with the Spanish team Fagor, and they had not prolonged his contract. Thevenet contacted him about joining RMO but on certain conditions. Before signing his one-year contract he was made to write a letter of resignation. In this way the sponsors craftily worked their way around a French Federation rule according to which the minimum length of a contract was a year. Because Patrick had not performed for the first half of the season, his letter of resignation was produced and he was fired. He was quite bitter when he rode his last race, the Midi Libre stage race, with us. I couldn't help getting the impression that he in some way resented us, as if we were somehow responsible for what had happened.

It was during the Midi Libre that I learnt of my selection for the Tour. I was really pleased, for I had been hoping ever since the Dauphine; but now it was official. On returning to Grenoble I planned some big training spins that took in some of the Tour's biggest climbs: Lauteret, Galibier, Granon and Izoard. I took notes on the gradient, surface and gear requirement for each mountain, convinced this could be a help three weeks later. I set my heart on winning one of these mountain stages, for in my mind I was still a climber.

A week before the Tour we rode a four-day stage race in Brittany. We were told to take it easy, and to use it just as training, but I was feeling good. On the first stage I managed to get into a break of seven riders and we sprinted out the stage win between us. I led into the last corner with the finish two hundred metres slightly uphill. As I cornered, my right pedal hit the ground, lifting the back wheel and as it landed the rear tyre rolled off and I slid into the gutter. I escaped with a few scrapes, but I was disgusted, for I had felt sure of at worst finishing third. The stage was marked by Bernard Hinault's abandoning the race. He sat at the back of the bunch from the start and frowned whenever anyone came near him. The 'Blaireau' was a weird fellow: he frightened me. I was always afraid of crashing in front of him and bringing him down. Sometimes he would attack, and the bunch would string out in a long line behind him. Then he would sit up and start laughing at us, mocking us. He had a certain presence, a sort of godlike aura. He was a great champion, but I didn't like him.

There were just five days separating the start of the Tour from the finish of the Armorique. As the Tour was starting in Paris and we had to be at the hotel two days before the start, Stephen Roche invited me to stay with him for the three days between the two races. I had planned to take it easy – but it was never easy to train with Stephen, and I can remember being most uncomfortable at his side on our training rides. He had had a lousy year, with his knee giving him all sorts of problems, and was unsure about riding the Tour until the last minute, when he said 'Yes'. As the countdown to the Tour started, I began to feel more and more nervous. There would be three Irishmen in the Tour: Martin Earley was riding for Fagor, Stephen for Carrera and I for RMO. There should have been four, but a crash in the Tour of Switzerland had ruled out Seán Kelly. As we drove into Paris I felt my rendezvous with destiny was arriving. I had dreamt of this as a kid. Now it was here.

10 TOUR DE FRANCE

FRIDAY, JULY 4, 1986: PROLOGUE, PARIS

Today was special. The crowds, the atmosphere, the whole size of the race – all hit me for the first time. I rode a lousy prologue – I was far too nervous. Nearly fell off the ramp as I was cycling down it, and I could not feel my legs. I am rooming with Barteau, which is a bit of a pain because nobody on the team wants to room with him. Oh well, I suppose somebody had to draw the short straw. He is a bit of a mouth and is still living off his 1984 Tour, when he held the 'maillot jaune' for thirteen stages. We were given five new jerseys and five new pairs of shorts and five new pairs of gloves. The waiter asked me if I could get him a pair of gloves as a souvenir. These fellows have no idea.

SATURDAY: STAGE 1+2, PARIS

Today was a split stage. In the morning we had an 88-kilometre road stage around the streets of Paris, and in the afternoon a 55-kilometre team time trial. The bunch is huge, 210 starters, and I found it hard to stay at the front. There were a lot of crashes but I avoided them all. I should have worn a crash hat, but it's no good for the image. The team time trial was hard. I rode strongly and never missed a turn. Barteau was dropped near the end, was outside the time limit and has been eliminated. Tonight there was a big row between Thevenet and Barteau in the hotel. Barteau was angry that the team did not wait for him when he ran into difficulty. Thevenet replied that he must have ridden the last ten kilometres at two kilometres an hour to get eliminated. Barteau told the press that Thevenet was a bad directeur sportif. Thevenet replied that he might not be the world's greatest directeur sportif but it was a fact that he could find no one on the team wanting to share a room with Barteau. No one said anything at the dinner table about Barteau's elimination but secretly we were all glad. He has gone home now, and I guess that means I will be getting a new room mate. 'It's an ill wind . . .'

SUNDAY: STAGE 3, LIEVIN

We left Paris this morning going north to the industrial mining town of Lievin near Lille. Before the start it was bucketing down. We, the English speakers Yates, Lauritzen, Earley, were sheltering under a tent drinking coffee. The mood was sombre as we contemplated six hours in the rain. Paul Sherwen, a veteran of seven Tours but now working for Channel 4, came over to our table and sat down. He looked at our faces and knew exactly what we were thinking. 'Never mind lads, only four more Sundays to go.' And at first I laughed but then started thinking about it – and Christ, he was right: there were four more Sundays to go, and for the first time the horrific length of the race hit me. Punctured near the finish but was going good, and had no trouble getting back on. The rain stopped almost as soon as we left Paris but my gear was still filthy dirty. Had to scrub it over the bathroom sink. It's desperately hard trying to get the stains out of these white jerseys. God I'm starting to sound like an old one in an ad. for washing powder. Am rooming with Jean Louis Gauthier. He doesn't say much but he showed me a great way of wringing out the wet jersey. You roll it up in a bathroom towel and wring it in the towel. It comes out nearly dry. Only three more Sundays.

MONDAY: STAGE 4, EVREUX

Our man Regis Simon made a great effort today. He broke away alone for over 100 kilometres and was caught just fifteen kilometres from the line. The finish was so incredibly hard, everyone was on the rivet. Tried to do some blocking for Regis and nearly got into a fight with some of Stephen's Carrera team but Stephen told me I was in the wrong, so I backed down. I noticed that the Belgian rider Eddy Schepers never leaves his side. He protects him from the wind, and when it's not windy he surveys him as a faithful watchdog surveys his master, waiting on the next command. I wish I were Schepers.

TUESDAY: STAGE 5, VILLERS SUR MER

A strange thing happened tonight. There was a knock on the door just before dinner and I answered it. It was someone wanting to see Jean Louis so I let him in. There was something about him: I knew I had seen him before somewhere. It came to me just as Jean Louis introduced us: 'Raymond Martin'. In 1980 this man had been third best climber and won a stage in this very race. Then, he and Jean Louis had been team mates. Now, Martin was working for a sock manufacturer. He asked Jean Louis about his projects for the future, when he retired at the end of the year. Jean Louis had no idea what he was going to work at, he just hoped something interesting would turn up. And then it dawned on me that one day I too would have to return to a normal life. My childhood fantasy of earning enough money on which to live happily ever after went out of the window as Martin spoke.

Jean Louis Gauthier. He is an extraordinary fellow. So honest and noble. He says it will be his last Tour. In 1980 he had won a stage. In 1983 he had held the yellow jersey and yet he still had regrets. He regretted that he had never cycled down the Champs Elysées in the service of the winner of the Tour de France.

The first night I don't think we exchanged more than two words, just 'Goodnight', and then 'Good morning'. I did not know him too well before the race. I just knew that he was our best domestique, was the oldest rider, and was respected by everyone on the team. Everyone except Bernard Vallet. He didn't like Vallet, and I found this a bit hard to understand. He must have liked me, for we have roomed together for three days now. I know if he disliked me I'd have been put somewhere else. The second night we talked a bit more and then a bit more and now I feel totally at ease with him. He is very helpful. When Martin left, I asked him about his decision to stop at the end of the season and if he would leave the sport content. He replied that he was unhappy with his career. In 1983 he had had a great year and received lots of good offers from other teams to change. But he was a loyal person and he stuck with his old sponsor. He realised now that it was a mistake. He said that in the last few years he had lost the will to win, had become too comfortable in the role of domestique, and had been too satisfied helping others. I suppose it happens. If you work as a domestique long enough then you end up losing the urge to win for yourself. I made a mental note to avoid this happening to me.

WEDNESDAY: STAGE 6, CHERBOURG

Today was incredible. From the drop of the flag we went like hell. At times I was hanging on by the skin of my teeth right down the back of the bunch. You know you are at the back, because you hear the engines of over a hundred cars and motorbikes following the peloton. It's very irritating, because you get the impression that they are all looking at you. I was more than happy to arrive in the coastal town, still in the bunch. Had tea with my cousin Theresa Byrne and her husband Mick, this evening at the hotel. Nice to get a bit of support.

THURSDAY: STAGE 7, ST HILAIRE DU HARCOUET

Ninth! Ninth on a stage of the Tour de France. Today I justified my existence. This was what it's all for. This was the thrill of professional cycling. To be in the front of the race in a twelve-man break. To have Messrs Levitan and Goddet behind you in their red race directors' car. To have the helicopter buzzing over your head and the television motorbike zooming in and projecting your image across the world. I imagined my mother and father doing somersaults in front of the TV back in Dublin, as Phil Ligett the Channel 4 commentator shouted, 'Paul Kimmage is magnificent, this has never happened in the Tour de France before! Can he do it? Can the Dubliner win the stage?' As I pedalled my way to St Hilaire I could hear him, and it made me pedal harder. My God, it was wonderful. I was suffering terribly in the front, but I was there, giving it my all. With five hundred metres to go I was there, sprinting for a stage win in the Tour de France. I believed, I believed. My legs were so desperately tired, but I believed in the miracle that would propel me across the line in front of the others. But I made a mess of it. Got into a lovely position second from the front, but was caught on the hop as the others swept past and boxed me in. The crafty Belgian Ludo Peeters won the sprint. I was ninth. I was worth a place in the top five, but I had messed it up. I am now the best-placed rider in the team. Thevenet came into the room tonight and said he was very pleased with me. I blew a good chance today, but I'm sure there will be others.

FRIDAY: STAGE 8, NANTES

Felt tired all day. Must have been the efforts of yesterday. Was not able to do much about helping the team. Felt a bit guilty about that, and talked to Gauthier about it. He said there was no need to feel guilty if I was tired and unable to help. Liked him even more after this. He is becoming my big brother on this race.

SATURDAY: STAGE 9, NANTES TIME TRIAL

Today I had a rendezvous with reality. I had hoped for much and came away with so little. Thevenet had warned me, but I hadn't listened: 'Don't ride too hard, save your strength for the stages to come.' Wasn't he forgetting that I was the best-placed rider in the team? Damn it, I had worked hard for the team for over a week: today was my chance to do something for myself. A good ride would have pushed me into the top thirty. I set out to give it my all. I did. I have never ridden so hard in a time trial. When it was over I almost collapsed with exhaustion. I cycled back to the hotel but could hardly get the pedals around. I was sore all over. My buttocks ached from the effort of using the big time-trial gear. On arriving at the hotel I marched straight to my bed and threw myself on it. The top riders were finishing. Bernard Hinault had the best time. He had beaten me by eight minutes. Eight minutes in 61 kilometres, and here I was, exhausted on the hotel bed; and there he was, fresh as a fucking daisy, chatting out at me through the TV screen. That's when I realised the world had separated us. I had been taking the usual multi-vitamins since the start of the race. I had refused all injections, but as I watched Hinault I realised that it wasn't possible to continue in this way. I was on my hands and knees after nine stages: how could I possibly complete the fourteen that remained? Tonight I told Thevenet I was knackered. He asked me if I was looking after myself. He seemed surprised that I had not taken any injections. He brought me to Emile's room and suggested a B_{12} injection. Emile looked at me and smiled. He was very kind, I had expected an 'I told you so,' but none came, and I was grateful for this. I dropped my shorts and abandoned my virginity without a second thought. I fought off guilt waves flowing from my brain. 'This wasn't doping, it was just getting even with the others.' However, I was a bit suspicious that the others were putting stronger stuff than B_{12} in their syringes. But B_{12} was as far as I was prepared to go – for the moment. I asked Jean Louis about the use of hormones, for I knew that cortisone and testosterone were being widely used. He warned me off them immediately and without hesitation. 'That stuff is shit, it's dangerous, messes up the system. Stay away from it.'

SUNDAY: STAGE 10, POITIERS

I felt really bad at the start, was sure I was going to get dropped. But as the stage went on I started coming round a bit and it was an easy enough day until the last 60 kilometres. LeMond was in trouble today. He had a bout of diarrhoea. He rode by me with 30 kilometres to go, surrounded by his domestiques bringing him to the front. God, the smell was terrible. It was rolling down his legs. I know if it was me I would stop. I mean, it is only a bike race. But then again I am not capable of winning it. He is, and I suppose that's the difference.

Stephen rode a great time trial yesterday and is now third. Don't know how he does it, for a few days earlier he assured me he was having trouble with his left knee. He said he was riding on one leg. I wish I had his bad leg.

MONDAY: STAGE 11, BORDEAUX
Another long stage, 260 kilometres. They wear you out, these long flat stages, hour after hour in the saddle. Tomorrow we enter the mountains. I prefer the mountains. Jean Louis's wife and child came to the hotel tonight. She is very nice, and I made a special effort to be polite.

TUESDAY: STAGE 12, PAU
War. Today was war. We lost two men. Bruno Huger and Jean Louis Gauthier both abandoned. Jean Louis's quitting was a big blow. We started the stage at Bayonne, and from the drop of the flag it was war. Attack followed attack on the roller-coaster, leg-breaking Basque roads. A large group went clear, there was a fierce pursuit and then it settled for a while. Just after it settled I talked to Jean Louis and asked him how he felt. He looked shaken, and he told me he was shagged and having a really bad day. Soon after that, we attacked the first big mountain (col) of the Tour and I never saw him again. After the stage I cycled back to the hotel with Bernard Vallet. I expressed my concern for Gauthier and it was Vallet who told me he had quit. Gauthier had been dropped on the first col and was chasing alone, twenty minutes behind, when he punctured. He could have taken a spare wheel from the broom wagon but decided to pack it in.

I couldn't believe he had quit. I entered our room at the hotel and he was there, already showered and dressed in ordinary clothes. I walked over to him, put my hand on his shoulder and said 'Shit'. I couldn't think of any other word to console him. I showered and slipped out of the room for a cup of tea and to give him time to think by himself. I went for massage and then returned to the room, and we watched the TV highlights of the stage as on any other night. But this time we watched in silence. I now realised just how upset he was. He just sat there, in that same position with a sad, empty expression on his face. I rose and suggested we go down to dinner, but he didn't follow. Halfway through the meal I mentioned to the lads that Jean Louis was very upset. Claveyrolat, who had been on the same team at La Redoute, left the table to bring him down. Half an hour later he returned alone. Gauthier had told Claveyrolat that he was ashamed, that he could not bear to eat with the team. He didn't eat tonight. He must be starving for his last meal was at nine thirty this morning and he had raced 150 kilometres before climbing off. Before sleeping he said just three words to me: 'Bonne nuit, Paul'.

WEDNESDAY: STAGE 13, LUCHON
He woke early and I heard him sneak down for breakfast. When I eventually dragged myself out of bed he was back in the room and had his bags packed. He gave me a few vitamin tablets he said he would no longer be needing, and then we shook hands and said goodbye. I felt we were close friends. Here was a guy who had ridden seven Tours and finished them all. But all that seems to be no consolation to him now. Before coming into the race I was 100 per cent determined to finish. Thinking of Gauthier I feel almost ashamed of myself. My 100 per cent determination is not nearly enough.

Today was so desperately hard again. I felt dead at the bottom of the first col, the Tourmalet, and was instantly left behind. But after 3 kilometers of struggling I suddenly felt the strength to pedal faster and I upped the pace. I caught a group, left them behind and caught another. I couldn't believe it when I saw Stephen in a group of stragglers. He was suffering really badly and I felt desperately sorry for him. Damn it, I was getting used to being left behind on the big climbs but this was a new experience for him. I threw my arm around him and tried to console him. I should have waited with him but I felt a new thrust of power and I wanted to see just how far it could carry me. I went across to the next group and rode really strongly up the rest of the Tourmalet. I got a bit of a fright on the descent. I was going too fast as I entered this long, sweeping bend in a sort of half tunnel and I bounced off the wall but incredibly managed to stay up. I rode hard in the valley that brought us to the bottom of the second col, the Aspin. I climbed this with the same vigour as I had climbed Tourmalet but it was on the third climb, Peyresourde, that I started running out of steam. The final two kilometres were never-ending and I crawled over the top. Stephen's group caught me as we were about to start the last climb, the 13-kilometre rise to the ski station, Superbagnères, with the stage finishing at the top. This time Stephen was encouraging me and I realised I had made a big mistake. It would have been much wiser to have stayed with Stephen's group on the Tourmalet but instead I had set off like an idiot on the glory trail and burnt off the little reserves that my body still possessed. Superbagnères was Calvary, but I made it. Tonight we are staying in an old school dormitory. Its an awful kip, but I'm so tired I don't mind where I sleep.

THURSDAY: STAGE 14, BLAGNAC

Today I realised just how tired I am. Some idiot attacked just before the feeding station and there was chaos. I grabbed my feeding bag and threw it over my back. The attack split the bunch into one long line and I was last man and too occupied to transfer the food from the bag to my jersey pockets. Thevenet drove up beside me and told me to quickly move to the front. I pulled out and started making my way up the line. I passed five guys when all of a sudden I realised I hadn't got the strength to go any further and I started slipping back, only to end up back where I had started from. The five guys I passed started laughing when they saw me going backwards, and I could not blame them. The chase lasted over 25 kilometres, and it was a half an hour before I could empty my musette and we settled down. I am looking forward to the rest day but it's another four hard stages away.

FRIDAY; STAGE 15, NîMES

It's so dreadfully hot tonight. My body is sweating all the time and I know I won't sleep too well. After dinner I went for an ice cream with Clavet, Castaing and Dede. We had to sneak out of the hotel, as Thevenet does not take too kindly to us eating ice cream. It was good fun, but irritating to watch the holidaymakers enjoying themselves in the bars and cafés of this bright, ancient Roman town. How many times have we cycled by lake shores, crammed with people enjoying themselves? Or been applauded by sunbathers in scanty bathing costumes? Is it worth it?

SATURDAY: STAGE 15, GAP

Today we arrived in the Alps and tomorrow is the first Alpine stage. The air is cooler and cleaner here than the hot and sticky stuff at Nîmes. Castaing's face is all bloated. I am not sure what it is, but perhaps he has been dabbling with cortisone and got his doses wrong? The other lads are giving him a hard time about it. Phoned my parents in Dublin. Da was out, so I talked to my mother. She says my father has bought a plane ticket for Paris and is coming over to the finish. This made me angry. He should know better than to presume I will finish this race. At the moment I am not sure of anything. I take it day by day. I've been surviving ever since the time trial at Nantes. Getting to Paris is all Thevenet expects of me, but I'm not sure if I can.

SUNDAY:STAGE 16, BRIANÇON

This was to have been my stage. The one I trained specially for. What a joke. What a cruel joke. At least I know now that I'm not a climber and never will be. A strange thing happened at the finish. I crossed the line and Thevenet was waiting for me. He put his arm around me and told me I had made it, I was inside the time limit. And for a few seconds I was disappointed. I was so exhausted, so knackered that I would gladly have accepted being eliminated. Elimination would end the nightmare of getting up each day to face another six hours of this bloody, endless torture. Today was easily the hardest day of my life. I was in trouble right from the start on an insignificant little third-category climb that was nothing compared to the three giants, Vars, Izoard and Granon that awaited us.

I tried to get myself together for Vars. I talked to Stephen just before it and he told me to start the climb at the front of the bunch. I followed him and attacked the first hairpins in the best possible position. Then the pressure went on, not a big attack, just an increase in pressure. I felt for the gear lever, pushing it downwards, trying to make things easier. But I was going backwards. I tried to hold on, but it was no use. I looked for the top of the mountain and the lines of spectators showed me exactly how far I had to go. 'Christ, I'm not sure I can make it.' I kept slipping backwards and all the time one minor detail was troubling my brain. Of the three giants Vars was the easiest.

But curiously I felt much better on Izoard. I was in a big group of twenty-five riders and I could have left them behind on the 15-kilometre monster. But I remembered the Tourmalet and decided to stay with them until the bottom of the Granon. We descended into Briançon and then rode out to the bottom of the last mountain. The Granon was so desperately steep. Out training I had sailed up it but now I was dying. The training reconnaissance was now a big disadvantage, for I knew exactly how hard it was. I said to myself 'I can't make this.' The good sensations I had had on the Izoard had now disappeared, and I slipped to last in the group. Our second team car was behind me. At the bottom of the climb they had stopped to pick up a fellow called Robert who works with RMO in Grenoble. He was standing on the front seat shouting at me through the sun roof. Three of the twelve kilometres had passed, I was dying. Spectators started to push me. Robert, who knew nothing about cycling shouted at the people not to push me. It is illegal to take a push and Robert thought he was doing the right thing. I turned around to face him in a rage. I said 'Robert, for fuck's sake, let them push me.' He was stunned, then realised his error and started shouting at the people to push me. I was pushed all the way up the climb but the last kilometre was still hell. My two hands on the tops of the handlebars, my head had dropped between my arms and I could hardly lift it to seek out the line. When I crossed the line, Thevenet was waiting. 'You made it Paul, a couple of minutes inside the limit.' 'Fuck.' I was sorry I had made it. Tomorrow I must start all over again.

MONDAY:STAGE 17, ALPE D'HUEZ

Emile gave it to me before the start. A caffeine tablet. He told me to take it immediately the stage started, at the bottom of the highest climb of the race, the Col de Galibier. Normally I would have thrown it away, but this time I put it in my pocket. Some bastard attacked as soon as we left the town, and I had absolutely nothing in my legs and was instantly dropped. I panicked and reached for the tablet in my pocket hoping for some miracle; but nothing happened. I wanted to stop. I wanted to get off the bike and kiss the road and sit down and weep my tears of defeat, but I remembered Stephen's words, spoken to me before the start: 'Whatever happens, finish. If you are eliminated, then there is no shame – but don't abandon.' So I pedalled on.

I started feeling better after the Galibier. Was it the caffeine? I don't know. I just know I was going better. I caught the French rider Bruno Cornillet in the valley before the day's second climb, 'Croix de Fer'. At the start of the race Cornillet had worn the white jersey of the best Tour 'débutant'. Now he was, like me, on his last legs. Although I had never spoken a word to him in my life it turned out he knew my name. It was 'Paul this, and Paul that'. All because he wanted me to ride with him, he didn't want to be left on his own. I knew how lousy it was to be left alone, and so I decided to stay with him. There was a small third-category climb just before Croix de Fer. I was going much better than him and started to pull away. He was desperate and started begging me to stay, saying that there was a long valley up ahead and that it would be better if we stayed together. I knew there was no such valley, that he was lying but I understood why he lied, so I waited. On Croix de Fer he was crawling, totally wasted. Every time I turned the pedals I pulled away from him. A spectator at the side of the road shouted that we were 25 minutes behind the leaders, Hinault and LeMond. I realised it would be touch and go for the time limit.

I looked at Bruno, he had raced a good race for sixteen days but was now reduced to this – a crawling, begging shadow. I was surprised he did not abandon and let me get on with it. My look said I had to go, and he understood. 'Allez Paul,' he said and I left him. I rode as hard as I could till the finish at Alpe D'Huez. I had a fierce urge to piss on the descent of the Croix but I knew that every second was now precious if I was to beat the time limit so I pissed off the bike at 60 kilometres an hour. I arrived at the Alpe just three minutes inside the time limit. Cornillet arrived fourteen minutes behind me. He was eliminated.

TUESDAY: REST DAY, ALPE D'HUEZ

I feel so pleased I have made it this far. It feels wonderful to still be part of the race. Rode for an hour this morning to stop the legs getting stiff. The afternoon was spent hand washing my gear for I have no more clean shorts or jerseys. Had a good chat with Martin. He told me he was knackered at the bottom of the Alpe yesterday when this large German 'fraulein' came to his rescue. She grabbed him and started pushing him up the mountain. She had huge breasts, which swung freely as she ran. But she was crouched over Martin and her left breast kept hitting him in the face. 'Schnell, schnell!' she cried, and Martin kept encouraging her. He didn't know whether to laugh or cry.

Only five more stages to go, I must hang on.

WEDNESDAY: STAGE 19, St ETIENNE

Thank God, Hinault controlled things today. He went to the front of the bunch and no one dared attack. The rest day hasn't done me much good. I felt desperately tired. Was left behind when the pressure went on with thirty to go, but finished in a big group.

THURSDAY: STAGE 20, St ETIENNE TIME TRIAL

I paced myself well over the 35 kilometres, hurting but not flogging myself. Today was almost a second rest day. Only three more stages. If I get over tomorrow's mountain stage to the Puy de Dôme I should make it to Paris.

FRIDAY: STAGE 21, PUY DE DÔME

Hinault controlled things again today and the race started with just 50 kilometres to go, which suited me fine. The Puy is a savagely steep 5 kilometre ramp but I rode up it OK. I think I can make it now.

SATURDAY: STAGE 22, NEVERS

A nightmare. I was the only rider in the whole peloton to be left behind when the pressure went on, 20 kilometres from the finish. The

Above: My father winning the last stage of the Ras Tailteann 1963 in the Phoenix Park
Below left: My brother Raphael winning a stage of the Ras Tailteann in Carrick on Suir in June '83. Second is Sean Kelly's brother Vincent
Below right: Ras Tailteann '83 — my only ever ride in the race they call the 'big one'

Above: *Racing towards the yellow jersey in the Milk Race '83 with Sean Yates on my wheel*
Below left: *Milk Race '83, the race that nearly made me a star — accepting the yellow jersey*
Below right: *Milk Race '83 — crossing the finish line at Harrogate having lost 13 minutes and the yellow jersey*

Above left: *On the attack with Frenchman Christian Sobota in the colours of my French club C.C. Wasquehal, June '85*
Above right: *Dede Chappuis – St Etienne time trial, Tour de France, 1986*
Below: *Brand new anorak. Grand Bornand '86 – my first meeting with the RMO team.* LEFT TO RIGHT: *Jean Louis Gauthier, myself, Bruno Huger, Christian Mogore, Michel Vermote, Bernard Thevenet, Thierry Claveyrolat, Simon Regis, Patrick Clerc, Marcel Russenberger, Pierre Le Bigaut, Francis Castaing, Vincent Barteau, Gilles Mas, Per Pedersen, Jean Claude Vallaeys, Bernard Vallet, André Chappuis*

Above: *Cornering, Tour de France '86*
Below: *Tough at the top. After finishing the stage to Alpe d'Huez, '86*

shame of it, I am totally knackered. But the real problem is tomorrow. The lads have been telling me that the speed on the Champs Elysées is something incredible. What if I'm left behind in front of millions of TV spectators – and worse, in front of my father, who will be in the crowd? God, the shame of it! 'No one gets dropped on the Champs Elysées,' they said. But damn it, I was the only one to be dropped today. After dinner there was a small meeting in one of the rooms. One or two of the lads were preparing syringes. Cutting them down to size, preparing them for the white amphetamines they would use the next day. I was astonished. 'What about the controls?' They smiled. Safe smiles. 'Tomorrow is the last stage of the race. Only the stage winners and leaders will be controlled. There is no random test. That's why no one gets dropped on the Champs Elysées.' I was tempted, so desperately tempted. They offered me a charge, explaining that I could take it in tablet form if I preferred. I refused, and said I needed time to think. I did not despise them. They were my friends. I understood. Hadn't we suffered enough? They wanted to help me. I wanted to accept their help, but that bloody conscience of mine was stopping me. I had never smoked behind my father's back. Had always been dependable and good. I had an acute sense of right and wrong. Taking drugs was wrong. The only merit I had now was finishing this race. If I did it with the help of amphetamines I could never forgive myself. But it was so tempting. I so wanted to be one of the boys.

SUNDAY:STAGE 23, CHAMPS ELYSÉES
It was a great stage. A fun stage. The triumphant ride into Paris. During the long 252 kilometre ride to the capital a bottle of champagne was passed around the bunch. There was the singing of the Tour song 'Oh, Champs Elysées' and spirits were high. I got more and more nervous as we approached Paris and the speed went up. I saw one of the lads taking his stuff. It was so terribly simple. The metal tube was opened. The plastic cap, protecting the needle, was taken off and held between the teeth. The right sleeve of the jersey was rolled back and the needle was slipped into the skin of the shoulder and with a squeeze of the sawn-off piston the amphetamines were pushed in. The plastic cap was replaced on the needle and the syringe was put back in the tube and into the pocket. Beautifully done and so terribly simple. One of the lads offered me a tablet but I refused, and lied that I was feeling fine.

We could see the Eiffel Tower. What a wonderful sight. We raced along the bank of the Seine, passed the huge mass of metal then swung left into Place de la Concorde and onto the Champs Elysées. The roar from the crowd sent goose-pimples through my legs and though we raced up and down at over 60 kilometres an hour I felt no pain. I was so overjoyed at having made it, so overcome with the magnificence of it all that I didn't feel the pedals. The finish line was crossed and we ground to a halt. Bernard Vallet stopped beside me and embraced me. He had tears in his eyes. 'Now you know what it is to ride the Tour de France.' My father was standing just a little further on. He threw his arms around me. I was so pleased he was here to share my triumph. It was the happiest day of my life. Two hundred and ten riders had started. One hundred and thirty-two had finished. I was 131st. I had survived. I was a 'Giant of the Road'.

11 THE ARMS RACE

The Tour was a great education. I learnt so much about myself and about the real world of professional cycling. Every race before the Tour had been almost child's play when compared to 'La Grande Boucle'. The Tour was the ultimate. The one hundred per cent race. Finishing it had instilled in me a certain sense of pride. It took a hard man to finish, and I now had my 'hard man's licence'. I had expected it would be hard, but it was so much harder. I felt like abandoning a hundred times in the last week but I didn't give in. I couldn't, for I felt my survival as a professional bike rider depended on getting to Paris. RMO were a small team, but at the end of the season the weak men would be sacked and new blood brought in. Monsieur Braillon was not pumping money into cycling to play in the second division. Big names would be signed and small names sacked to make room for them. I had a contract for two years, so I was assured of my place for 1987 but already I was thinking ahead to 1988. I may not have been the classiest bike rider in the world, but I had other qualities. Courage, guts and honesty. In a year's time Thevenet would remember not that I had finished the Tour on my hands and knees but that I'd finished.

I had made some bad mistakes. I had been desperately naive in thinking I could ride a Tour de France on two multi-vitamin tablets each morning. The Tour de France was no ordinary race. It made superhuman demands on the human body. Riding six hours a day for twenty-three days was not possible without vitamin supplements, mineral supplements, chemicals to clean out a tired liver, medication to take the hardness out of rock-hard leg muscles. Taken in tablet form the medication passed through the stomach and liver. This was extra work for already overworked organs, and the result was that much of the benefit of the product was lost. Injections avoided this, and were therefore much more efficient. A syringe did not always mean doping. In a perfect world it would be possible to ride the Tour without taking a single medication – so long as everyone else did the same. But this was not a perfect world. We were not doping, we were taking care of ourselves, replacing what was being sweated daily out of our bodies. The substances taken were not on the proscribed list, so how could we be doping? And yet one thing was becoming clear to me: As soon as you started playing, as soon as you accepted the taking of medicaments, the line between what was legal and what was illegal became very fine. The line between taking care of yourself and doping became very, very thin. Most fellows cross it without ever realising they have. They just follow the advice of a team mate or soigneur. 'So and so swears by this, anytime he wants to do a ride he takes it.' And even though the rider himself may not want to take the product, doubting perhaps its legality, the thought of being disadvantaged changes his mind. It's a bit like an 'arms race': 'Laurents got an intercontinental missile in his arse today, I'd better get one or I'll be blitzed.' And before they know it they are in the middle of a very dangerous game. By accepting an injection on the night of the Nantes time trial, I had indeed entered the 'dope stadium'. I was, however, firm in my commitment to stay off the playing field as far as illegal substances were concerned. Could this last? I hoped so.

On the night the Tour finished we were back on the Champs Elysées, but this time dressed in shirt and tie and pressed pants. It felt great to be able to wear normal clothes again. For a month we had spent our days with a sweaty jersey on our backs and the greasy leather chamois of our racing shorts on our bums while at nights we were obliged to wear the drab old team tracksuit. Champagne was the beverage of the 'soirée' as we clinked our glasses to half-naked cabaret girls at the Millionaires' Club. It was a great night. Next day, I returned to Grenoble. As a way of trimming down travelling expenses it was decided that Dede and I travel home with the equipment truck. The journey was long and tedious, as we had a long detour to drop Dede at his home in Rumilly before finally arriving in Grenoble. There was no tickertape welcome awaiting me. The football centre was empty, as most of the apprentices were on summer holidays, but as I entered my room I got a sharp surprise. A young black footballer was lying on Ribeiro's bed, and I noticed immediately that my personal belongings were not as I had left them. His name was Charles and he explained to me that Ribeiro had flown back to Brazil for two months and that he had been ordered to take his bed. This Charles seemed a nice enough fellow, but I was furious. After a month's suffering, what a way to travel home and what a home to come home to! I would have to look for an apartment of my own, for the centre was becoming impossible to live in. I just had to get out of there. It would take time to find a suitable flat, but there was no question of me spending my two week's holidays with these arrogant brats. I decided to return home to Dublin.

I had not seen Ann for six months, as she had spent the summer working in New York. I had phoned her from a coin box in Nantes on her birthday and she had spent much of the five minutes crying. New York was not working out; she was finding it hard to get work. Like thousands of others, she had gone there without a student's working visa and had no social security number. She had gone in the hope of raising money to pay for her studies, but her tears told me she would barely cover her travel expenses. I told her to go home. She arrived home two days before I did. It felt good to be back. To be once again surrounded by the warmth of one's family. To have your girlfriend throw her arms around you and tell you she loved you. It made it all so worthwhile – the emptiness of the football centre was a million miles away. I felt like a 'star'.

There were two city-centre 'criterium' races on in Dublin and Cork. Professional races with Kelly and Roche both riding. Sean, Stephen and Martin were all managed by a Dublin businessman called Frank Quinn. I was always sceptical about managers who scratched their backsides and demanded ten per cent but Frank was different. He had a great human quality about him. He cared, and this was important to me. At the start of the year he had offered me his services, and I accepted. In my four years of professionalism I think it is the only manager–rider relationship which finished with the rider owing the manager money, but that's the way Frank is. He phoned the race organisers, informed them I was available and asked about a contract for the two races. It was very fair and on a par with what a new professional would get in France – about £250 per race. They offered him a pittance, claiming their budgets were all tied up. I felt really let down, insulted even. The organisers had flown over a load of continental pros for the events and here I was, one of only four professionals in the country, one of only five Irishmen ever to have ridden the Tour de France – and they could find no place for me. There was no place for Martin, either. It was despicable. This took a lot of the good out of being home. I no longer felt quite the star and was almost looking forward to going back.

Thevenet phoned me in Dublin at the end of the two weeks and told me to fly straight to Amsterdam for the Tour of Holland. The flat, open plains did not suit me, and I spent a very uncomfortable week. It was such a come-down from the glories of the Tour and, not at all motivated, I abandoned with a stage to go. Of the four RMO riders present, only I had ridden the Tour. The other Tour riders were in France riding criteriums.

Criteriums were a tradition in August in France. The Tour would generate huge interest for cycle racing in July, but in August there was nothing. The criteriums were a means of avoiding the cold turkey syndrome. A way of weaning off an addicted public until the autumn classics. The mayor of some small village would decide he wanted the stars of the Tour de France in his town and he would contact a criterium manager. The manager would submit the price of engaging thirty professionals and the mayor would hand over the money. The manager then set about contacting the riders. He would sign up three or four real big names, the Tour winner if possible, the French champion, and two or three Tour stage winners. Most of the mayor's cash would be spent on these, for these were the men that drew the crowds. The rest of the peloton was made up of usually twenty-five small-timers or domestiques. It was at criteriums that the poorly paid domestique made most of his money. For the two to three-hour street race he was paid about £350. It wasn't a hundred per cent profit. It was the rider's job to look after his own accommodation, travel and food. To economise, most domestiques travelled together. It was not uncommon for them to race in Brittany, finish about midnight then jump into a car and drive to the next race at the opposite end of the country. To save time, and money, the pre-race meal was usually a bag of chips and a sausage roll bought from a chip van at the side of the road. If there was a possibility of getting a few hour's sleep a cheap and often sleazy hotel would be found – anything to save a few francs. As a result, on arriving at the criterium they were often in no condition to race – but this was a minor detail. Amphetamines were wonderful for motivating a tired domestique to climb once again into the saddle. And as there were never any controls it was at criteriums that abuse was highest. The drugs were never used in the pursuit of victory, because all of the criteriums were fixed. The people came to see the star winning, so the star always won. That way the punters went away happy, and would return next year. No, the amphetamines were an insurance. An insurance that riders would 'perform'. The small riders were expected to animate the race. The routine was to attack off the front for a few laps, milk the applause and then let the star bring you back. By doing this you felt uninhibited when, at the end of the night, you approached the manager and asked for the contract. Contracts were always paid after the event. Amphetamines insured you got paid.

During the Tour Vallet had promised me he would find me a few contracts. He was a big name and had a lot of pull with the criterium managers but it was like a lot of the promises he made – empty. I reckon I am the only rider to have finished the Tour in 1986 who never rode one single criterium. It was one thing being a 'petit coureur' and French, but quite another being a 'petit coureur' and Irish. They could ring up the criterium managers and demand favours; but I hated crawling, and besides I was afraid. I knew that the criterium would draw me close to the temptations of drugs and I didn't want that. I was afraid of being tempted, too many complications. If one of the lads offered me a charge, in good faith, before a criterium, how could I possibly refuse without offending them? I didn't want to offend them. I still wanted desperately to be just one of the boys. If I refused a charge, I knew they would never totally accept me. And so being absent from the criteriums suited me just fine.

At the end of August we rode Paris–Bourges, a two-day stage race. It was my first contact with Gauthier since the day he had abandoned in the Tour. He was in good form and told me privately that he had received an offer to race with the Z Peugeot team in 1987. He had decided to accept. I was surprised as I felt sure he had made up his mind to retire. He had, but talking about retiring was one thing, actually doing it was another. There were not an awful lot of avenues open to a 32-year-old former 'maillot jaune' of the Tour de France. He had had one or two offers of employment but none that pleased him. The local amateur club from his region had made him an attractive offer if he wore their colours for a year but the thought of racing again as an amateur disturbed him. It was hard for me to imagine why he would want to leave RMO for Peugeot but I suppose it was because he had raced with other, better teams before. We were a small team. It's a bit like the first division footballer who is forced to play in a second division club. We were definitely second division, Peugeot were playing in the first: so it was normal for him to want to play for them.

There was a nice, relaxed atmosphere at Paris–Bourges. Dede had been offered a new contract for 1987 and this cheered him up greatly. And when Dede was happy, we all were. He was always the life and soul of the party. I was knackered after the first stage and decided to go to bed early. I was not rooming with Gauthier but with one of the others, whose identity must remain secret. I had slept solidly for more than an hour when my room mate came in and woke me. 'Paul I have a girl, and I'm on to a sure thing. In a few minutes I'm going to bring her up. You just keep your eyes closed and pretend to be asleep.' I laughed and told him I was knackered and to stop pulling my leg and he went out. Five minutes later he was back again with the girl. There was a slight hesitation when she saw my sleeping body in the adjoining bed. 'That's Kimmage, the Irishman, he's a very heavy sleeper,' he assured her. I was lying there with my eyes closed, paralysed in a state of total disbelief. He was serious. Oh, my God, he was serious. He was going to have intercourse with this girl on a bed that was almost touching my own.

At first they talked. She was competing in the women's race to be held next day. She asked him about his life as a professional and marvelled at his prowess. He played her along beautifully and this went on for fifteen minutes – then the clothes came off. The two bodies flopped down on the room's second single bed, which I repeat was almost touching my own. I kept my eyes glued shut, I never saw the girl's face, never saw the girl's anything. I didn't have to, the groaning and grunting of their lustful bodies left nothing to the imagination. My team mate was exceptionally noisy. 'The bastard's doing it on purpose.' The positions changed, the action restarted and suddenly I could feel this leg kicking me through the sheets. It was his leg. 'The dog, he's definitely doing it on purpose.' I thought about pretending to wake up, but this would only cause embarrassment all round. 'How could he do this?' During dope controls I felt embarrassed when the commissars stared at me while I was urinating. How could he possibly have intercourse with a girl when there was someone else in almost the same bed? I couldn't believe it. Then I noticed the smell – a desperate burning smell that I couldn't quite place. What the hell could possibly be burning?

The act terminated, they lay motionless for five minutes and then she asked him if she could take a shower. He escorted her to the bathroom and carefully closed the door. He ran over to my bed and shook me by the shoulder. 'What about that, Polo, do you want a go now?' I insulted him, but this only seemed to please him more. 'What the hell is burning?' To dim the light in the room, he had placed a towel over the bedside lamp, but the heat from the bulb was so intense that the towel was burning. He ran over to it, lifted the smouldering remains off the bulb and threw it out of the window. His partner finished her shower and re-entered the bedroom, no doubt amazed at the sleeping powers of the Irishman still unconscious on the other bed. He bid her goodnight and she left the room.

Next day as we started the second stage he was still euphoric about his conquest. He would ride up behind me and imitate his sexual grunting of the previous night, and then burst into a fit of laughter. Then he would go around the bunch telling all his mates about it and bring them to me for verification. The typical reaction was, 'I wouldn't have let him into the room unless I was sure of getting a go.' Or, 'I would have woken up, pushed him off and jumped on myself.' I don't know if all sportsmen are as gross as this. Not all cyclists are, but most of them are. They are all gentlemen, but there is this crude, savage side to them. I don't know if it's the demands of the sport that cultivate it, but it certainly exists. A typical example is the following:

Pierre: 'What's up with Louis, he's not sprinting very well?'

Serge: 'Yes, he had a bad crash while going for the stage win last week, and as he wasn't wearing gloves he ripped all the skin off both hands.'

Pierre: 'That's bad luck, I'm sure he'd have won a few stages here, he was going really well.'

Serge: 'Yes, but the worst part is that he can't even masturbate.'

I didn't ride well at Paris–Bourges. I didn't ride well in any of the end-of-season races. The Tour had taken a lot out of me and I was just going through the motions at races in August. September was another quiet month. I rode three one-day French classics before lining up for Paris–Brussels, which was to be my last race of the season. I didn't want to ride, but was told I had to make up the numbers because the team needed ten starters to be paid the travelling expenses from the race organisers. The night before the race I talked to Gauthier, who told me of how he had abandoned the year before. The day before the race he put his bike in the car and drove to a little village 50 kilometres from the start at Senlis. He parked the car and then cycled back to the team hotel. Next day he raced the 50 kilometres from Senlis to the village, abandoned down a narrow side street as the peloton traversed the village, jumped into his car and drove home. It was too late for me to try the same stunt but I planned something else. On the morning of the race I signed on the start sheet, dressed in my shorts and jersey. Just as the race was about to start, I hid in the toilet of a café across the road. When I was sure they had gone I discreetly slipped out of the café, jumped into the car and headed for Calais and the ferry to Dover.

I crossed to England and caught another ferry to Dublin. Home. My first season was over. Well, not quite.

The Tour of Ireland, or Nissan Classic, was due to start a week late but RMO were not sending a team so I wasn't racing it. Stephen had planned to ride it on a composite team, but his knee was still giving him trouble and he pulled out. This left a place to be filled. Frank phoned the team's sponsors, Ever Ready, and proposed me as a replacement. They agreed, and on the day I arrived home, Frank phoned me and told me I was riding the Nissan. I was a little bit short of condition and spent the three days prior to the race in frantic last-minute training. The team was made up of two Belgians, Jef Lieckens and Carlo Bomans, two Englishmen, Sean Yates and Tony Doyle and myself. On the first stage to Galway, it rained heavily. The bunch was in one long line and was being buffeted by strong cross winds as we raced along the Oranmore road to Galway. I had bad stomach cramps and felt really weak. I was dropped. It was a cruel disappointment. I would have to ride into Galway and complete the small circuit on my own, minutes behind the whole bunch. I knew my mother and father were waiting for me and I felt quite ashamed. Just before arriving on to the circuit I rode past the team hotel. I thought very seriously about getting off and making some excuse. Any excuse. anything to avoid the shame of riding the circuit on my own. But I kept going, Ever Ready were paying me a contract. By abandoning it, I would not be honouring it and this would not be professional. I finished the stage in a foul humour and cursed myself.

The rest of the week went off much better and I started to ride quite well. After the third stage to Cork I roomed with Sean Yates. I liked Sean. When I was an amateur he had helped me take the yellow jersey in the Tour of Britain Milk Race. He is one of the nicest and most down-to-earth blokes I have ever met in the game. He had a little gadget for examining blood. You pricked your finger for the sample, placed the droplet on a slide and examined it through a sort of small microscope. I asked him to test me and on examining my droplet, he said I was lacking in iron. I asked if he had any with him and he prepared me a syringe with vitamins and iron. Sean, like most of the pros, rarely went to the soigneur if he felt he needed something. He would simply do it himself. The idea of sticking a needle in myself repulsed me and I asked Sean if he would do it for me. He refused. 'You have to learn some time. Now is as good a time as any to start.' He gave me a piece of cotton with methylated spirits and the syringe, or 'flèche' as it was known in the trade, and I went to the bathroom and closed the door. The door was always closed just in case anyone walked in. I often wondered about my Father walking in and seeing me with a syringe in my hand. What would I have said? 'Eehh! Sorry, Da, this is not what you think.' No the door was always closed.

The syringe had to be inserted in the muscle of the buttock at about the same height as the coccyx. We had a choice of buttock, left or right, but it was equally painful. I had watched the lads do it before. There were two methods. The most painful was to place the point of the needle against the skin and slowly start pressing. Or, you could throw the syringe like a dart, so that it quickly penetrated the flesh. I decided to opt for the second method. I stood for at least ten minutes, making several efforts to throw the syringe, but each time being incapable of releasing it. This infuriated me. When finally I found the courage to do it, I was so tense and my buttock muscle so contracted that when the needle hit the flesh it bounced off and fell to the dirty bathroom floor. Furious, I picked it up, squeezed the piston and squirted the liquid down the toilet bowl. I threw the empty syringe in the bin and left the bathroom, cursing my head off. Sean had a huge grin on his face and offered to make me another one, but I refused. I later retrieved the syringe from the bathroom bin, as it was a golden rule never to leave anything that might surprise the cleaning maid. But I was thoroughly disgusted with myself.

The Nissan finished on the Sunday in Dublin. I tried to put up a bit of show in front of my home crowd as we dashed up and down O'Connell Street, but I ultimately failed to make any real impression. Galway was forgotten, and I could at least hold my head high again. This time the season was over and I wasn't sorry. I needed a break.

12 QUALIFIED PRO

The winter months were spent in Dublin. This was the fun part of being a pro, the three months spent at home at the end of every season. I enjoyed a high profile in my native land. My notoriety had started when I was an amateur. Now, as a professional, I was part of an elite band. There were just four professional cyclists in the country. Sean Kelly was the world's number 1 and Stephen Roche not far behind him. Martin Earley had won a stage in the Tour of Italy and Paul Kimmage had finished, well, 131st in the Tour de France. Cycling was becoming more and more popular with the media and as a result more familiar to the ordinary man in the street. I enjoyed cashing in on my new fame. I was invited by cycling clubs throughout the country to give coaching talks and lectures on the life of a pro. There was often a five-minute television slot here or a radio slot there and gradually I was building up a name for myself. There was no money to be made at it, but it made me feel important, as if I was something. So at the end of my break I always found it hard returning to France, where I was nothing.

I left Ireland on the ninth of January after a phone call from Thevenet. He had organised a pre-season training camp at Gruissan on the French Riviera. I caught the ferry to England and drove to Stoke, where I stayed the night with Martin. The next stage saw me on a stopover at Paris with my good friends Jean and Ginette Beaufils. And from there I drove to Gruissan. There were eight new faces on the team. Gauthier, Le Bigaut, Barteau, Russemberger, Mogore and Castaing were replaced by six Frenchmen, an Italian and an American. Jean Claude Colotti, Jean François Rault, Dante Rezze, Patrice Esnault, Vincent Lavenu and Michel Bibollet were the French newcomers. Pierangelo Bincolleto was the Italian and the 1984 Olympic champion Alexi Grewal the American.

Alexi was to be one of the leaders for the year. He had ridden one or two races with us on a trial basis in 1986 – although it is important to point out that it was Alexi who was giving RMO the trial. He seemed to like it, so he signed up full-time for 1987. Thevenet thought very highly of him, but I knew there was no way it would work. Physically he had the capabilities to be an asset to any pro team on the continent. But mentally Alexi was never going to fit into our team or any European team.

I shared a room with him at the training camp. He had this fear that his body would run down if he didn't eat enough. Half an hour before dinner he used to light up this small portable gas stove that he brought with him from the States. He boiled water and cooked and ate about half a ton of spaghetti. When he had finished he would come to the dining room and eat a normal dinner with the rest of us. He was a great man for stretching and yoga. Sometimes I would walk into the room to find him standing on his head or lying on the floor on a special piece of wood that massaged his back. On the team training rides, he would often ride a hundred metres behind the group on his own because he felt he was training better. And because he was Alexi Grewal he got away with it. He was paid 35,000 dollars a month, which kind of dwarfed the £500 a month that I was earning.

I found him to be the most eccentric, obnoxious person I have ever met, and yet I liked him. I despised many of the traditional European cycling values but my survival depended on toeing the line. I could never open my mouth. That's what I admired most about Alexi: nothing and nobody intimidated him.

I knew he wouldn't stick it. Alexi was too American, too inflexible. But his biggest problem was his fragile health. He was incredibly vulnerable to picking up colds which would soon develop into bronchitis, putting him out of action for weeks. Good health is one of the primary assets of being a pro. If Alexi had had the same health as Sean Kelly he would have gone a long way. But in the six months he spent with the team he was constantly sick, and I don't remember him ever riding well. By June he had had enough and returned to the States.

Of the other new guys, Colotti was the one I liked best. He was a year older than me but had only started to race four years earlier. I had been racing since I was eleven years old and the difference showed in our attitude to training and racing. He had a huge appetite for training and an infectious enthusiasm for the sport. It was all new and exciting to him but I had seen it all before. I was more laid back. Too laid back.

In the opening months of the season, while I struggled desperately to find any sort of decent form, Colotti blossomed – earning regular top ten placings and winning the French classic, the Tour de Vendée. His success frustrated me. I didn't begrudge him, it was just that I couldn't understand why it never happened to me.

The start of the new season was soured by two deaths in the peloton. The Spaniard Vincente Mata lapsed into a coma and died shortly after crashing in the 'Trophy Luis Puig' in Spain. A week later the second death occurred. I was a witness. It was in the Tour de Haut Var. There was a short hill not long after the start, and the descent was narrow and twisting but not too dangerous. We were strung out in a long line. I was fifth from the front, on the wheel of Thierry Marie, when suddenly the Hitachi rider in front of him fell off. We both managed to avoid running into him, and it didn't look a heavy fall. But when I looked back he was lying motionless in the middle of the road. Michael Goffin, a Belgian, lapsed into a coma and died two weeks later. I was fully aware that it was a dangerous sport, but deaths were uncommon. But the two deaths in the month of February made us all feel a little uncomfortable about the risks involved. There was no way I wanted to die on the bike. I started to wear my crash hat for a few races after that. But the dangers were soon forgotten, and although my crash hat was always a part of my baggage it was rarely taken out of my suitcase. 'Que sera, sera.'

The opening month of the season was a disaster. I rode pretty badly in almost every race I entered, so it was pretty logical that I did not get selected for Paris–Nice in March. On returning to Grenoble I immediately set about trying to find an apartment, as there was no way I was going to stick another year at the football centre. Clavet told me about a two-roomed flat that was vacant in his town, Vizille, which was just 12 kilometres outside Grenoble. I paid it a visit and decided to take it. The hassle of moving didn't do my physical condition any good, and I missed a lot of training. As a result I was in poor condition when I returned to competition for two races in Belgium. I abandoned both of them and this started a run of seven abandonments, one after another. I managed to stop the rot at the Grand Prix of Rennes where I finished seventeenth and succeeded in getting my name in *L'Equipe*. This was important. Thevenet was starting to lose patience with me and the result showed at least that I existed. Things improved from then on. I finished 51st in my favourite Classic, Liège – Bastogne – Liège, and returned to Ireland shortly after for the wedding of my brother Raphael.

It was not a triumphant homecoming. Kelly, Roche and Earley had all had fantastic starts to their seasons. Mine had been a disaster. I started to worry about the future. My two-year contract with the team was up at the end of the year, and unless I improved dramatically, I'd be lucky if they offered me another one. What would I do? Jobs were almost impossible to find in Dublin. There was not much demand for ex-professional cyclists, especially unsuccessful ones. On the day before I returned to France I had lunch with my friend David Walsh. David was a journalist with the *Sunday Tribune* and also worked for *Magill*, an Irish current affairs magazine. When I finished the Tour in 1986 he asked me to write an account of the race, or more particularly my struggles in the race, for *Magill*. The story seemed to go down quite well with anyone who read it. I had written other stories for an Irish cycling magazine in my amateur days and I liked expressing myself by means of a pen. I often wished I had entered University and tried for a degree in journalism instead of dashing off to France for a professional cyclist's contract. David suggested that there were plenty of opportunities to write freelance cycling stories on the continent. He encouraged me to continue on the bike, and made me feel much more optimistic for the future.

I made my comeback at the Grand Prix of Frankfurt, where I rode quite well. Two important stage races were coming up, Quatre Jours de Dunkirk and the Tour de Romandie. The 'Dauphine' was just a month away and I knew that my selection for it depended on a good performance in one of the two stage races. I preferred Romandie to the Quatre Jours and managed to convince Thevenet to send me there. Stephen was riding it, and it was my first opportunity to talk to him, as up until then we had rarely raced together. He was having a dream of a season and was clearly back on top after his troubles of last year. I made a special effort to impress him during the race, as my secret ambition was to ride by his side in the same team – but only if I was good enough. I was proud of my independence at RMO. I had won my contract there on my own steam and without the help of either Kelly or Roche. But the plan was eventually to team up with one of my famous compatriots but on my terms. I wouldn't accept charity. If I wasn't good enough to be offered another contract by RMO then I wasn't good enough to join Kelly or Roche. Stephen's good form continued in Romandie where he won easily.

On the night before the last stage I shared a room with Bernard Vallet. It was my first time ever to share a room with him. It was almost an honour. I admired him, for he was suave and classy and had always been nice to me. He told me he was pleased with my performance and that he would make sure that I had my place on the team to ride the 'Dauphine'. Having the confidence of Vallet was a great advantage, for I knew he pulled a lot of weight with the sponsor Braillon and with Thevenet. He then asked me about my impressions of Thevenet as a directeur sportif. I knew they were friends but because I liked Thevenet I found no reason to lie and told him exactly what I thought.

'Bernard has one or two organisational problems but he has great human qualities which compensate largely for his faults. I like him. He is a good directeur.'

I was a little puzzled as to his reason for questioning my impression of Thevenet. Jacques Michaud was directing the team in Switzerland, while Thevenet was looking after the Dunkirk squad. Was Vallet conducting an opinion poll behind Thevenet's back, or with his approval? I was quite unprepared for what followed.

'Braillon has asked me to take over as directeur sportif of the team next year.'

Silence. Ah . . . all is revealed. He looked at me, trying to gauge my reaction. I was shocked, but tried not to show it. I had expected Vallet to join Thevenet next year as his assistant – but not as his replacement.

'I want to accept, but I am in a bit of bother because Thevenet and I are good friends.'

Why was he confiding in me about this? I could see he was getting high just talking about it. He must have been dying to tell someone, and I just happened to be around when the dam burst. He asked me to keep our conversation secret, saying that he needed time to make his decision. But he wasn't fooling me. His decision was already made. He would take the job, but he just needed time to find a way of knifing Thevenet as painlessly as possible.

My good form in Switzerland had gained me selection for the Dauphine. Outside of the Tour, it was my favourite race. I lived in the region and felt compelled to perform well in my 'back garden'. There was always so much at stake in the Dauphine but this year especially so. A good performance meant a place in the Tour de France team. A place in the Tour team enhanced my chances of being offered a new contract, so I was not lacking in motivation. I had super form for the eight-day event, but I used my form cleverly. Even with super form I knew I was not capable of winning a stage. But I was capable of helping Claveyrolat or Vallet to win one. This was what was important about being a domestique. It was better to put all your efforts into helping a team mate to win than trying and failing to win yourself. Second or third. Fifth or sixth. These places have no value for a pro team. Winning is everything. I knew I was capable of getting placed on stages, but decided it was in my best interests to sacrifice myself for the leaders. Vallet and Claveyrolat were on form. Vallet would more than likely be directeur sportif the following year. Clavet was my friend. For the eight stages I put myself totally at their disposition. I protected them from the wind, rode at their side in the mountains, fetched their drinks, waited with them when they stopped to piss, pushed them and willed them to success. They rewarded me with praise each night in front of Thevenet at the dinner table.

'Did you see the work Paul did for us today? He was extraordinary.'

The only regret I had was for my parents. They came over from Ireland on two week's holiday to see the race with my youngest brother Christopher. My only bad day of the race was on the first mountain stage to Modane. It was a scorching hot day and I cracked early on the Col du Glandon. I knew my parents were waiting for me at the top. I dreaded passing them so far down the field, and in my frustration I composed a speech that explained my role of domestique. On seeing them at the side of the road I planned to stop and say, 'Da, I'm sorry. Look at me. This is the reality. This is what I am. I'm not a star and never will be. I am a water carrier, a domestique, a nothing.' I never got to say the prepared words. He was standing 2 kilometres from the top, with a bottle of water. I smiled, pulled in and filled my 'bidon'. He said I was doing fine, and pushed me off, encouraging me further. His enthusiasm lightened my heart and my speech was cancelled.

The following day we crossed three mountains. At the summit of the second, the Izoard, I was just behind the leading group. Only Claveyrolat from our team was in front of me. Thevenet ordered me to wait on Vallet, who was chasing behind with two other team mates, Mas and Simon. I went down the descent like a madman and we rejoined the front group in the valley. Three riders had broken clear and I was ordered to the front to chase. I rode my heart out until the first hairpins of the day's last mountain, the Col de Vars, where I soon cracked and was dropped. My work was not in vain, for Thierry won the stage and moved up to fourth overall. That night Thevenet came into the room. He praised me for my team work and told me to prepare myself for the Tour de France.

'I hope you are going to stay with us next year.'

He was offering me a contract. I was surprised and delighted.

'Bah oui, j'espère (I hope so)'.

'Good. Think about your salary and come back to me next week with a figure. If you wish, you can sign on for two years.'

I was thrilled. A new contract. Lots of good amateurs turn professional but half of them never last longer then the duration of their first contract. The first contract is an apprenticeship. The second one is a confirmation of qualification. I had been offered a second contract: I was a qualified pro.

The day after the finish of the Dauphine, I left for the Tour of Luxembourg. I didn't want to go. The Dauphine had been very hard and had taken a lot out of me, but the team were committed to riding both in Luxembourg and at another stage race in Brittany so I had no choice. I don't know how I ever made it through the first stage. It was a short-circuit race in the city centre and there was lashing rain which turned the oily roads into a skating rink. I was knackered, and spent the entire evening at the back of the bunch, counting down the laps to the finish. It was on nights like that when racing a bike was not sport, but just a job. An obligation to earn an honest crust. To survive, you must put the race and the suffering out of your mind. You must think of good times. It rained every single day in Luxembourg, so I was thinking of good times for almost a week. I was climbing really strongly and finished the race in good form about fifteenth and best of our team.

I had ten days off after Luxembourg. The problem of my salary was bothering me. Thevenet had asked me how much I wanted. This was awkward. I would have preferred him to make me an offer. I am not a good businessman and don't like asking for money and had no idea of how much I was worth. One thing was very clear to me. This job was far too hard to be worth only the £500 a month I was then being paid. At a meeting with Thevenet at the team headquarters in Grenoble I asked for double, £1,000 a month. He scratched his head, and said I was asking for too much. He offered me £900. I accepted, but decided to sign for just one year. This was a bit of a gamble. I was sacrificing the security of a two-year contract. But if I rode really well, I would be free to negotiate a higher wage and the gamble would be worth it.

Things were going well. With my contract and Tour ticket in the bag, I returned to competition for the Midi Libre stage race. Seven riders were assured of places in the team for the Tour. Along with me there was Vallet, Claveyrolat, Colotti, Vermote, Esnault and Mas. The remaining two places were to be fought out between Dede, Simon, Rault, Pedersen and Bibolet. The Midi Libre was the final selection race for the two places. The atmosphere in the team was not good. The battle for the placings strained relationships between the five. Only a blind man could fail to notice the back-stabbing as some of the team tried to score points with Thevenet at the expense of others. I was a little disgusted at this, but then I suppose it was easy for me to talk. Perhaps if I was fighting for my place I would be the same?

For the second time in a month I was selected at random for dope control. Had I a junkie's head? I don't know: it just seemed a bit of a coincidence. It was after the third stage, and I was a little bit worried as I had taken a vitamin C and caffeine tablet before the start. But the doses would have been quickly sweated through my body and Clavet assured me I had nothing to worry about. With two stages to go, Patrice Esnault took over the race lead. I was quite pleased with myself, as I had bust a gut in the breakaway to ensure that Esnault took the leader's jersey. The next day was a time trial and he managed to hang on to his slim advantage over the Spaniard Julien Gorospe. Just one day to defend the jersey: things could not have been better. The last stage was split into two parts: 100 kilometres in the morning and 90 in the afternoon. Because it was a split stage and the last day, we knew there would be no random dope controls on either the morning or the afternoon stage. Esnault, as race leader, would be controlled. So would the winners of both the stages. But the significant thing was that there was no random control. The job of protecting the lead was not Esnault's responsibility; it was his team's. With no random control they, we, could charge up to protect his lead, knowing we wouldn't be asked to pee.

I felt most uncomfortable on learning all of this. I wanted to do everything I could so that Esnault would win, but I drew the line at charging up for him. If I wasn't prepared to do it for myself then I wasn't going to do it for someone else. What disturbed me most was the attitude of some of my team mates. Some certainly disapproved but a few were almost rejoicing about the fact that they had a green light to be merry the next day. And to make matters worse, one in particular put pressure on me to toe the line. He said it was part of the job. That Esnault had made the supreme effort of defending his lead in the time trial and that it was the duty of his team to defend for him on the last day. I felt he was putting a gun to my head. I refused. Others refused also, but we were a minority. I felt a bit guilty, but most of all I felt angry at being placed in such a dilemma. Why on earth were there no controls. Did the organisers not realise the pressure they were putting on riders like myself? Esnault hung on and won the Midi Libre. It was the first stage race the team had ever won but the repercussions of the last day had left a bitter taste in my mouth.

My non-eligibility for the French road race championships meant I had ten days off before the Tour. The days were spent resting on the shore of the lake at Laffrey, 7 kilometres above Vizille, with Ann. She had just graduated from University with a teaching degree, and had come to live with me until the end of the season. Three weeks later I would once again be at the lake shore of Laffrey, but this time as a Tour de France rider, looking at the sunbathers as I cycled by. I treasured every minute.

13 TOUR '87

JULY 1: WEST BERLIN, PROLOGUE

Today I rode faster than twenty-one other pros in the 6-kilometre prologue time trial. There were 185 riders who rode faster than me – so I can't say I'm exactly delighted with my first day on the race. Still, it feels so wonderful to be part of it all. It's so big and colourful and exciting. A man from Irish radio interviewed me today. The Tour is getting big coverage back home this year, so I must try to keep my face up there. We have not trained well the last two days. Most of the time has been spent trying to find quiet roads, but inevitably we end up staring at the wall or trying to ride through Checkpoint Charlie. Dede seems happy enough, though. He found this park with women sunbathing almost nude. Today was Colotti's birthday, and we ate this huge cake to celebrate. I must have put on weight, for the food here in Novotel is brilliant.

JULY 2: WEST BERLIN, STAGE 1+2

It's always a bit worrying when you discover you are not going as well as you thought. Today I discovered it. It was in the afternoon team time trial stage. I started it with the conviction that I'd show the lads just why I was one of the best domestiques in France, but things didn't quite work out. I spent the last 20 kilometres swinging off the back with Clavet.

The morning stage was chaotic. Everyone was extremely nervous and the stage was incredibly fast. We covered the 105 kilometres at an average speed of 48 kilometres an hour. Inevitably there was a huge crash that completely blocked the road. Two riders got tangled up together and fell. Normally everyone else would have avoided them, but because we were riding so hard most people had their heads down. Again, normally we would have been alerted by the noise of metal

93

scraping off the ground but the television helicopter was down so low over our heads that we couldn't hear a thing. At least forty hit the deck, and an Italian was carted off to hospital. One down. Jean Claude got off to a great start and is wearing the red jersey of leader in the sprints competition. I suppose we will have to help him to defend it, as it's good publicity. He is also the French TV mascot for the race. Every day he is interviewed after the race on live TV and asked how his day went. That's more publicity. He is doing well for himself.

JULY 3: TRANSFER

Today we flew over the Wall and back to the West. Whenever we make these transfers by plane I am reminded of the Munich air disaster that wiped out the Manchester United football team. What would have happened if our jet carrying 200 of the world's best cyclists had crashed? Well, obviously, the cancellation of the Tour. But not everyone would be sorry. The riders not selected for the Tour would be jumping up and down with relief. The world-ranked 201 would be thrilled, as he would suddenly become the world's number 1. And 200 bottles of champagne would simultaneously pop in the homes of until then ambitious but frustrated amateurs. It's a morbid thought, but the consequences never cease to fascinate me.

JULY 4: STUTTGART

The holiday is over. What a stage! Oh, my God, what a stage! It was so unbelievably hot and so incredibly hard. Tonight I feel as if we are in the third week of the race, not the third day. It was up and down for 219 kilometres and at the finish there were bodies everywhere. One big 22-man group got away in the last hour. We had no one in it but we were all too knackered to chase. Mottet, one of the favourites for the race, was up there but his rivals did nothing to chase. They couldn't: at the end it was a case of every man for himself, just to finish. It was action all day from the gun. There was always someone on the attack and someone else ready to chase – until the end, that is. The pace was so fast that we could not go back for bottles from the cars, and near the end I had to give Kelly a drink, as he hadn't a drop in his bidon. I don't understand why he didn't command his domestiques to fetch him one. I'm sure he could, with someone like me in his team. My leaders may not be the best in the world but they are seldom thirsty. Funnily enough I was actually riding better than most of my team mates. They all suffered from the heat. So did I. During the stage I thought of a great idea for Treets. You know, the chocolates that melt in your mouth, not in your hand. The idea was to have a Tour rider carrying a Treet in his jersey pocket and to take it out during the boiling hot stage, and it not be melted. Am I going mad?

JULY 5: STRASBOURG
Another split stage. In the morning an 80-kilometre sprint to Pforzheim and in the afternoon a 112-kilometre run to Strasbourg. We didn't need a frontier to tell us we had crossed into France. We could judge from the surface of the road and from the reaction of the crowds. In Germany we had great crowds. They cheered us with air horns and shouting, just like you'd find at a football match. In France it was the traditional polite applause and accordion music as we cycled towards Strasbourg. I have left home exactly a week now and we have only just entered France. The really hot weather continues and there are already a lot of tired bodies in the peloton. Nine have quit the race after just five stages, and if we continue at this pace there won't be a hundred riders in Paris.

JULY 6: EPINAL
The first mountain stage with the first-category Col de Kreuzweg and the second category Col du Donon. I lost contact late on the Kreuzweg but managed to get back on before Donon, where I held on. But it was too far to the finish and we eased up, enabling most of those dropped to regain contact. It was the first real cease-fire of the race, so no one was complaining. The last 50 kilometres were very hard and fast and I was lucky to avoid the huge crash 20 kilometres from the finish.

We are staying in Hôtel Ibis. We hate these hotels: the rooms are so small that there is never any room to open the suitcase. The team doctors came tonight and put me on a glucose drip. I felt so tired that I wasn't refusing. I hope there was only glucose in the bottle, but I am not sure and too tired to ask. When the drip was finished they gave me a sleeping tablet. I don't like taking them, but they tell me a good night's sleep is essential to recovery and I need to recover.

JULY 7: TROYES
I am rooming with Vallet tonight. This year we are changing almost every night, so that we are never with the same bloke two nights in a row. I don't like rooming with Vallet. I feel I must always put on a show for him. I insisted that he have the big bed because I know he expects to be offered it. I refuse to complain when he leaves the light in the room on until after eleven at night and I feel almost obliged to get

up and leave the room when I feel like farting. I am nearly sure, now, that he has agreed to take over from Thevenet at the end of the year. Braillon was in our room tonight and they were talking business. I pretended not to listen.

JULY 8: EPINAY
A relatively easy day. A relatively easy day is one with a slow start, a really fast bit in the middle, a short lull and the last 60 kilometres covered in an hour. We had to drive to Orléans for tomorrow's start after the stage which was a bit tiring. Orléans is Esnault's home town, and he has a crowd of supporters in the hotel tonight. He is supposed to be our leader here, but I am riding better than him, myself. I wouldn't mind if he gave a hand with the chores. But a leader is always a leader, even when he is not riding as well as a domestique. Today I bust a gut to get him a bottle, and when I brought it to him he didn't want it. It is the last one he will get.

JULY 9: RENAZE
Colotti is still holding on to his sprint leader's jersey. Today I led him out on three occasions, and tonight we are rooming together and he gave me a jersey as a souvenir. Highlight of the day was the crash, 12 kilometres from the finish. We had been riding on good, wide roads all day, but for some inexplicable reason the organisers brought us on a criss-cross of small, narrow roads for the last 30 kilometres, so crashes were inevitable. This one was different, because there was almost a fight after it. The Colombians are responsible for most of the crashes in the bunch. The majority have very poor bike control, and now every time there is a crash someone cries 'Bloody Colombians!' I'm not sure today's crash was their fault, but it happened at a very bad time, when most of us were knackered and roasted by the sun. A Belgian threw his bidon at a Colombian, hitting him in the back of the head. He was immediately set upon by two other Colombians, and things got a bit out of control.

JULY 10: FUTUROSCOPE TIME TRIAL
What a long time trial: 88 kilometres to be ridden alone. Lucho Herrera was off a minute behind me, and he caught me after 26 kilometres. I rode hard, but not flat out as the memories of Nantes were still fresh in my mind. Stephen won, and I think I lost about 16 minutes, which is phenomenal. I think if my life had depended on it I could have ridden 6 minutes faster, but no more. I feel a bit small

tonight. The hotel is showing pornographic videos, and you can walk into any of the rooms and it will be on. I reckon there will be a few tired bodies tomorrow.

JULY 11: CHAUMEIL
Today was probably the hardest stage of the race so far. It was 255 kilometres, but up and down all day on tiny roads with the tar melting off them from the hot sun. My feet are killing me. They expand in the heat, and the pressure of the buckle of the toe-strap left me limping after the stage. Colotti nearly cracked mentally today, and I had to nurse him through. Physically, I didn't feel too bad; but for anyone who went all out in yesterday's time trial it must have been hell.

JULY 12: BORDEAUX
We lost Sean Kelly today. We had ridden hard for the opening 50 kilometres, when the pace dropped. I was dying for a piss, and stopped as soon as I recognised the ceasefire. The Team cars had just started to pass me, when suddenly they all braked and I heard the word 'chute' ('crash') from the race radio. As soon as the word was spoken the team mechanics jumped from the cars with a pair of wheels and ran to the pile of tangled bodies up the road. I didn't panic, as crashes happened every day; so I finished my widdle and casually set off in pursuit. As I passed Thevenet, he told me not to hang around, as there had been an attack. The race radio was announcing the names of those who had crashed. Kelly was riding at the back and surrounded by three team mates when I made contact. His face was screwed up in pain, and he was riding with one hand off the bars. The doctors' car drove up alongside and sprayed his shoulder with a pain-killer but it didn't seem to be having much effect. The bunch slowed and we made contact, but he never stirred from the back and it was obvious to me that he could not continue in his present state. I approached him and gave him a gentle pat on the back as a gesture of solidarity, and then one by one the team leaders dropped back to pay their respects. He was distanced as soon as the road started to rise, and he abandoned in tears shortly after. I felt really disappointed for him. He was having a lousy Tour, and that morning he had made a rare appearance at the coffee table for a joke and a chat. It wasn't the same without him.

Signed a new one-year contract with Braillon at the hotel tonight.

JULY 13: PAU
The teddy bear's picnic. The words of the children's nursery rhyme

kept repeating themselves in my mind as we cycled out of Bayonne. Today was the Colombians' day: the first Pyrenean stage of the race. With their dark skin and large eyes they remind me of teddy bears. Today was their day – the teddy bears' picnic.

If you go down to the woods today . . .

I was in good form riding out of Bayonne. I like the mountain stages and I have always a little hope in the back of my mind of one day winning one. I started badly on the first climb, the first-category Col de Burdincurutcheta, but soon found my climbing legs and went through the struggling bodies like a warm knife through butter. I was with the top group going over the top of the second-category Bargargui and felt this was going to be the day. Clavet, Mas and I were the only three from the team still up there, and I felt wonderful as we started the descent. Then it all went wrong. Someone attacked on the descent, and we went down it at a fierce pace. The tar had melted on some of the corners, making them treacherously slippy, and I knew there would soon be trouble with overheating rims. The rims overheat from constant braking, and there are two possible consequences: either the glue that sticks the tyre to the rim melts, and the tyre rolls off the rim, or the heat of the rim makes the tyre explode. Three-quarters of the way down I started to feel my tyres swaying a bit on the rims but I could hear tyres exploding all over the place. I was descending behind a Carrera when suddenly, as we entered a hairpin, his front tyre exploded off the rim and he crashed.

'Fuck. I'm going to crash.' I swung out the bars and tried to avoid him, but there was nowhere for me to go, and I hit him and flipped just off the edge of the road. Five seconds of the world turning upside-down, of total lack of control, and I come to a halt. Oh, it's always a great feeling to open your eyes after a crash. My knee is stinging a bit but I'm OK. I try to get up, but I'm trapped under my bike and I burn my hand on the hot front rim. The tyre has rolled off and I will need a change. Behind, there was chaos as, one by one, riders started piling into the back of us. The Belgian Henrick De Vos didn't have time to brake: he went straight off the cliff edge, landing 60 feet below us. Team cars screeched to a halt behind, the panicking race doctors slid down the side to rescue poor De Vos – who I felt sure was dead. Thevenet and Coval both came to my rescue. Thevenet reached me first and he screamed at the mechanic, who had run further down the road, to come back and change the wheel. But the front rim was so hot that he burned his hand as he tried to get it out.

I jumped back on the bike dazed but only slightly grazed. There were bodies everywhere on the descent, absolute carnage, and I joined Kim Andersen and Miguel Indurain. We were descending a long straight bit of road at about 60 kilometres an hour when one of the team cars overtook and came so close that he clipped Indurain's handlebars with the side of the car, and God knows how the Spaniard managed to stay upright. This latest incident had a strange effect on me. I sat up and decided to take no more chances on the descent. 'These people are all insane. It's only a fucking bike race. To hell with them.'

I finished the stage with a big gruppetto, and I am feeling fine tonight. Twelve riders abandoned, including Vermotte from our team. De Vos was lifted from the side of the mountain in a helicopter. He has a fractured skull, but his life is not in danger so he is lucky. Colotti had a really bad day today and barely scraped through. I feel a bit guilty at not having waited with him. He is the only one from the team getting any publicity, as he is still sprint leader so I will stay with him tomorrow.

JULY 14: LUZ ARDIDEN

The team doctors came to the hotel last night. This morning before the stage they came into the room. They started preparing a syringe with a small ampoule of something or other. I asked what it was and was told 'synacthen'. I hadn't got a clue what that was, but I didn't like the sound of it so I said I did not want any. It was a bit embarrassing, but the doctor bowed to my wish and didn't insist – he gave it to my room mate instead.

(Synacthen is common, even a 'lightweight', among many of the hormonal products used in the peloton. It is a medicament that simulates 24 of the 39 amino acids that constitute a molecule of l'A.C.T.H., which stimulate the production of cortisone in the body. It therefore commands the body to produce its own cortisone. The other way of increasing cortisone in the body is to take it directly. Kenacort is a synthetic cortisone, and a product widely used in the peloton. It is banned but detection is a problem – the body produces cortisone naturally, and some people produce more than others, so finding a norm is difficult.)

I have been sorely tempted to experiment with stuff during the race; but fear the secondary effects of cortisone abuse, so I have decided not to enter that little game. And yet I am tempted. I know I will improve, for I've seen the improvements in others, but it's doping and I'm afraid of where it will lead me. The old argument that a doped ass won't win the Derby is a true, but a dangerous one. I know that by taking stuff I'll never win the Tour. But physically I would improve. And by improving I would gain in confidence and maybe start winning races. That would earn me more money – which is all that counts at the end of the day. Maybe it's my upbringing – the terrible attacks of conscience whenever I do anything wrong. Maybe it's my natural intelligence – the knowledge that at the end of the day I will have to stop and find a job, and that good health is really the only wealth that we have. I suppose it's a mixture of both. Either way, it's a road I don't want to go down.

Colotti was on his hands and knees today. He was the first to be dropped on the climb of the Col de Marie Blanque just after the start. I waited with him. I felt so strong, riding at his side. Stronger than I've ever felt in any mountain stage of the Tour. But maybe I was fooling myself. Maybe it was because he was so weak that I felt so good. I don't know. Dede waited with us as well. I felt sure he was done and just wanted friendly company for the day. We dragged Colotti over the mountain and then set off in pursuit of the descent. There was thick fog on the descent, and I overshot one of the first hairpins but didn't fall off. I felt he was going to abandon the second mountain, 'Aubisque', but he held on. In the valley before Luz Ardiden I rode along as hard as I could at the front of the group. We caught Jean Louis Gauthier, Adri Van der Poel and Van Poppel and I paced them to the bottom of the climb to the ski station. We made the time limit with 10 minutes to spare and Colotti went on French TV and said he would never have made it without Kimmage and Chappuis.

We are staying in a real kip tonight. I think it's an old schoolhouse.

JULY 15: BLAGNAC
What a terrible day! Had trouble with my stomach, cramps. There was a cloudburst with 40 kilometres to go, and I have never seen so much water on the roads. At one stage you would have drowned on toppling over. The bunch split to pieces under an attack from Mottet and Fignon. We had to ride really hard to avoid being eliminated. The American Seven Eleven rider has a phrase that sums the race up. 'It sucks.'

JULY 16: MILLAU
Colotti abandoned. It was early in the stage and he complained of problems with his left knee. Dede and I waited with him on two occasions when he was dropped at the start, but on the third time he

decided to call it a day. He was devastated and in tears as he climbed off, and I felt sorry for him. He had tried so hard – too hard – in the first ten days, and he was still wearing the sprint leader's jersey. But his lead was being eaten away and he had not won a sprint for three days. He was physically drained, but it's a pity he could not hang on, for in two days we have the rest day.

Clavet was also in trouble. He has picked up bronchitis from yesterday's bad weather, and he was dropped with 40 kilometres to go. Dede waited with him.

JULY 17: AVIGNON

The stomach pains continue and are getting worse, if anything. Today was a nightmare: 240 kilometres, with a big climb just after the start. We started like rockets, and I was in big trouble on the climb and only held on by the skin of my teeth. Vallet started shouting near the end for us to attack, but the guy's dreaming. He was as quiet as a mouse for the first ten days, when he was hanging on, but now that he is going better we are supposed to attack. I didn't feel much like attacking, and got dropped near the finish in the cross-winds. Ann was at the finish. She came down with Clavet's wife Myriam. She is staying the weekend, for tomorrow is the rest day, and on Sunday there is the time trial up Mont Ventoux. Thevenet tells us that he shouldn't really be allowing the wives to stay in the hotel with us. At meal times we are forbidden to eat together. The riders eat at one table. The wives eat at another. Tradition has it so. Tradition sucks.

JULY 18: AVIGNON, REST DAY

Thank God it's a rest day, for there is no way I would be capable of riding a stage. I spent the morning in bed: the cramps are subsiding but I feel terribly weak. Ann washed my gear and in the afternoon I went out with Paul Sherwen to turn the legs a bit. We did about 40 kilometres around the vineyards of Châteauneuf du Pape. I have started to appreciate wine now, and can look around me with a new interest. Most of the lads rode up the Ventoux but I was too weak to contemplate it. The doctors are treating me, and I feel a little better tonight.

JULY 19: CARPENTRAS–MONT VENTOUX TIME TRIAL

The Giant of Provence. A mountain made famous by the death of a famous English cyclist, Tom Simpson. In between the effort of trying to ride up the mountain I tried hard to pick out the memorial statue to him as I neared the top but it was hidden behind the thousands of spectators who had come to cheer the modern-day heroes. I felt quite OK, after a shaky start, and finished 118th of the 164 still in the race. I seem to have recovered from my stomach bug and that gives me new optimism for finishing the race.

JULY 20: VILLARD DE LANS

Clavet and Esnault both packed it in today. The team is down to just five men and morale is low. Poor Clavet, I feel sorry for him. Tomorrow we ride through his home town, my adopted town, Vizille. The mayor of the town sent leaflets to all the inhabitants asking them to to come out to cheer the two 'local' men, Claveyrolat and Kimmage. But Clavet won't be around now for the 'party'. He has locked himself in his room, and there is no talking him out of it. The television showed his tearful abandoning this evening. I suppose it must make great television, but it's still a bit much.

I had one of my better days. I felt good from the start and was never under any serious pressure. It's a great day for the Irish for Stephen is the new maillot jaune. He becomes only the third Irishman ever to have worn the famous tunic. I'm very happy for him, although I would like to get to talk to him more. He is too busy trying to win the race.

JULY 21: L'ALPE D'HUEZ

If, in later years, I am asked what the greatest thrill in my life has been, I will hesitate between two replies. It would either be arriving on the Champs Elysées after a hard Tour, or riding through the thousands of screaming voices to the ski station of L'Alpe d'Huez. I was too knackered to appreciate it last year – so tired that all I ever saw of the 13-kilometre rise was the 5 feet of rising tarmac before me. But today was different, and I was going quite well. Martin and I both rode out of Villard de Lans at Stephen's side. Proud to be Irish sounds so corny but damn it, I was proud to be Irish. It was one of the hardest stages of the race, with seven climbs. I got clear with a group on the day's first climb, the Placette, and as far as I remember it was my first time in twenty stages to get into a breakaway. It didn't last long, for the Carreras reeled us in on the descent. I stayed with the top men over the second-category Cucheron and the first-category Coq. I must admit to being highly motivated, for I wanted to be in a good position going through Vizille. I led through the village and crucified myself to stay at the front for 2 kilometres of the 7 kilometre Côte de Laffrey on the outskirts of the town. I got lots of cheers, and my name was sprayed all over the climb. I know the road to the Alpe like the back of my hand, and that's always a big help. I enjoyed the twenty-one hairpins of the mountain. I was able to settle into a rhythm and ride up at my own pace, and it was almost a pleasure to suffer in this way. At the top Stephen had lost the jersey to Pedro Delgado. 'Perico' is in the same hotel as us tonight. I like him: he is natural and has an honest smile. I didn't see Ann today, although she told me on the phone tonight that she was on the Laffrey. Frank arrived from Dublin and is a bit disappointed about Kelly.

14 JULY 22

It is 7.45 at the Hotel Christina. I have been lying awake for fifteen minutes now. It's nice to lie here and rest. Soon it will be time to get up. Another stage, another day. I didn't sleep well last night. I woke at least four times but each time managed to doze off again within five to ten minutes. I put it down to sleeping at altitude. I never noticed the problem until I heard Mas and Vallet complaining that they never slept well at altitude. This set me worrying that I wouldn't sleep well at altitude and, consequently, I don't. Frank walks in and I close my eyes, pretending to sleep. He taps my shoulder and whispers softly 'Allez Polo, c'est l'heure.' I drag myself out of bed and walk out on to the veranda. The view of the Alpe on this fresh sunny morning is breath-taking. Below, the soigneurs are busy loading suitcases while the hiss of an air compressor inflating a hundred tyres announces that the mechanics too are at work. Which reminds me that it's time for me to start. After washing and shaving I go down for breakfast. Coffee, fresh croissants and jam. It's the favourite part of my breakfast. Normally we are not allowed croissants. The myth is that they are too fattening. Typical of the French: it's OK to eat half a ton of cheese in the evenings but not OK to eat croissants in the morning. I have lost three kilos on this race, so I decide to ignore the frowning brows and reach for a second. The food here is really good. The steak is tender and the spaghetti 'al dente' and for once eating is eating, and not fuelling up as is often the case. A yogurt, a fruit salad, and a stroll outside to see what's happening.

The soigneurs are starting to panic. They urge me to return to the room to pack my suitcase. The suitcase is a mess. I'm not a very organised person. For 'organised' you can substitute 'tidy'. I throw a day's kit on to the bed and pile everything else into the case and close it with great difficulty. It is then left outside the door to be picked up by

Above: *Smiles before the miles: riding out with Stephen and Martin Earley in the '87 Tour*
Below: *Shades, suntan: I'm looking pretty cool this morning with Martin and Stephen at Orléans — '87 Tour*

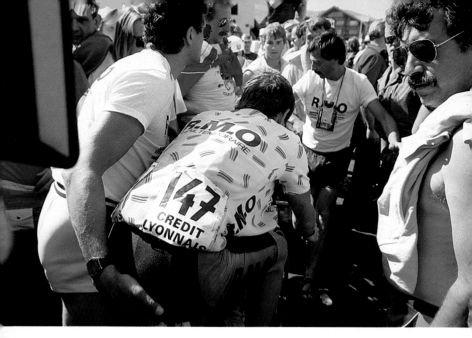

Above: *Helping hand: Bernard Thevenet always stood on the finish line until all of his riders came in. He had to wait 35 minutes for me here at L'Alpe d'Huez — '86 Tour*
Below: *Alone on the mountain: struggling on the Galibier — '86 Tour*

Above: Nearing the end of my pain: 100 metres from the finish line of the
Mount Ventoux time trial — '87 Tour
Below: The heroes: without Roche and Kelly I would never have survived
my four years in the professional peloton

Above left: One of the good guys: my friend Jean Claude Colotti at Orcières time trial, '89 Tour
Above right: World Championship, Villach '87. One of the great memories — Stephen will soon be World Champion
Below: And now the end is near: the Aubisque mountain, '89 Tour — Stephen's last day on the race. The Fagor riders (from left to right): Kimmage, Biondi, Roche, Lavenu and Schepers (his back)

the soigneur on his next passage. There is just time to study the race bible and the battleground for today's stage. Five mountains: Lauteret, Galibier, Telegraph, Madeleine and the summit finish of La Plagne. Hmmm . . . the Galibier. Visions of last year's tour and my struggling body on its steep slopes disturb my mind. But I am riding much better this year, so there shouldn't be any problem.

The stage start is in the village of Bourg d'Oisans, twenty-one hairpins below us. A few years ago it used to start here at the Alpe and be neutralised to the bottom. But the riders were forced to brake constantly behind the race director's car, and the wheel rims overheated, causing dozens of punctures and blow-outs. Now, everyone descends in cars. As usual I am the last to leave the hotel. Thevenet blows the car horn for me to hurry. His is the only team car left and it's full. He drives with Vallet beside him in the front seat. I am squashed in the back between the mechanic Coval and Yves Hezard, an ex-pro and a good friend of Thevenet's. With the exception of Coval, each of us has raced up the Alpe in the Tour and it is the topic of conversation as we descend.

'What used to impress me most,' says Hezard, 'was arriving at the bottom and looking up to see the lines and lines of spectators almost directly above you.'

'I don't remember ever having the strength to look up,' Thevenet replies jokingly and we all laugh.

As we descend we notice the hordes of cycling tourists of every shape and size sweating and panting their way up the mountain.

'They are all timing themselves,' says Thevenet. 'They know exactly how long it took Roche and Delgado to climb yesterday and tonight they will compare times and work out exactly how many pros they'd have beaten on the stage.'

Like all Tour de France stage 'departs', Bourg d'Oisans is crammed with spectators and it is with great difficulty that we find a parking spot. The routine never changes. Get out of the car, collect the race food from the soigneurs' car and the bike from the mechanics. Check that the brake blocks are not too close to the wheels and that both wheels are well tightened. This is purely a personal thing. I hate having the brake blocks too close to the rims in case they rub and I'm always afraid of an untightened front wheel popping out of the forks at 60 on a mountain descent. I ride to the signing-on podium and spend the thirty minutes before the start chatting and drinking coffee with Martin at one of the hospitality tables. We meet at the same table each morning. Sean Yates, Adrian Timmis and Allan Peiper are with

Martin at 'our' table as I arrive. Conversation is as it always is. Of the day before, of how knackered we all are and of how we are all looking forward to finishing in Paris. Our chief concern today is that the hostilities don't start too early on the road to La Plagne. But then again that's our chief concern every day. Pedro Delgado, the race leader, arrives at an adjoining table. The table where all the Spanish riders sit. The Spanish table. He is pestered by autograph hunters and requests from journalists and has no time to drink coffee. Being famous can be such a pain. The high pitch of the race starter's whistle beckons us to line up. The excited spectators shout the names of their favourites. 'Tiens, il y a Roche! Allez Roche!' 'Le voilà Delgado! Bravo Pedro!' No one ever shouts my name but this morning a spectator taps me on the shoulder.

'Bonjour, I'm a friend of Dante Rezze,' he said, shaking my hand.

'Ah, OK,' I reply.

What being a friend of Dante Rezze has to do with shaking my hand is beyond me, but these things often happen on the Tour. The starter's flag is dropped, and I ride out through the valley talking to Martin. He is changing teams at the end of the year and is getting a bit of hassle from Fagor, his current employers, so his morale is a bit low. My own worries are of a different nature. The amazing thing about being a bike rider is that you always know from the first turn of the pedals what sort of a day you are going to have. Or is it the same in every sport? Can Serge Blanco tell by pulling on his rugger boots if he is going to score five tries or play a stinker? It's something I must find out. This morning, I was in no doubts. My legs were tired and very heavy. It would be a bad day.

'Have you ridden up the Lauteret from this side before?'

Martin shakes his head for 'no'.

'It's a long bastard.'

Soon we turn left and the climb begins. There are climbs you like and climbs you hate. I like the Alpe d'Huez. I hate the Lauteret. It is 33 kilometres long, is badly surfaced and I never ride well on it. After just one kilometre I am sweating. My arms and face are dripping and I feel most uncomfortable.

'Shit, I should have brought a caffeine tablet.'

The pace is fast but bearable when we enter the first of five tunnels on the climb. It is unlit. The riders in the front accelerate, safe from all obstruction. Behind, it is chaos. It is almost impossible to see the wheel in front and we are forced to ride through at a snail's pace. On coming out of the tunnel we are 45 seconds behind the 'tête' of the peloton. I chase hard for 2 kilometres with Peiper to rejoin. The chase confirms my earlier impressions. I am having a really bad day. Others are suffering too.

'Did you see the guy that crashed in the tunnel?'

I look across. It's Dede.

'No, didn't see a thing.'

'He was covered in blood.'

A race official's motorbike moves up alongside and we learn that the Dutch rider Nijboer has abandoned and is being taken to hospital. We enter another tunnel and another Dutchman, Solleveld, falls off just in front of me – but this time without serious injury. Fignon stops for a pee. Martin decides it's a good idea and stops with him. Jean François Bernard stops, and with him his watchdog Dominique Garde. And for 2 kilometres we ramble along and I am thankful for the common sense being shown. Then it happens. The attack. Shouts and whistles go round the bunch and I look up to see who it is. Yes it's him. Chozas. He does this every year, the Spanish bastard. Takes off at the start of a hard mountain stage when everyone is content to take it easy. The million dollar question is: will they chase him? If they do, it will blow the race apart. If they don't, we shall ramble along for a good bit longer until someone decides it's a reasonable time to start racing. I look up, waiting for a reaction. I can hear it. The imaginary fuse burning on the end of the imaginary dynamite. More cries. Two more riders dash off the front. The chase is on. Badooom!

The peloton stretches out in one long line, and all I can do is try to hang on. Those with tired legs are soon in difficulty. The points leader, Van Poppel, is dropped along with eight others including Peiper and the Swiss Zimmerman. The chase intensifies. I am directly behind Dede. He lets the gap open.

'Allez Dede!'

'I am sick of this bloody race.'

I ride past. I look around and he is 20 or 30 metres behind. I'm suffering but am surprised and encouraged at my ability to close the gaps opening all over the place. There are just 5 kilometres to the top of the Lauteret, then we swing left immediately to start the 8-kilometre ascent of the Galibier. Martin is in trouble. He lets the gap open, and I ride up behind him.

'Hang on, it's too early to lose contact.'

We take turns at trying to reduce the deficit. We close to 30 metres, 20, then I pass him and grit my teeth in one last effort to make the junction. But suddenly I run out of gas. I can't make it and can no longer stay with Martin. My legs are turning, but without power. The tiredness mounts from my legs to my arms, and soon it has paralysed my whole body. I look up just as Martin makes contact. And then the group pulls away.

The Van Poppel group catches me. I grit my teeth and take my place in the slipstream of the last rider. We pass the café at the top of the Lauteret and turn left to start the Galibier. I am finding it harder and harder to stay with the group. My body feels so empty, and morale is tumbling. One length, two, and I lose contact with the group. Panic, desperation and the realisation that I am in big trouble. Rault catches me and shouts for me to stay with him.

'Go on, the Tour is finished for me.'

Why did I say that? Thevenet passes me in the team car.

'Paul you must try to get up to Van Poppel's group.'

I look across to him and shake my head and he drives past. The pedals turn but with no conviction. Self-pity is now the abiding sentiment, and once that starts there is no hope. I am doomed. I see a banner, 'ROCHE EARLEY KIMMAGE', and my friend Seamus Downey standing under it. I look to him and shake my head, and then feel angry with myself for giving up. Dede catches me.

'Allez Paul!'

'No Dede, go on leave me.'

But he insists on staying with me, so I scream abuse at him to leave me alone. He does. Michaud is behind now, in the second team car. Tears fill my eyes. I decide to try again. I begin to ride faster, deciding not to give up. But the effort lasts just one kilometre. My legs are just empty. A rider passes me on the right at twice my speed. I look across to see who it is. It's a bearded tourist, riding up the mountain with pannier bags on his bike. A bloody Fred. Michaud drives up alongside and tells the tourist to get off his bike. But the damage is done, and I am now completely demoralised. Spectators are now pushing me, and Michaud realises that I'm cooked and drives past saying that he will shortly return. I look behind. The broom wagon is just 500 metres back, with just two riders in front of it. It is drawing me in like a giant magnet.

I am resigned now to abandon, as I know there is no way I will make the time limit in my present state. I pass the statue of the Tour founder Henri Desgrange. It's as good a place as any to get off, but there are too many spectators. Allochio, an Italian and Gorospe, a Spaniard pass me just before the summit and leave me. The broom wagon is now directly behind. The descent of the Galibier is twisting and dangerous but I take no risks. There is an icy wind blowing up from the valley below and it freezes me as I drop. Down through the village of Valloire and then the short 5-kilometre climb of the Telegraph. Oh God, that feeling of jadedness when I am asked once again for effort. There is nothing in my legs. I look for a place to end it. A place void of people so that I can retire with dignity. I stop on the right-hand side of the road after a kilometre of climbing. I have cracked. It is over. The broom wagon and ambulance stop behind me. I stand, head bent down over my bike, as a nurse descends from the ambulance and offers her sympathies. A commissar gets out of the broom wagon and unpins the two race numbers from my back. 'C'est dure', he sighs, as he completes this unpleasant duty. People further up the mountain come running down to witness the excitement. There are ohs and ahs as I climb into the bus, and then cheers as I am driven away. I feel numb and dazed and cold. I wrap myself in a blanket and ask the commissar how many abandonments there have been. Four.

We catch Gorospe and Allochio at the feeding station at St Jean de Maurienne. Gorospe abandons. The commissar gets out to remove his numbers. He gets into one of his team cars. Michaud is waiting for me. He tells me I must stay in the broom wagon until the end of the stage. I nod, accepting my punishment. He gives me a bag of food and drives off. We catch Allochio at the bottom of the Madeleine. My eyelids are so heavy and I must fight to stay awake, but there is no fight left in me and exhausted I fall asleep. I wake half an hour later near the summit of the mountain. It's like waking from a bad dream and encountering a nightmare. I can't come to terms with the fact that I am in the bus. What am I doing here? How the fuck could I have abandoned the Tour de France? Oh God, what have I done?

My body has warmed up now, so I discard the blanket. Some spectators recognise my jersey in the back of the broom wagon. 'Look, an RMO has abandoned.' I pull the blanket around myself again, this time to hide my identity. I am in disgrace.

The final climb to La Plagne seems unending. The nearer we get to the finish the worse I feel. We drive past a huge Irish tricolour flag with the names of the four Irishmen on it. Ashamed, I must look away. We pass the little red triangle that signifies the last kilometre and arrive at the finish line. As usual it's chaotic. The race announcer Daniel Mangeas announces the list of the day's abandonments. His voice is soft and sad. The tones are those you would expect from a man announcing a list of soldiers killed in a war. I leave the bus and walk, head down, to the team car. Coval is at the wheel. 'Thevenet is gone looking for you.' I sit in the front seat and Thevenet returns five minutes later. He knows exactly how I am feeling and his words are chosen carefully.

'Ah Polo. You gave it all you could. We can ask no more of you.'

The kind words have the effect of an aquarium just shattered by the blows of a hammer. Three hours of caged-in disappointment, anguish and shame come flowing out as I break down and weep as I have not done for a long, long time. There is a short drive to the hotel. Thankfully I am rooming with Dede. He tries his hardest to sympathise, but it really isn't easy and I realise exactly how Gauthier felt at Pau a year earlier. Dede goes off for massage and I am happy to be left alone. Alone with my thoughts. I have failed.

I left La Plagne the very next morning about half an hour before the start of the stage. The team equipment truck was to leave me at the station at Albertville, where I could catch a train to Grenoble. There were cars everywhere and we got stuck in a traffic jam just outside La Plagne. Some teams had stayed in the valley below and had to drive back up the mountain. The Carrera car stopped opposite us and Stephen was in the front seat. I tried to hide, hoping he would not see me but he did and immediately rolled down the window. I smiled a false smile. He grinned that typical Roche grin and shouted playfully.

'Oh, Kimmage, what are you doing there?'

This hurt. It hurt badly, but I tried not to show it. He recognised the hurt.

'Take it easy for a few days, Paul, but get back on your bike as quickly as possible.'

The words were sincere and greatly appreciated. The cars in front started to move, and our conversation was interrupted.

'Good luck to you Stephen.'

Although it was only 70 kilometres away, it was two train rides and a bus journey back to Vizille. Ann was waiting at the flat. I had not phoned and this had hurt her. I was narky and tired. She felt hurt and upset. We had a huge row as soon as I entered the flat. She was quite right to be angry, but my disappointment had been so complete that I could not bring myself to pick up a phone to talk about it.

Back in Ireland the whole country was following Stephen's bid to win cycling's biggest prize. I couldn't bear to watch any of it during those final three days. On the day of the race-deciding time trial at Dijon I was out shopping with Ann. I remember walking by a furniture shop with a television set in the window. It was the live broadcast of the time trial that drew my attention. I had left the house

110

to avoid watching it, but as I passed the shop the temptation was too much. I stood in front of the window and watched as the screen split showing Delgado and Roche and the time gap that separated them. Stephen was winning the Tour. The next day, Sunday, we took the train to Paris. I had promised Thevenet I would come up for the end-of-Tour team night out. But as I arrived at the Sofitel I was sorry I had come. It wasn't the same. I couldn't rid myself of the feeling of guilt. The feeling that I had sinned.

Just before we went out to dinner Stephen, the triumphant Tour winner, arrived back at the hotel. He was surrounded by a million people, which suited me because I wanted to avoid him. I felt compelled to approach him and congratulate him, but the revulsion I felt about having quit was stronger. But there was another factor. I was happy he had won, but I was also jealous. Jealous that he had made it to the top of the world, while I had just fallen off it. He was a star now, and I could find no likeness to the Roche I had adored as a youngster. So I decided to stay clear of him. But the most incredible thing happened. He was being jostled from all sides and was pushed and shoved across the marble floor until he was right under my nose. He had a warm greeting for me, and I felt instantly ashamed. I put my arms around him and congratulated him as best I could. And then he was whisked away on a tidal wave of handshakes.

I didn't touch my bike for nine days. Just couldn't face the thought of throwing my leg over it. On the Friday after the Tour the phone rang late in the night. It was Jacques Chevegeon, a criterium manager. He said he had a place for me at a criterium at Château Chinon on Monday and would pay me £250 if I turned up. I agreed and put the phone down. I was sorry I had agreed. I had been off the bike for nine days. I would surely get the hell knocked out of me at a criterium where ninety per cent of the guys would be charged up. I dreaded facing another hammering – another humiliating slap on the face in front of thousands of spectators. But I had given my word. Early on Monday morning I loaded the car and headed for Château Chinon.

15 ONE OF THE BOYS

Château Chinon was a 4-hour drive from the flat in Vizille. I arrived at 11.30, three and a half hours before the race – but I like giving myself plenty of time. The town is smothered in a thick, wet fog and it's hard to avoid the Monday morning blues. I expected it to be much bigger, but it's really quite small. Too small to accommodate the hundreds of spectators' cars already choking the streets. Still, the locals don't mind, especially 'les commerçants': it's the only traffic jam of the year, and the bars and cafes are full. I parked in the main street and waited. I did not really know what to do, but Vallet and Claveyrolat would soon arrive and I planned to follow them. After spending half an hour in the car I recognised their two cars driving through the town. They had come from Bordeaux where they had raced a criterium the day before. Vallet has not been home for nearly six weeks now. The day after the Tour finished he set off from Paris and has ridden a criterium a day for eight days now. Nine days and thousands of kilometres of driving from one small village to another. I'm not sure how much he gets per race but I know he will go home with about six grand in his pocket – which is what I earn in a year. His wife and two daughters are travelling with him and they look almost as tired as he does. Claveyrolat is travelling with Colotti. Jean Claude is completely shagged and has also had a hard week.

The greeting is as it always is, a handshake and a smile. I follow them to a small hotel at the end of the main street. It's a typical criterium hotel. Run-down and cheap, but clean. Two rooms have been reserved and we will also eat lunch here before the race. Most of the riders are eating and changing here. But first the bikes must be prepared. I take mine from the car boot and put the wheels in and inflate the tyres. The bike is spotless. I washed it yesterday, making sure it was shining for my first criterium race. Appearances are everything. If I make a good impression today then the criterium manager might offer me one or two others. The other lads' bikes are not so clean, still caked in the grime of the Bordeaux criterium. But a wipe of a cloth makes them presentable. It feels strange, being responsible once again for the cleanliness and good working order of your own bike.

Lunch is simple and light, and digestion is helped by the constant good humour to be found whenever cyclists eat together. Outside the fog is lifting and the roads are starting to dry. The Château Chinon criterium, 'Le Critérium de France', is one of the most prestigious in the country. It is one of the few modern-day criteriums where spectators must pay an entry fee on to the circuit to watch – 35 francs. They are still coming into the town in droves and as I look down on them from the hotel bedroom I feel pressure. Today I am not just a professional cyclist: I'm a performer. These people are paying to see me perform. In a normal race you don't give a damn about what the guy at the side of the road thinks. Some are very abusive. It is not uncommon to be insulted as a lazy bastard or an over-paid lout by a spectator peeved with the fact that we are taking it easy. People are not happy unless they see us riding by at 60 kilometres an hour with our eyes in the backs of our heads. Or grovelling up some mountain on our hands and knees. If they insult us, then we feel justified in insulting them in return. I mean, nobody forced them to stand at the side of the road. Today is different: today they are paying to see a spectacle, and therefore we are obliged to perform. What if I can't? What if I'm unable to follow the others? The lads say that Château Chinon is one of the hardest criteriums with a climb each time on the short 2-kilometre lap. The Tour left me so terribly bitter. Didn't ride my bike for nine days after it. Couldn't face it. But I will surely pay the price today. I'll probably be dropped. Will the manager still pay me my contract? Will I have the neck to approach him for it? I shouldn't have come here – but hell, I need the money. Ann is living with me now. There's more expense, more responsibility. I never had that responsibility before. We won nothing in the Tour this year, a pittance. I need the money. It's the only reason I'm here.

We change into our strip. There are five of us in the room. I apply grease to the chamois leather of my racing shorts and pull them on to my bare bum, the cold grease sending a shiver up through my body. A bit like putting on wet swimming togs. I pull on a short-sleeved woollen vest, a pair of white ankle socks, two short-fingered leather mitts, cycling shoes and finally the white RMO jersey of my sponsor. I sit on the bed watching the others get ready, waiting for the moment. I know it has to happen. I'm waiting for it to happen. Fuck it, I want it to happen. The pressure – I can't take this pressure. It happens: the smiles . . . a bag is produced. In it, small white ampoules of amphetamines and a handful of short syringes. A glance is thrown in my direction. My 'chastity' is well known within the team but it is only polite to offer. I scratch my head and breathe in deeply. If I walk out through the door with only the hotel lunch in my system I will crack mentally. As a result I will probably be dropped and ridiculed after two laps. I can't face any more humiliation. The pressure. I need the money. I nod in acceptance.

My syringe is prepared. As it's my first time it is decided that 7 cc will be enough. Ten to fifteen is the average dose, but the real hard men often use double or treble this. Amphetamines work strongly for about two to three hours, after which the effects diminish. The criterium will last just two hours, which means we can take them in the privacy of the hotel room before going out to the start. I roll back the sleeve of my jersey. No turning back now. The needle is slipped under the skin of my left shoulder. I'm charged. One of my ambitions had always been to leave the sport without ever having taken anything. I got a certain satisfaction in casting myself as the pure white hero fighting to hold on to my virginity in an evil black world. But that was over now. To hell with the past.

They told me to remain perfectly still. They said I would soon feel the urge to talk and jump around the place, but that I must refrain from all excessive talk and gestures. People had eyes. If they saw the normally calm and withdrawn Paul Kimmage arriving at the street shaking hands and patting everyone on the back they would put two and two together. I didn't want that. My mind was clear and lucid, but after five minutes I started to feel the first effects. A little buzz. It got stronger and stronger and was soon a big buzz. It turned my head a bit at first, but then it manifested itself in a new way: aggression. I felt a terrible urge to get on the bike and make it bend under me. I felt invincible, that nothing could defeat me. The lads started joking about the effects the charge would have on me.

'You will drive back to Vizille like Fangio and tonight, you won't be able to sleep a wink. Your wife will have a great time.'

I laugh with them. Someone says he will give me a sleeping tablet for later. But sleeping is the last thing on my mind. I'm ready for action.

'Come on lads, let's get to the start.'

More laughter. We pick up the machines from the hotel garage and cycle the 2 kilometres to the start. My head is clear. I can't let anyone notice anything different. I must remain calm. I must remain calm. I must remain calm. Then I hear it. The voice. The voice calling out my name. An Irish voice. Jesus an Irish voice calling for me, and here I am charged up to the gills. Stay calm. Stay calm. I turn around to see who it is. He is young – and yes, I recognise him from somewhere but can't quite place him. We start talking. Paul, don't look him in the eye. If he sees the dilated pupils he will cop it straight away. I try not to look him in the eye. The name comes to me: Gareth Donahue, a young Irish amateur cyclist racing with a local French team. I said I had to rush and would talk to him again after the race. Of all the luck. The one time in my life I charge up, and I run into someone who knows me. The finish line is crowded. We must sign on at the podium and collect our numbers. There is a metal crowd-control barrier blocking the entrance to the podium. I am in full buzz and, feeling full of energy, I decide to jump it. I clear it by at least 10 feet but land on my backside. I look up to see if anyone has noticed. Thierry Clavet is fighting hard to hold back his laughter.

'For God's sake, take it easy, Polo.'

I signed on at the podium, making a special effort at calmness. Most of the lads were sitting on the chairs pinning their numbers on, so I joined them. My fingers were rattling a bit as I tried to pin mine on, but I eventually managed to do it. We were called to the line. The peloton was made up of twenty-five pros and six of the best local amateurs. Charly Mottet and Jean François Bernard were the two stars – the men the crowd had come to see. I presumed one of them was to win, but no one had said anything to me. I asked Clavet what the story was, but even he was confused. There seemed to be a bit of a problem between Mottet and Bernard – both wanted to win. Because he had ridden best in the Tour, Jean François Bernard would normally have been designated to win. But 'Jeff', lived in the region and there was an unwritten rule that the local man never won in front of his home crowd. This is to avoid any crowd suspicion of the rigging of the race. The Peugeot rider Gilbert Duclos is boss. He acts as mediator between the different leaders and then informs the smaller riders how the race is to be won. He controls things during the race. If a small rider steps out of line by attacking when he isn't supposed to attack, it is Duclos who will kick his arse. Punishment for a big offence is a word in the ear of the criterium manager. The offender would then have to wait a bit before he was offered another criterium contract. First, second and third were always designated, but anyone could race for the other placings. Sometimes the leaders don't agree and a free-for-all is announced, resulting in the victory of a smaller rider. Daddies don't always appreciate explaining to their sons how Joe Bloggs managed to beat Charly Mottet when Charly Mottet is supposed to be the best. So it is in the interests of all the riders to toe the line by having a good, 'organised' race, where everyone goes away happy. But although the race is organised this doesn't necessarily make it easier. It's not that easy to fool the crowd. Unless they see the stars whizzing by at 60 kilometres an hour they won't be happy. There is nothing false about the average lap speed, which rarely falls below 50 kilometres an hour. There is nothing false about the grimacing faces. It is just the result that is, well, 'doctored'. Duclos rides up to me on the first lap.

'It's Mottet in front of Bernard and Colotti. D'accord (OK)?'

'D'accord.'

There is no way I'm going to rock the boat. If he tells me to dive off and fake crashing, I'll do it. If he wants me to make a spectacle by riding around with my shorts around my ankles I'll do it. I just want the money. I just want to be one of the boys.

The race is one of the easiest I have ever ridden. I am never under pressure. I have such absolute confidence that I won't get dropped, and I'm able to attack off the front and contribute to the spectacle. This is all that matters to me. To be able to perform. To merit the few quid I have come for. I am prominent in several breakaways. Each time, we ride hard to build up a good lead and then ease up without making it look too obvious. Duclos controls things masterfully. Physically I feel the effort. I feel the pedals, the shortness of breath on the climb, but mentally I'm so strong that it's never a problem. My mind has been stimulated. Stimulated by amphetamines. I believe I'm invincible, therefore I am.

Bernard and Mottet break clear with three laps to go. Bernard is still not happy about not being allowed to win so they fight out a straight sprint and Jeff just edges Charly out. The gap between them is so close that I'm wondering if indeed it was a straight sprint, but anyway this is unimportant. The crowd have been given a good race and go away happy. We ride back to the hotel. After showering and changing we divide the room and lunch bill between us. I offer to pay for the 'charge'. Amphetamines are hard to come by and very expensive. An average charge costs about fifty pounds but I am not surprised when the offer is refused. It is rare that money passes hands between the riders. It's a case of 'See me right today, and I'll see you right tomorrow.' I have joined the club, and it feels almost satisfying to have done so.

The club contract cheques are distributed in a room of the town hall. We line up and enter the room one by one and receive our envelope from a member of the organising committee, under the watchful eye of the criterium manager. Sometimes the bastards make you wait until after the race reception. They know well that you might have 300 kilometres of a drive home, but expect you to shake hands and talk small talk to the locals before they hand over the hard-earned few bob. This is the fault of the criterium manager. They cream off ten to twelve per cent of all the riders' contracts, and also demand a large chunk from the race budget of the organising committee. They are parasites, and I despise them. They exploit the smaller riders, paying then small amounts, knowing too well that the poor sod has no choice but to accept. Real scum.

A large crowd of enthusiasts gathers outside the town hall, and I sign a hundred autographs on the way back to the car. Clavet and Colotti are also going home, but Vallet is engaged at a criterium somewhere else next day. Clavet gives me some advice as I get into the car.

'You will probably feel guilty later on. It happens to us all, you must not blame yourself. It's just part of the job.'

I thank him but forget to ask for the sleeping tablet. He catches me an hour later and we race for five minutes, but I don't feel comfortable driving at speed so I let him go. The drive back seems much shorter but not short enough to avoid the pangs of conscience stinging my brain. After the upper there is inevitably the downer. It is after twelve when I arrive home, and Ann is in bed but awake. I decide to tell her of my day's activities. All of them. She is lenient.

'You did what you thought was best. As long as it does not become a habit there is no harm done.'

This was said to comfort me, to ease the guilt. But her attitude annoyed me. It was too casual. I mean, I had taken drugs, cheated myself of my honour. How could she be so casual about something so serious? I wanted to be told off, to be chastised. We had a row, and she turned her back to me and fell asleep. I lay there, my two eyes glaring out of my head like two headlights. I was a million miles from sleep. The events of the day were turning in my head, the arguments for and against crossing my head like a tennis ball in an seemingly never-ending rally. The 'against' were hitting beautifully.

'Where was the logic in taking a charge for a race that was fixed? Where was the benefit? You realise now that you'll never be able to ride a criterium without taking something? And more than likely they'll find you dead in some hotel room in five years' time with a syringe sticking out of your arm and your eyes bulging out of your head. And the lads will crowd around your tombstone and later raise a glass to you and praise you for being one of them. One of the boys.'

But the 'fors' returned with some lovely volleys.

'No, that's rubbish. You've sat on the fence long enough. Aren't you forgetting how vulnerable you felt before the race? If you hadn't taken it you would have been slaughtered. You didn't do it to cheat. You did it to survive. To fight the battle with the same arms as everyone else.'

Over and back. Over and back. The last thing I remember is the 'fors' being two sets up and then the lights going out.

16 THE FAB FOUR

The repression of amphetamines through dope controls has had varying consequences. The use of the drug in the major tours and championships is minimal, almost non-existent. It is number one on the controllers' list and is easily detectable. The current trend is towards a different area of doping – hormones. They are natural: the body produces them, and so detection of hormone abuse is difficult. The 'sin' is not in taking illegal products, but in getting caught. Hormones, when used intelligently, offer the security of undetectability. The abuse is frightening.

An amphetamine charge lasts roughly three hours and is then flushed out of the system. Frequent use can result in addiction and maybe one or two problems with heart rhythm – but nothing too serious. Hormones are different. They don't flush out after three hours. They screw up the body's chemistry, lingering in the system for months, even years. Abuse can result in cancer and death. I was tempted many times to try hormones. I could see their beneficial effects on other members of the team but the consequences of abuse scared me, and I never touched them. I did, however, dabble with amphetamines.

I used them twice in criteriums shortly after Château Chinon. In twenty months of professionalism I had stayed clean but, incredibly, in the space of two weeks I charged on three occasions. It becomes so easy to slip into a routine. Once you experience the feeling of invincibility, it is so hard to race with just 'Vittel' in your bottle – especially when you see the others taking stuff.

I had always taken pride in my strength of character and my new habit started to worry me. I was losing control of my ability to say 'No', and on analysing the problem I decided never again to put myself in the position of riding a critérium without having trained. It was difficult at first but I managed to hold out. Even so, I never felt comfortable starting a criterium without at least two vitamin C tablets in my drinking bottle. I suppose it was doping, but at least it was legal. In my two final years in the peloton I stayed clean, but I am not particularly proud of this. There were many reasons why I never again touched it – a guilty conscience was the principal one but there were other factors. I suppose you could say I was 'chicken'. The fear of being caught terrified me. The scandal it would have caused back in good old Catholic Ireland would have ruined me for life. I couldn't bear to bring that shame on my parents. But there was another factor. I was not prepared actually to stick the needle into my own arm. When my team mates did it, I would look away. It was not a fear of pain or of needles, it was just the act of doping oneself that I found repellent. Another reason was the acquiring of the amphetamines. I had heard stories of police raids on riders' cars, and this scared me. I hadn't the balls to purchase and transport the stuff myself, and there was no way I could continue borrowing it from others. This would have given me a bad name among them – and above all, I wanted to be liked.

Back in Ireland, Stephen's Tour triumph was celebrated as a national victory. He was welcomed home to scenes of incredible adulation in an open-top bus tour of Dublin. Cycling was 'the' sport, and winning the Tour made Stephen the greatest sportsman the country had ever produced – and one of the most popular. I felt sorry for Kelly. Before Roche's Tour win Kelly had always been regarded as the country's number one cyclist. July 1987 must have been the most miserable month of his life. On the 12th he crashed out of the Tour, and to have sat at home injured and watch another Irishman wipe out everything he had ever done with one triumph must have been unbearable.

If Kelly was in agony then Roche was very much in ecstasy. For years he had played second fiddle to the 'King', but every dog has his day and this was Stephen's. He could have been forgiven for making the most of it, but he refrained from proclaiming himself as the country's greatest, which was most admirable.

'People should not say I have won this race and Sean had won that. They should look at our careers and say that between us we have won every race on the continent worth winning.'

When I look back on the nice things he has said and done throughout his career, it is to his eternal credit that he was nicest in his finest hour.

I met up with Kelly again in August. He was making his return to competition in the five-day Kelloggs Tour of Britain. My first words to him were those of consolation and encouragement and I think he appreciated it. I liked him and admired him more than any other rider in the peloton. It was not always this way. Before I turned professional I never understood him: I'm still not quite sure that I do, but I'd go as far as saying that in those early days I actually disliked him. I found him solemn, a machine with no heart and no personality. He was the world's number one who could have helped me when I was struggling for my contract, but didn't. Ireland was split between the supporters of Kelly and those of Roche: the 'Kelly' men and the 'Roche' men. I was definitely a Roche man. It has taken me four years of professionalism to break down the complex layers of 'l'homme' Kelly. Talking to him was never easy. It still isn't. You must make an effort to reach him, but once you do, then the effort is worth it. He is colourful, has a caring heart and a great personality. I am grateful now that he didn't help with my contract when I was struggling as an amateur. It made me fight harder. I earned it under my own steam, which is the only way.

I remember riding the Criterium International in my first year. I was eliminated in the Sunday morning mountain stage and as a result was exempt from the final-stage time trial in the afternoon. I left for the airport to fly back to Lille before the time trial finished and just as the plane was about to close its door Kelly ran in, still in his racing gear. He had just won the final time trial, clinching the race, but had no time to change – there was just one evening flight to Lille, and his wife Linda was picking him up and driving to their home in Brussels. We had to change flights at Lyon and he bought me dinner. We dined and talked, and being with him was such a thrill that I completely forgot about the lousy weekend I'd had.

The justification for the writing of this book was that it would tell of the unglamorous life of the 'back room' boy. The account of the life of an unknown among many unknowns who pass most of their lives in the professional peloton without ever making a name for themselves. But, on reflection, I realise that I was not a domestique like the others. I had one great advantage. I shared a friendship and a comradeship with two of cycling's greatest ever riders. It is a privilege that only now becomes apparent to me as I look back on the August of 1987.

Martin and I both profited enormously from the euphoria of Stephen's triumph on returning to Ireland for three city-centre races at the end of that month. I will remember for the rest of my life the night of the first race in Dublin.

It wasn't easy. I hated city-centre races – one-hour dashes on tight circuits – and we were totally unused to this type of racing on the continent. I just hadn't the speed to perform well in them. None of us had – except Sean. But because it was Dublin, and Stephen had just won the Tour, I expected that the opposition, all British apart from Aussie Allan Peiper, would have no objections to fixing it for Stephen to win. I was wrong. We had a meeting among riders before the race. Sean spoke on our behalf and suggested we come to an arrangement for Stephen to win. He was backed up by Peiper and by Paul Sherwen. Paul had been a pro for seven years on the continent, but was riding his last season with Raleigh in England. He tried to convince his compatriots that everyone would benefit from a Roche win. The spectators would applaud it and the future of the event would be assured by it. But the appeals fell on deaf ears. The 'English pros' argued that city-centre races were their bread and butter. They wanted financial compensation in return for a Roche victory.

Their attitude disgusted me. I walked out of the room before a solution had been reached. I had never liked the English pros, big-headed sods who thought having a pro licence made them pro-fessional. I despised them for their pettiness. They were not worthy of polishing Roche's shoes, and yet here they were, laying down the law – in Dublin. Pathetic. I waited for the three lads to come out of the meeting. The English pros had agreed to let Stephen win – in return for £1,000. The race was incredibly fast and I remember gritting my teeth so hard that I chipped one, sprinting out of the last corner and going into the finishing straight. Stephen won, and most people went away happy – but not all of them went away.

After the finish we showered in one of the Georgian houses directly behind the finishing line on St Stephen's Green. There was a post-race reception at Jurys Hotel but the view from our room told us that getting there would be a problem. Hundreds of people were banked at the entrance to the house waiting for us to come down. When we did, it was chaos. They all wanted autographs and they were shouting, screaming, touching. I felt like one of the 'fab' four coming out of a concert in the sixties – a Beatle. We needed protection from the Gardai to get from the house to our manager Frank Quinn's car, and flashing blue lights and screaming sirens cleared the road for our drive to the hotel.

The second race was held in Wexford on the following evening. We left Dublin in the morning and rode some of the way for training. The world championships were just twelve days away. Again, as in

Dublin, there was a riders' meeting before the race. We weren't invited, and the English lads met among themselves to divide up the spoils. No one approached us about it, which we felt was most unreasonable. Stephen had paid to win in Dublin, and we felt it only right that we be recompensed in a similar way for an English triumph in Wexford. Being ignored irritated the two lads and we decided to pull out all the stops for an Irish win. At the end of another fast race Stephen led Sean out along the Wexford seafront, and Kelly swept by for the victory. It is questionable whether Kelly got as much pleasure out of winning two Paris–Roubaix races as he did in sprinting to victory that night on the seafront, for he was truly delighted and we all shared his pleasure. After showering at the hotel, we decided that a celebration was in order. A few pints in some quiet bar would have suited us fine, but it was impossible to leave the hotel. There was no such thing as a quiet bar for Kelly and Roche. They were instantly recognised anywhere they went, so we stayed at the hotel. We ordered fresh fruit salad, sandwiches, tea and coffee and a few drinks to be brought up to the rooms. I roomed with Martin and Sean with Stephen, but our entourage included Frank Quinn, his assistant Margaret Walsh, Kelly's brother-in-law Gerard Grant and Stephen's brother-in-law Peter. The bedrooms were too small to hold a party, so we laid out the trays of food and drink on the corridor outside and sat together on the carpeted floor. It was a great night. We talked and joked and made plans for Cork.

I don't know if the English riders saw it as we did, but for us the three race series had developed into Ireland versus England – especially now that we were winning two nil. We were outnumbered ten to one but this sweetened the challenge, for two aces were always going to beat forty jokers. We did indeed look on them as jokers, with the exception of Sherwen and John Herety, who had both served hard apprenticeships on the continent and as such knew what real pro racing was about. They had 'played in the first division'. But it was never easy beating the jokers in these city-centre races. I wasn't capable of it, neither was Martin. Stephen could win only by breaking clear alone and there was no way they would let him away in Cork. Kelly was our only hope, and all our efforts were to help him.

We rode some of the way down next morning and talked about the next challenge. Martin and I were to control the race for as long as possible by keeping the pace high and closing down any breakaway attempts. Stephen was to save himself for a lone assault in the last few laps and, that failing, would act as lead-out man for Kelly in the final sprint. The tactics worked well, right up to the last lap. Stephen hit the front, riding as hard as he could, with Kelly on his wheel. Sean came through going into the last corner and Roche followed him round. Kelly started sprinting, Roche made no effort to follow him, and, realising the danger Englishman Mark Walsham tried to go past; but in his haste he rode into the Tour de France winner. There was a huge crash, bodies everywhere. I cornered seconds after the impact and couldn't believe it. I picked out the yellow jersey of Stephen in the middle of the tangled bodies and gingerly picked my way around the groaning heap. Walsham and some of the other crash victims threatened violence towards Stephen, claiming he had closed the door and had deliberately caused the crash. Walsham and Co. were forgetting that they were in Ireland and that Stephen Roche was sacred here. If they had put a finger on him they'd have been lynched. In the turmoil of the crash, Kelly's victory almost went unnoticed. Unnoticed to all except Roche, that is. He made a fake effort at cooling tempers on both sides.

'After all, lads, the score is Ireland 3 England nil, and the match is over.'

Talk about adding fuel to the flames!

Martin returned to Dublin after the race, and from there took a flight back to Manchester and returned to his home near Stoke. Stephen, Sean and I flew back to the continent early next morning. We had spent five days together and those five days will remain in my memory as my happiest five days in professional cycling. We teamed up again twelve days later in Villach, Austria for the world championships.

Villach was more serious. Sean wanted badly to save a disastrous season by winning the rainbow jersey. It was the one single-day race which has always eluded him and he trained particularly hard for it. Stephen was much more relaxed about it all. When you have just won the Giro and the Tour de France, nobody expects another performance in the world championships. His life had turned into a perpetual series of product promotion, press interviews, signing autographs and shaking hands. He had come to Villach to get back into serious racing and to give Kelly a bit of a dig-out. The difference in attitudes showed at the hotel on the day before the race. In the morning we trained on the circuit. World championships are very special. There is a great atmosphere generated among the thousands of bike lovers from all over Europe congregating to cheer on their favourites in the annual feast of cycling. The circuit was hard, and the long drag after the finish was more difficult than first announced. I liked it, and knew I could ride well here. I felt very proud riding with the three lads. Sean and Stephen rode at the front, flanked by Martin and me. I could not help noticing the ease with which Stephen pedalled. Kelly noticed it too, but neither of us thought he had the form to be world champion. Lunch was followed by a long discussion on the choice of gear to be used. We spent most of the afternoon in bed snoozing and reading – except for Stephen, that is. Some journalists had come looking for interviews and he spent his afternoon talking to them in the garden of the hotel. At meal times he would leave his food to answer telephone calls and other requests, and he wasn't a bit serious about the race. I started to feel the pressure in the evening. None of the Irish supporters came to the hotel. It was the night before battle, and they knew better.

The rooming arrangements were the same as in Ireland. Sean shared with Stephen and Martin with me. I liked rooming with Martin. As amateurs we had roomed many times together on Irish teams, but then we were rivals and it was often difficult to be honest. Now it was different. We were both professionals and no longer rivals. I had the edge on him as an amateur but he was now the better professional. I was unbelievably nervous before going to bed. Two of my brothers, Raphael and Kevin, had come over from Ireland and would be on the circuit tomorrow. I did not want to let them down by riding badly. But I was also very excited. My last appearance at a world championship was two years after my sixth place in the amateur race in Italy. I had lost any illusions about ever winning the Tour de France but I secretly dreamed about one day being world champion. I polished my shoes before getting into bed, and had them shining. Normally I am not one for polishing shoes, but this was the world championships, and in my excitement I brushed them till they were sparkling. My enthusiasm irritated Martin, who was trying not to let the build-up start until the morning of the race. He offered me a sleeping tablet. I accepted. We slept like logs.

I love the sound of rain splattering off the windows when I'm cosy in bed. For a while I enjoyed the sound. My senses were still numbed with sleep and I could have been anywhere. In my childhood bed back in Dublin. In my wife's bed back in Grenoble. All I knew was that I was in bed and that it was raining outside and that I liked being in bed when it was raining outside. But slowly the messages from my ear found a receptive brain cell and the splattering sounds were analysed more carefully. I wasn't just anywhere: I was in the Hotel Piber in

Villach. The rain that was battering the window would soon be making its way into every pore of my skin, chilling me, making me uncomfortable. 'Oh, my God, I'm a professional cyclist . . . And it's the morning of the world championships . . . FUCK IT'S RAINING . . . I HATE RAIN.'

How unlucky can you get? In the run-up we had three days of beautiful sunny weather, but now it was not simply raining but bucketing down. All of my enthusiasm went out of the wet window. I hate rain. I never ride well in it. I'm not sure I talked over breakfast.

I was in serious difficulty for the first half of the race. I had been given new wheels and the rims were smooth, making it hard for my brake pads to get any sort of grip. Slowing on the descent was a problem, and for a while I felt very insecure. The other three sat near the front of the bunch, watching, controlling, waiting. Stephen came back to me to encourage me to come to the front. My only wish was to abandon, but I couldn't let my brothers down – as they had spent their hard-earned money on coming over to see me – so I tried to follow him. The ease with which he cut his way through the bunch was heart-breaking. His incredibly efficient style. So graceful, so beautiful to watch – like a long-legged woman walking down the street. It was as if the bicycle was an extension of his hips. The rain stopped after about three hours, and slowly my stiffened leg muscles started to heat up again and I at last felt the urge to race. After eighteen laps the hill after the finish line started to feel like a small col. Cracks started appearing in the diminishing bunch, and amazingly I found myself closing gaps instead of opening them. With 60 kilometres to go a four-man group that included two favourites, Dutchman Teun Van Vliet and reigning champion Moreno Argentin, went clear. The French took up the chase, aided by a quarter of the Irish team, Martin Earley, and the gap started to narrow. I sat near the front, waiting for a sign of weakness from Martin. The four were retrieved and the attacks followed. Martin, exhausted from his chase, retired – he had done his work. I moved up on Kelly's shoulder and told him I was available for short-range chasing. He nodded, and I set about closing down any serious break without a green jersey. As the bell rang, announcing the last lap, the decisive move went clear. It was on the climb, and I was shattered and really suffering. I looked up to the glorious sight of two green jerseys bridging the gap. Behind, the race was over, and we all knew it. I tuned my ear to the p.a. system and tried to work out what was happening up front. I said a prayer that Kelly might win. With both of them up front they had a great chance. The logical tactic was for Stephen to hold it together for Sean in the sprint. I strained my ears as we turned into the finishing straight. The p.a. announced the winner.

'Steven Rooks, Champion du Monde.'

There was a huge roar from the crowd. 'Did he say Roche or Rooks?' I wasn't sure. Rooks, the Dutchman, was also in the break. 'I think he said Rooks.' I didn't bother to sprint. It was seconds after crossing the line that I discovered the truth. I bumped into Irish journalist John Brennan as he scurried across for a few words from the new world champion.

'He's done it. The bastard's done it.'

'Who?'

'Roche.'

'No, you're joking?'

He wasn't joking.

I made my way through the crowd to our pit area. Stephen had been whisked off for the medal ceremony, but our pit was still crowded. Kelly was giving his story to journalists, Martin was having the back patted off him by almost every Irish supporter on the circuit and there were scenes of great joy all around the pit. I too wacked him across the back and then threw my arms around Kelly and congratulated him on his fine performance. I really wished it could have been him on the winner's rostrum, but I suppose it's the one title he is destined never to win. We pulled on some warm clothes and cycled back to the hotel, where it took some solid scrubbing under the shower to remove the grime and dirt from seven hours of racing from my legs. Stephen arrived about an hour later. He looked resplendent in his new rainbow jersey, but the magnitude of his achievement had not yet sunken in. He had done something that only one other man in the whole world had done. In winning the Tour of Italy, the Tour de France and the world championships in the same year he had equalled Eddy Merckx.

The celebrations went on late into the next morning. Most of the supporters came around to the hotel, and it was a great night to be Irish. I felt very privileged to be part of it all, as it's something I can tell my children and my grandchildren. I can see myself in my rocking chair by the fire, forty years from now with grandson on my knee.

'Tell me about the day you helped Stephen Roche to be world champion, Granda.'

And I will tell it – without doubt exaggerating my contribution to the victory.

'And where did you finish, Granda?'

'Well, son, I was so tired after all my work that I could only finish forty-fourth.'

And I'll smile, and memories of the day will warm me more than any fire.

My good performance at the world championships gave me great confidence for the end-of-season races. I particularly wanted to do well in the Nissan Classic in Ireland in October. Thevenet was particularly kind. He allowed me to choose the four riders to accompany me on the race as a reward for my good year. I chose the four that I was closest to: André Chappuis, Jean Claude Colotti, Thierry Claveyrolat and Per Pedersen.

I went into the race as team leader – the only time in my life that I held such a responsibility. On the second stage I asked Thierry and Jean Claude to ride over the Vee climb as hard as possible in an effort to break up the race. I sat in their slipstream and they set a pace which blew the race apart. This was a new kind of pressure, one I had not experienced before. My normal role was to do what they were now doing for me – the donkey work. But the pace they set was so fierce that I began to wonder if I had the legs to continue the effort, once they finished their effort. If I cracked, then I would be the laughing-stock of the bunch. Joel Pelier attacked just after the hairpin, and I bridged the gap. Eleven others joined us, and for those behind it was curtains, for we soon had a gap of over ten minutes – I had detonated the vital move in the five-day race. I so wanted the break to succeed that I did too much work and was knackered by the time I got to the stage finish at St Patrick's Hill in Cork, so I was not placed highly on the stage. The following day was a hard loop around the Ring of Kerry to Tralee and I did another good ride, moving to seventh overall. The stage was won by Sean Yates in a solo break which I rate as one of the best rides I ever saw in my time with the pros. The fourth stage was a team time trial. Dede and Clavet packed it in after getting dropped after the Vee on the second stage, and spent the rest of the week buying Aran sweaters and drinking pints of Guinness. So we were down to just three men for the trial. I slipped a place to eighth, which I held on to until the finish of the race in O'Connell Street in Dublin. I felt very satisfied with my performance, for the organisers had put together a high-class field. Sean won, Stephen was second, Martin was sixth and I was eighth – it was another week of being 'fab'.

The wedding day is supposed to be a great day in a couple's life. I enjoyed my wedding day, but only after the church ceremony; for I was so nervous that I bungled the 'for richer, for poorer, in sickness and in health' bit – still, it got a good laugh. We were married in Ann's parish church in Balscadden in North County Dublin on October 23. Most bike riders get married in October. It's the month that the season ends, the time for drink and fun and relaxation and, well, marriages. I had been going out with Ann for five years and I was twenty five-years old and she twenty two so we both reckoned we were 'ripe'. I invited the other 'Beatles' to the wedding. Sean was tied up and couldn't come, but Martin and Stephen were both present. From RMO I asked the four that had ridden with me on the Nissan, but Dede was the only one to come. Stephen's presence was a big surprise. He was besieged with requests for functions and promotions all over the country, and I honestly didn't expect him to turn up. While we were being married word got round that Stephen Roche was in Balscadden church, and village kids and housewives from the area converged on us when the ceremony was over, looking for his autograph. Stephen felt a bit worried that his popularity might detract from what was essentially 'our day' – but on the contrary, his presence created a carnival atmosphere that made it all more enjoyable.

We honeymooned in Connemara and Clare and I returned to France two weeks later to pass the winter in our flat in Vizille. Nineteen eighty-seven had been very satisfying. I was sure I would continue to improve. I was wrong: it was the summit of my career.

17 COFFEE AT ELEVEN

The village of Vizille lies 12 kilometres outside Grenoble on the road to Gap. It's a typically rural French village but can claim a certain notoriety because it was from here that the French Revolution started two hundred years ago. A magnificent château, a former residence of French presidents, dominates the village square, and life and traffic circulation in the village revolves around it. The 'Café de la Gare' is ideally placed, and lies 50 metres opposite the château and its magnificent park. It's a typically French café. From seven to eight it serves mostly coffee, nearly always black, and croissants. Just before twelve there will be a rush on 'pastis', the aniseed drink that is the aperitif of the French labourer. From one to two it's coffee time again; but the afternoons are calm until just before seven when there will be another rush on pastis.

I got to study the patterns quite well during 1988. There was a great view from the terrace and I studied Vizille and its inhabitants and its château in falling snow and falling rain, in grey skies and in blue. I watched green leaves turn to falling leaves – always from the terrace. From my chair and an empty row of coffee cups I studied them. The old men playing 'boules' in the shade of the sixteen sycamore trees. The old woman hastily loading a basket of groceries on to her bicycle as the rain started to fall. The village idlers doing the rounds from one cafe to another, scrounging drink. The buzz of traffic clogging up the square. At every hour of the day, on every day of the year, you could be sure there was something happening in the village square. Which is precisely why I went there so often. It was an escape. I found immense tranquillity from buying a cup of coffee and sitting on the terrace with it. Watching, analysing, thinking and inevitably searching for a way out. A job. I spent more time on the terrace of the Café de la Gare that year than I did racing my bike. It was a bad year.

Everything had been rosy at the end of 1987 – too rosy. It was in the months of November and December that I let it slip. Because I had had a hard season I felt I needed a good break. I did, but I just got carried away. When I should have been sweating it out in the weights room, I was off touring the wine cellars of the vineyards of Avignon. Wine was a passion: smelling it, tasting it, buying it and especially drinking it. I had the reputation in the team of being a 'gourmet' – a connoisseur of good food and wine. A hard man for the drink and the crack. I impressed with my knowledge of 'grands crus', and I found a new pleasure in being impressive. I got too cocky. I became great friends with Colotti. He advised me to watch my weight and to train hard. I advised him on the wines he should stock his cellar with. I rode the odd cyclo-cross, did a little jogging; but it wasn't enough.

The year started with a training camp and a 'let's get to know each other' week just before Christmas. It was Bernard Vallet's opening act as the new directeur sportif of the team. Thevenet had been disposed of ever so tidily and ruthlessly. He was first offered the job of 'team manager'. The manager is in charge of team administration. He co-ordinates travel to races, deals with race organisers for expenses and acts as public relations officer. It's a 'cosy' number, and although he would have preferred to stay on as directeur sportif, the post of manager held a certain attraction for him. He accepted, and Vallet's promotion as directeur sportif was announced to the French press. The dust was allowed to settle for six weeks, and then Monsieur Braillon informed Thevenet that he had reconsidered and that his services were no longer required. Thevenet's dismissal was an embarrassment to Vallet. They had been friends, and when questioned about it Vallet got himself out of the corner by explaining that it was Monsieur Braillon's decision. Thevenet claimed unfair dismissal, and won his case before the courts. Monsieur Braillon was forced to pay him a year's salary – about £30,000.

The training camp at Autrans, a cross-country ski resort in the Vercors mountains, was fun – even though there was no snow. The core of the team remained the same and there were just five changes. Bincoletto, Lavenu, Grewal, Peillon and Huger were replaced by Frank Pineau, Eric Salomon, Hartmut Bolts, Alex Pedersen and Patrick Vallet (no relation to Bernard). We played indoor football, swam at the local pool, jogged and did some mountain biking. In between sports outings we were photographed, measured for our new clothes and examined by doctors. At night we had team talks from the new chief. Vallet gave some great team talks.

He told us he was confident that we were going to have a great year. He intended to run the team like the captain of a ship. We were all in the same boat, and we must all row together for the team's success. If he'd known the words of 'The Soldier's Song' I'm sure he'd have sung it.

We're on the road. . .

And it worked. We believed him. We left Autrans convinced we had a good directeur sportif and that everything was 'rosy in the garden'. A day later we were of a different opinion.

Looking back on it I am reminded of those gory 'Friday the Thirteenth' movies. You know, the 'just when you thought it was safe to go back in the water' stuff. In our case Freddie, or Carrie, or Gory attacked us in the shape of a newspaper article.

L'Equipe, the French sports daily, had sent a journalist to Autrans to cover the training week. The journalist, Guy Roger, did a half-page interview with Vallet and it was published a day after we returned home. To say it shocked me is an understatement. It had the effect of Carrie's hand coming up from the grave. It was a question-and-answer piece – no room for misinterpretation. Vallet was questioned about the 'faiblesse', or 'weakness', of his new team. He replied.

I will be frank. Of the eighteen riders in the team, half were signed before I took control (i.e. by Thevenet). I personally wouldn't have done it. I believe also that none of the eight would have found jobs in any other French team either.

I remember reading the interview over breakfast. I interrupted my bowl of porridge and did a quick calculation. I was one of those who had signed under Thevenet. Was he referring to me? Surely not.

He didn't criticise everyone. He had glowing praise for two of his signings, two of the new pros.

I am pleased to have signed Hartmut Bolts and Alex Pedersen, who finished second and third respectively, in the last amateur world championships. These two have the right approach. I haven't seen them pedal yet but their mentality and behaviour are those of real pros. They will help the others to get the finger out.

I had expectected criticism from Vallet at some stage in the year but not before we had even turned a pedal. I picked up the phone and rang headquarters for an explanation. Vallet was not around but Jacques Michaud the assistant directeur sportif was. Yes, he had seen *L'Equipe*. No, there was no need to worry about it, all lies. He said that a letter of explanation from Vallet was already in the post and to make no further comments to anyone until reading the letter.

Sure enough, the letter arrived next day. Vallet told us to pay no attention to the lies written by Guy Roger, whose only interest was to upset the normal running of the team.

I didn't believe him. Any advantage Guy Roger could gain from rocking the RMO boat was beyond my comprehension. No, I was quite sure that Vallet had said it all right. Not intentionally, of course, and perhaps he just got carried away. Being in *L'Equipe* is all that ever matters to a lot of French pro's. Vallet could now give them half-page interviews – in my view he loved it. He loved the power, being the centre of attention. It seemed to me that in his first interview as a directeur sportif he wanted to make an 'I'm a tough guy' impression. He made an impression all right.

Two days before writing this chapter I met up with Guy Roger at the Grenoble Six, a track event. I had always wondered about the famous interview and asked him if he had altered any of Vallet's words. Roger assured me over the heads of his two children that he had written the piece word for word. Bolts and Pedersen last week came to the end of the two-year contract signed with Vallet. He fired them both.

I accept that the job of directeur sportif is a difficult one, and that harsh decisions are often necessary for the good of the team. I don't blame Bernard Vallet for my failure at RMO in 1988. He was the epitome of what a good directeur sportif should be. A superb organiser, he has a total understanding of professional racing and is a good motivator. He was certainly better at the job than Thevenet. But Thevenet had a quality that made up for his organisational faults – his sincerity. In my opinion Vallet didn't know the meaning of the word. I think he was as two-faced as they come.

I was fully prepared for a hard start to the 1988 season. I knew I would have problems, but it didn't worry me too much. I had had problems early in 1986 and 1987, but each time I had hit form at the right moment to win a place in the team for the Tour. I felt that 1988 would be the same – that it would take me two months to hit form.

February, March and April were disastrous months. I just couldn't get going, found it impossible even to finish races and abandoned one after another. But in May, in the Grand Prix of Wallonie in Belgium, I started putting it together. I could feel good form coming on. I had trained really hard for it, and felt good except for one thing – I had this maddening itch around my arse. I couldn't understand it, but put off getting it seen to, as it was a bit embarrassing. The day after Wallonie, we lined up for a three-stage two-day race, the Tour de L'Oise just north of Paris. It opened with a short 80 kilometre stage but I was totally knackered, and suffered from stomach trouble. I was dropped with 30 kilometres to go and lost nine minutes. I was terribly depressed at this latest setback, and couldn't understand it as I had ridden so well in Wallonie the day before. I was rooming with Frank Pineau. I had a shit at about nine and left the most dreadful smell behind me. Frank complained that he had never experienced anything like it. He assured me there was something wrong with my insides. This got me thinking. The itch around my anal passage was driving me insane and had developed into a rash. Perhaps there was something wrong.

I started the stage next day but I had this persistent stomach cramp and was completely drained of strength, so I abandoned. I flew to Grenoble that night and on Monday morning paid a visit to the doctor. He looked at my bum and asked me to stick out my tongue.

'Champignons (mushrooms).'

'What's that?'

'It's a fungus that develops in the digestive tract. It's gone right through you from your tongue to your bum.'

I was told to stay off the bike until the rash had disappeared and he advised a break from competition for ten days. It was almost a relief to have been told there was something wrong with me. Until then, I just couldn't understand what was going wrong. Now I had a reason – an excuse. Even if the mushrooms were not totally responsible for my lack of form I had no problem convincing myself that they were. Coffee sales were up that week at the Café de la Gare.

I made a return to competition at the Tour de l'Armorique. I was still undergoing treatment but was feeling brand new, if a little behind physically. There was one place left to be filled in the team to ride the Dauphine, to be filled either by me or by Eric Salomon. I wanted to ride the Dauphine. It was my ticket for the Tour. But the mushrooms had set me back in my preparation. I rode with little flair at Armorique and Vallet offered the ride to Salomon.

I was disappointed, but had expected it. The day after the Armorique we stayed in Brittany for the Grand Prix of Plumelec. A single-day race, Plumelec is one of a series of French classics where there are never any controls. These races are know among the pros as the 'Grands Prix des Chaudières'. 'Chaud' means 'warm'. The word 'chaudière' is used for someone who heats, who warms up, who takes a charge. Mauleon–Moulin, Châteauroux–Limoges, GP of Plumelec, GP of Plouay, GP of Cannes – all are 'Grands Prix des Chaudières'. At the team meetings on the night before these classics the dialogue from the directeur sportif was always the same.

'Now lads, I can't say there won't be a control tomorrow but this is Plumelec.'

And there would be spontaneous laughter.

'We are all professionals, so it's up to each of us to conduct ourselves as such. If there is a surprise control and anyone is caught, I will do my best to protect you as far as the sponsor is concerned.'

I could never bring myself to charge up for the 'Chaudières' races and always went into them with an inferiority complex. As a result of not taking anything I felt disadvantaged and never bothered even to try to win. It was those high principles of mine: there was no way I could be happy winning a race, knowing I had charged for it. And yet I am forced to admit that a lot of it was purely psychological. In my first year I was as green as grass starting the GP of Plumelec. I didn't realise it was a 'Chaudières'. I felt I was riding on the same level as everyone else, so it didn't bother me. I finished eighth. But three years later I was a man of the world. I knew what was going on but wasn't mentally strong enough still to try and win.

Plumelec is a five and a half hour race. It was a foul day, raining and miserable. Tired from the Armorique stage race, I was never going well. Half-way through the race, on one of the small back roads of the circuit, we were strung out in one long line. I was second last and Dede last. I knew he was getting it rough so I looked around to see how he was. His body and face were wet and mucky from the spray from the back wheels. He had something between his teeth – a needle. He bit the plastic cap off and I immediately understood what he was going to do next. I dropped behind him to push him as he injected himself with the white liquid, most probably amphetamine. This was to help him to get it over as quickly as possible so no one would see him.

To see him dirty, suffering and with that needle between his teeth turned my stomach. I wanted to get off and just leave the bike there and then. I abandoned the race and rode straight to the showers. I was disgusted. Not at Dede, he didn't know any better. He was simply playing by their rules, another innocent victim. No, I blamed the system. The race organisers, the directeurs sportifs, the sponsors – the men in power who knew what was going on but turned a blind eye to it. And when his career ended, the system would spit him out – a penniless ex-pro. The incident strengthened my conviction never to enter the drugs stadium. I would go as far as I could for as long as possible, but if it wasn't good enough then it was just too bad. If someone had offered me a decent job that Sunday in Plumelec I'd have taken it, there and then. But I had to keep trying. There were bills to be paid, responsibilities to be met – and a little flicker of hope of riding the Tour.

I believed right up until the last minute that I could still make the Tour team. It became almost an obsession. I used to take out this team poster and with a pen place crosses on the heads of those I felt had blown it. The heads of the fellows still in with a chance were marked with a question. With two weeks to go there were eight ticks on the poster. I was one of three question marks fighting for the last place. The other two were Frank Pineau and the German Hartmut Bolts.

The Midi Libre stage race was my last chance to prove myself. I worked like a Trojan for the others for the week and finished it off with third place on the final stage – a mountain stage. I was sure I had done enough. The decision was Vallet's. He said he'd make up his mind after the national championships a week before the start of the Tour. All of the European and Scandinavian countries hold their professional championships on the same date. Ireland does not hold a professional championship as we are only a handful of pros. I spent the day at home, hoping against hope that neither Pineau nor Bolts would ride well. Pineau didn't. Bolts became the professional champion of Germany. On Monday I drove to a meeting with Vallet to hear the decision. I don't know why I bothered. In the morning's *L'Equipe*, Vallet had lavished glowing praise on the new German champion. I should have read between the lines and realised that I hadn't made it. But I wanted the waiting to end. I wanted to be told. I was told.

It was to be a month's holiday at the 'Café de la Gare'.

Vallet told me to have a short break and to prepare myself for a good end of season. I was shattered. I cried on my way back to Vizille, and the depth of my disappointment surprised me. I phoned home the news to my parents and also to David Walsh at the *Sunday Tribune*. We had planned to write a book on the Tour together, a 'from the saddle' account of the three-week race; but with my non-selection the project went out the window. David asked me if I'd consider writing a short column for the *Tribune* on the four Sundays of the Tour. I had

Above: Leading the Nissan Classic 1986
Below: The Dublin Bus − RMO team for the Nissan Classic 1987. LEFT
TO RIGHT: *Thierry Claveyrolat, Per Pedersen, myself, André Chappuis,
Jean Claude Colotti*

Above left: Martin Earley and Sean Kelly riding for Kas in the tour of '88
Above right: Patrick Valcke
Below: Claveyrolat shares his supply of food — Nissan '87

Above: World Road Race championships, Belgium 1988. The rider in dark glasses, to my left, is Jorgen Pedersen
Below left: The pressure is on at the '88 World Championships Johnny Weltz of Denmark is number 52
Below right: Tour de France '86, Alpe d'Huez. Getting a massage from Emile and advice from Stephen Roche

Above left: *Tour de France '89. Montpellier, 13 July. The evening of my last race as a professional. Hours earlier I had abandoned the Tour and my career as a pro cyclist*
Above right: *Hill walking with Ann in the Alps, August '89*
Below: *A proud moment — accepting the prize as Irish Sports Journalist of the Year, December '89*

been writing on and off for 'Irish Cycling Review' for two years, but had never written for a newspaper before. David was taking a bit of a chance in getting me to write the column and stressed that I keep it short – about 500 words. If it was rubbish, then it would be just 500 words of rubbish and no one would notice too much. It was still a big responsibility, and on the morning I wrote the piece I regretted ever having agreed. I was unbearable. I ordered Ann out of the house and the slightest noise would drive me nuts. But writing it was only half the battle. I then had to read the piece over the phone to a copy-taker at the paper. Evelyn was very patient and understanding but even then I hated it. I kept waiting for her to say, 'Now, hold on a minute, son, this is rubbish.' But she never did, and my pieces got a good response. The first one was about being left out of the Tour. The second week I wrote about my hopes for Kelly doing well. And on the third week I did a piece which the *Tribune* entitled 'A picnicker's view of the Alpe d'Huez':

Alpe d'Heuz. Thirteen kilometres of strength-sapping ascensions. Twenty-one hairpin bends that climb to almost 6,000 feet. The blue riband of the Tour, a monument to its glorious history.

Driving up the Romanche Valley, or the Valley of the Dead as it is better known, I was filled with remorse. For this morning I was going to that famous battleground, not as rider but as spectator. My wife Ann and I set out at nine, convinced that the 32 kilometres from our house to the foot of the Alpe would take no more than an hour to drive. I had forgotten it was Bastille Day.

All of France was on holiday and we found ourselves stuck in a traffic jam 15 kilometres from Bourg d'Oisans, the town at the bottom of the climb. For twenty-five minutes we sat there without budging. Word came filtering back that the Gendarmes had closed the road early because of the huge volume of traffic.

We abandoned the car and walked the four kilometres to the police roadblock. It was too far to walk to the Alpe so we set up camp on a boring 300-metre flat stretch of road, a kilometre from the town of Rochatailee.

Sitting by the side of the road I soon realised that as a tour spectator I was a bit of a green-horn. We had no fold-up chairs to sit on. No white cotton caps to keep the sun off our heads and no transistor to keep us informed on how the race was going.

We did however remember the picnic basket. It soon became evident to me that many other people had lost hope of getting to the Alpe, as little by little our anonymous piece of road started to fill with picnicking families.

The hours slowly passed and I found myself becoming more and more frustrated at the lack of race information. I spotted a veteran Tour spectator across the road. He had the vital equipment and I decided to ask him if he had heard anything. He told me that Fignon had not started the stage and that Jean François Bernard had lost contact on the Col de la Madeleine and was trailing the leaders by five minutes.

I was amazed. Bernard had been my Tour favourite. The old spectator had no news of Kelly. I went back to Ann and we began eating lunch. I dropped my baguette when the old man raised his arm to me. Kelly was four minutes down. *Merde*! I was really disappointed.

Kelly had lost the Tour, for I knew that those four minutes would soon double and maybe even triple for they had not yet crossed the Glandon and there was still the Alpe to come. I thanked the old man for the last time. I had no more interest in crossing the road.

The publicity caravan arrived. I recognised the co-directeur sportif that I had had in 1986, Jean Claude Valaeys. He was throwing plastic bags and paper hats out of the window of his brightly coloured Peugeot. Never liked the guy.

The roadside nicely littered, we waited for the main act. Rooks and Delgado duly obliged and for 15 seconds we watched as the two heroes battled their way up the road, dwarfed by the swarm of TV cameras and photographers and race organisation vehicles. Group after group the shattered faces rolled by.

I shouted encouragement at Claveyrolat and Colotti, the two team mates I regarded as friends. But as my other team mates passed I held my breath in disrespectful silence.

Another group appeared. Three yellow and blue jerseys riding at the front. I knew immediately this was the Kelly group. I looked at my watch. Fifteen minutes had ticked past since Delgado and Rooks had gone by. Martin Earley was riding at the front of the group. I was pleased, for it was his place. It is ungraceful and unjust that the giants of the road be left isolated on the days they are ordinary men.

Sean was in the middle of the group. In our best Irish accents we shouted at the two of them but they did not look up.

Ann had seen what she had come to see and she started the long walk back to the car. Strangely, I found myself not wanting to leave. Two years previously I had ridden along this very stretch of road on this very same stage of the race. I was 35 minutes down and alone.

I can remember the encouragement that I received from those spectators who had waited. I felt duty bound to wait a while. If I had been riding I would have been in one of these groups. On a good day I might have been with the Kelly group. A bad day and I would have been in one of the groups that were now passing before my eyes, 42 minutes down.

I watched in silent homage. Still no sign of the last rider. I decided I would have to go as Ann would be waiting for me and I thought I felt a drop of rain. I felt guilty. I should not have left. The cock crowed three times as I walked back to my car.

I liked the Alpe piece. I was starting to relax a bit more and was even managing to sleep a little on the night before writing an article. But a day after the Alpe stage something happened that put an abrupt end to my series of articles on the race. The race leader Pedro Delgado was found positive at dope control.

18 RESCUED

The scandal rocked all of France. Pedro Delgado, 'maillot jaune – positif'. Riders testing positive was a not uncommon event in the Tour, but it was rare that the 'big fish' were caught. Delgado was the biggest fish in the pond. He had taken control of the race in the Alps, was second to Rooks on the Alpe D'Huez and he smashed all his rivals in the following day's 38-kilometre mountain time trial to Villard de Lans. Few doubted he would win the race when they entered the Pyrenees, no one did when they left. He was untouchable in the mountains – the tour had found its new champion. Or so we thought.

At Bordeaux, with just four stages to go before arriving on the Champs Elysées the bomb dropped. Jacques Chancel, a television journalist working on Antenne 2's nightly review of the race, screwed up his face at the end of the Bordeaux emission. He had something serious to tell us. He had heard, from a good source, of a positive dope test involving race leader Pedro Delgado. When a rider is called to dope control, the sample of urine he gives is put into two separate sealed bottles. The bottles are sent to a laboratory where one is tested. If traces of illegal substances are found, the rider is informed. The rider has the right to either accept the analysis or appeal. If he appeals, then the second bottle of urine is tested. If this second testing confirms the initial results then, and only then, can news of the positive test be released to the press.

This is not how it happened in the Delgado affair. Someone leaked news to Chancel that Delgado's first bottle had been positive *before* Delgado himself had even been told. Perhaps Chancel thought he was honouring his profession, but even so in my opinion it was still a despicable thing to do. Half the world knew of the findings of the first bottle before Delgado did. Journalists descended on him like vultures, but he confessed total innocence of the whole affair.

Next day, the race 'commissaires' were forced to clarify things. They denied having leaked anything to Chancel, but confirmed that traces of Probenacide, a masking drug for steroids, had been found in Delgado's urine after the Villard de Lans time trial stage. Delgado immediately appealed, and the second bottle was examined. For two days Delgado raced under tremendous pressure. The second bottle was opened, traces of Probenacide were again found – but the race leader was cleared. Incredible, no one had consulted the UCI's (Union des Cyclistes Internationals) list of prescribed substances. They had consulted the IOC's (International Olympic Committee's) list. Probenacide was on the IOC list but was not due to enter the UCI list till August, a month after the race ended. Delgado could not be found positive for taking a medicament that wasn't yet proscribed – he was 'blanchi', cleared.

It was a most unsavoury affair, and the race was ruined. Even though Delgado had been cleared, the presence of Probenacide in his urine was still unexplained. He had escaped on a technicality, but for many he was still guilty. It was a difficult time to be a professional cyclist. In the café in Vizille I was bombarded by the bar's clientele with demands for information. When I sat down for coffee the jokes would start.

'Hey Polo, you are used to something stronger than coffee for riding your bike.'

And they would all laugh. Few of them held any grudge against Delgado: 'Poor Pedro', that's what they all said, 'Poor Pedro'. The consensus among the pastis drinkers of the Café de la Gare was that it was humanly impossible to ride a race like the Tour without taking stuff. Most ordinary people in France were of the same opinion. Delgado was encouraged like never before from the roadside: 'Poor Pedro'.

He is one of the most likable 'leaders' in the peloton, and I was greatly surprised when news of his positive testing broke – surprised he had been caught, that is. The affair left me in an awkward situation. How could I possibly write another Tour article for the *Tribune* without mentioning the Delgado affair? Oh, I could have done it all right. A piece on my shock and horror that a fine rider like Delgado would do such a despicable thing and 'cheat' by taking drugs would probably have fitted in quite nicely. But I wasn't shocked, I knew what went on, and as soon as I picked up my pen I would have to be honest. I was not ready to write about the drug problems in the sport. They could not be explained in five hundred words. I talked it over with David and we decided that the best way out was to abandon the column. I forgot about journalism and went back to being a cyclist.

I got terribly depressed watching the Tour on television. I loved the race. Riding it, being part of the glorious circus, made the hardship and sacrifice of the pro life worthwhile. But watching it from an armchair was an act of self-destruction. Always the same old questions. What future have I in the game? I am not good enough to ride the Tour. Will they sack me at the end of the year? Will anyone else give me a job? What else can I do but cycle? The conclusion was always the same – I had no choice. Bills had to be paid and riding my bike was the only way of paying them. I dragged myself out training, and tried to get back into some sort of physical shape. Mentally it was very difficult and on the weekend that the Tour finished I hit rock bottom. I had arranged with Kelly to stay with him for a week to ride some kermesse races in Belgium. I stopped for lunch at a motorway café near Lille which was half an hour's drive from the border. It was an awful hole, really grotty, and I didn't eat too much. While eating I suddenly felt terribly alone. I started to think about the race. I hated racing in Belgium and knew I was going to get a terrible stuffing. This depressed me, and the more I thought about it the more it annoyed me to have to go. I was desperately short of racing practice and without competition there was no way I was going to have a good end of season. But I still didn't want to go. I even started to feel physically sick about it. I needed time to think, to work it all out. I went to a nearby shopping centre to try and get myself together. No, there was no way I could go to Belgium. I needed to talk to someone, I felt so terribly alone. Who could I ring? Ann was out. My parents in Dublin would not understand. I tried to ring David, but he wasn't at home. I rang Frank Quinn in Dublin and talked to his assistant Margaret. I don't know if anything I said to her made sense but I remember asking her to phone Kelly and to inform him I wouldn't be coming. I put down the phone and got into the car. I turned down the motorway and drove 300 kilometres back to my friends in Paris. It was as near as I have ever come to a nervous breakdown.

Frank phoned me later than night. He persuaded me to keep at it, and convinced me I should drive to Kelly's house in Brussels next day. I felt like a right idiot, knocking on Kelly's door, but I was welcomed as if nothing had happened. Sean and Linda were very kind and I raced next day and was back on the rails. During my stay, I made some interesting discoveries about the 'iron man'. One night we went for a sauna in a health club in Volvoorde. I never liked saunas, and Kelly insisted on rising the temperature by throwing water on the stones. We lasted fifteen minutes but had to get out. It had been incredibly hot and we were both so drained that we could hardly stand.

'Jaysus, Kelly, you look like death warmed up.'

And he laughed, but then said:

'Did you never feel this tired after finishing a race?'

I thought about it. Yes I had, but only once. It was in a prologue time trial of the Coors Classic in Boulder, Colorado a few weeks before the Olympic road race in L.A. The finish was at the top of a hard climb, and I remember losing consciousness about 50 metres before the line and waking up with a blanket around me five minutes later. It was the only time in my life I ever pushed myself beyond my limits.

'No, Sean, I can't remember ever being this tired. What about you?'

'Yes, regularly.'

I looked at him: he wasn't lying.

After a week of kermesse racing in Belgium I rejoined the team for a special classic in Montreal. I loved the circuit, the Olympic road race circuit of 1976, and rode well on it. I was in the thick of the action right from the start and got myself into the winning break, but I didn't have the distance in my legs so I abandoned before the finish. Still, I won over 1,500 dollars in sprint prizes so my team mates were very pleased with me. Unfortunately, neither Vallet or his assistant Jacques Michaud were at the race to witness my performance.

On returning to Grenoble, I visited team headquarters to ask about my programme of races for the end of the year. The team had ridden a lousy Tour. In its last week, Giles Mas, Regis Simon and Michel Biboillet were told by Vallet to look for a new job for the following year. Bibollet was particularly upset. At the start of the Tour, Vallet had told him not to go looking for another team, and that he would be signing him later in the race. Michel was delighted – security for another year. But signing-on day never arrived, and at the end of the race it looked as if Vallet had forgotten his promise. Michel was shown the door.

I didn't know if he was going to get rid of me. I asked him. He said he wasn't sure. He assured me that he personally wanted to keep me in the team, that I was a great team rider but that the sponsor Monsieur Braillon wanted only winners on the team. He told me of a new team that Patrick Valke and Stephen Roche were setting up. He said that Valke had assured him that he would take me on if Monsieur Braillon didn't want me. He told me that the ball was in my court, that it was up to me to convince Braillon in the two months of racing that remained that I was worthy of my place. So that was it: Vallet wanted me, Braillon didn't. Could I believe him? I was disappointed and confused. I desperately wanted to believe that Vallet wanted me in the team, but couldn't convince myself he wasn't lying. I told Colotti and Claveyrolat of my situation and both said they would canvass on my behalf. Colotti was very supportive, and argued with Vallet to keep me on. Vallet wouldn't commit himself, and for the month of August I lived in uncertainty. André had also been told to look for new employment. The news did not surprise him. He had ridden poorly all year and he was resigned to the fact his career was at an end – but he was still bitter.

I too became bitter. I resented the riders on the team who had signed contracts. Their 'I'm all right Jack' attitude sickened me, even though I fully realised that I had acted in the same way previously. I started to panic. What the hell was I going to do? A rider's career was measured in results. I had given three years of mine to helping others obtain results. Only RMO knew my worth as a team rider. I thought of asking Kelly or Roche for a dig-out, but decided against it. If they offered I would accept, but I would never go begging. My relationship with Vallet deteriorated. A week after returning from Montreal I got a new dose of 'champignons'. We were riding a two-day, Paris–Bourges, and I was so uncomfortable that I could hardly sit on the saddle, never mind race. Vallet was not very understanding, and I knew straight away there was no way I would be in an RMO jersey in 1989.

I treated the 'champignons', and they quickly disappeared; but I could not find any decent form. I went to the world championship in Belgium in September determined to do the ride of my life. I failed miserably, and abandoned with five laps to go. As in Austria the year before, I cried on entering our pit. But this time the tears were of bitterness and not joy. The season had been a complete and utter disaster.

It was Roche who came to my rescue. We went back to the hotel after the world championship ended and he called me into his room. 'Don't worry about next year, Paul, I'll look after you.' I thanked him, and gratefully accepted. Stephen was that type of fellow. If he promised, he delivered, and even though he didn't know who he'd be riding with I never once doubted that we'd be riding together for 1989. Some of my sacked team mates got word that I had found a saviour. They knew Stephen and I were good friends, and asked me to talk with him on their behalf. I didn't like Frank Pineau and told him to his face that I wouldn't speak for him. The two others, Mas and Rault, I liked. I just hadn't the heart to tell them that I couldn't canvass on my own behalf, never mind theirs, and promised them both I would talk to Stephen for them. I never did – just hadn't the balls. I was afraid he would think I was asking too much, so I said nothing. Jean François Rault rang Ann a few times and left his number for me to return the call but I never did. He never found a job. I would have liked to help him, but I was powerless.

I felt sorry for him. Six months earlier he had won the marathon classic Bordeaux–Paris. Vallet had kissed him and promised him the sun, moon and stars. He was promised the post of assistant director sportif for 1989. Jacques Michaud would be promoted to team manager. The squad needed a manager, as Vallet had signed Charly Mottet and was strengthening the squad. The French national champion Eric Caritoux came on the market, and Vallet offered him a deal. Caritoux agreed, but insisted that his former directeur sportif Christian Rumeau be given a job with the team. Caritoux signed, Rumeau was made assistant directeur sportif, Rault was given his marching orders. I thought they should've had the decency to keep him on for another year as a rider.

The Nissan Classic was my last race with the team. Unlike 1987, I wasn't allowed the pleasure of selecting the team and simply felt thankful to be in it myself. As a result, André and Clavet stayed at home. Jean Claude was picked, but his wife lost a baby the day before we travelled, so he couldn't come. He was replaced by Esnault, and the others on the team were the Belgian sprinter Michel Vermotte and the two Danes Alex and Per Pedersen. The day before the race I was visited at the hotel by the sports editor of the *Tribune*, Stephen Ryan. He wanted me to write a diary of the week for Sunday's paper. I agreed.

The Nissan Classic is a five-day race. For four days I rode my arse off. I desperately wanted to succeed in front of the 'home' crowd, and I tried hard on every single stage. Nothing went right. I punctured at the worst possible times, fell off on the climbs when my gears wouldn't work properly – and some little bastard stole a pair of brand new sunglasses from my hotel room. After two stages I was starting to feel pretty pissed off. On the morning of the third day I met a girl in a wheelchair just before the start. Her name was Deborah Kane. Her father Dave had raced with my father, and Deborah had once been the top female cyclist in the country. She was racing in England when she rode into a parked lorry. She suffered horrific injuries and was paralysed. We had a good chat before the third stage, and she smiled radiantly. I could not believe she could still smile. Her smile did something to me. I suddenly felt terribly fortunate. In my diary of the week I gave her a special mention for her great courage.

The last stage was a 70-mile loop around the streets of Dublin, to be televised live by RTE. The stage passed 5 miles from Coolock, where I had grown up as a kid, and the highlight of the day was the three laps around the beautiful Howth Head. I have always loved Howth Head. When I was a 14-year-old schoolboy with a head full of dreams I would train around it three times a week with my pal, Martin Earley. We dreamed on that hill. It was the Alpe d'Huez or the Galiber or the Tourmalet and we were Merckx and Thevenet and Van Impe. As we lined up for the start, Martin turned to Kelly and said 'Watch Kimmage today.' The flag dropped and I had but one aim: no one, but no one, was going to beat me over Howth Head.

Because of the live television coverage, attacks started from the gun, and the first loop in south side Dublin was really fast. By the time we crossed the Liffey the first selection had already been made and I was part of a forty-man leading group. I knew something was going to give as we dashed out along the seafront at Clontarf – it was just a matter of choosing the right attack. When Allan Peiper took off with Pascal Poisson, I didn't hesitate. These were two drivers, two strong men. I jumped across. We rode really hard, and I had a lead of about a minute approaching Howth harbour. We swung left up through the village and started the climb. There was a great crowd all the way up and I was cheered like I had never been cheered in my life. The cheers sent goose-pimples all over my body, and I didn't feel the pedals. I went to the front at the bottom and stayed there until we reached the summit. I was first over the Head. Vallet drove up alongside for the first time on the descent. He told me I was doing too much work and should ease up. I nodded in agreement but immediately forgot his orders. He was absolutely right. I was riding too hard, but he didn't understand. This was Howth. This was part of me. Nothing else mattered.

We completed three laps of the Head and headed east, and then south towards the finish in the city centre. I started to feel the pinch with 20 miles to go. We were joined by two Fagor riders, Sean Yates and John Carlsen. They were riding like trains, and I immediately knew there was no way we could be caught. On the run into the city centre Vallet drove up and told me to do some 'talking' to try and win the stage. I approached Sean, who was a good friend, and asked him if he was interested in doing a deal. He never answered me, so I understood that as meaning 'No'. I wasn't surprised. Yates and Peiper were great mates. I knew they would be working together so I didn't bother talking to Carlsen or Poisson. I was knackered when we got on to the circuit. Peiper broke clear, and won on his own. I was fifth, but the television exposure had made me a hero. I was interviewed after the stage and next day on a popular radio programme.

Dublin was my last race for RMO. Of my three years with the team the first two under Thevenet are the ones I will remember most. If Stephen had not rescued me I'm sure I'd have left the sport very, very, bitter; but joining a new team, Fagor, changed all that, and I could afford to be nostalgic.

It had always been my ambition to ride for at least one year on the same team as Kelly or Roche. By finding a place for me at Fagor, Stephen had saved my career. But I would never have accepted a place if I hadn't believed that I could be of some service to him. I wanted to survive on my own merit and didn't want to spend the rest of my cycling days suckling off Roche's generosity. To succeed I needed a good winter. I spent the winter in France. I was determined not to make the mistakes of the previous year, and set myself a strict training schedule involving diet, weights, jogging and mountain biking. We returned to Dublin for two weeks at Christmas. I was careful not to eat too much, and continued to train hard. During our two-week stay I met the editor of the *Sunday Tribune*, Vincent Browne. To my great surprise, he offered me a job with the paper. I tried not to show it, but was secretly delighted. But I had to refuse. I just didn't have the confidence to write full time, and wanted to devote just one last year completely to the bike. But I was so pleased he had asked me. The thought of one day going into journalism excited me. At last I had an escape route. It would be easier now to accept the hardship and suffering, knowing that at the end of it all I could find a good job. I returned to France very pleased.

I trained hard in the month of January. One morning I was out early in the suburbs of Grenoble. There was an icy fog and it was freezing cold. I came across a Ford transit van driving slowly in the opposite direction. It was painted black and had black glass on its two sides. It took a few seconds for me to realise it was a hearse. There was a coffin inside, and behind two people followed in a car. The scene chilled me to the bones. I decided there and then to leave the country as soon as my career as a bike rider was over. I didn't want to die in this place, to be brought to my resting-place in a clapped-out old Ford with just two people crying over me. My family and friends were in Ireland. As soon as it was over I would return there.

I met up with Fagor for a training camp at the end of the month. It was a very weak team. Most of the good riders had left after disagreements with the team's management. My old RMO team mates Regis Simon and Vincent Lavenu had also found jobs here so the ambience wasn't too bad. We rode six hours on our first spin and I was pretty knackered when it was over. Next day I was stuck to the road and turned home after just two hours. I felt drained and run-down. When I went for massage that night, the soigneur asked me if I wanted to take a B_{12} injection. I did. Silvano Davo was Italian. He had looked after Stephen at Carerra and had left with Stephen for Fagor. He was temperamental, as only Italians can be, but I liked him and was confident he would never give me any illegal medicaments or shit. Normally I would take my first vitamin injection three months into the season – but damn it, I needed it. So I took it and next day felt much better. While at the training camp I roomed with Stephen. It was great. I enjoyed being Roche's man, and wanted to be at his side at all times. I was surprised he wasn't sharing a room with Eddy Schepers, his loyal lieutenant of three years. Eddy was a rider of class, in his own right, and he was very level-headed and straight. I liked him.

On the last evening of the training camp a group of Belgian tourists sat down at the table next to us. As soon as they realised they were sitting with Stephen Roche they started pestering us. One fellow in particular was obnoxious. He was overweight, drunk and smoked like a trooper. I couldn't understand Stephen talking to them all night. When he came up to the room I asked him about it.

'Why didn't you tell them to fuck off?'

And he laughed.

'Paul, you just can't turn round and tell people to fuck off.'

And I thought about it and agreed with him.

'And anyway, Paul, did you see the big tanned guy? That was the Mexican Pancho Rodriguez, a former world middleweight champ. He's the Belgians' bodyguard.'

'Jaysus, just as well I kept my mouth shut.'

Next day we drove to Arles for the first race of the season. We were staying in the same hotel as RMO, and instinctively I found myself going to their list pinned to the wall beside the lift and examining it to see who was sharing with who. Clavet was sharing with Ribeiro – 'good enough for him'. Colotti was sharing with a new guy, Sanders. I paid a call to his room but as usual he was spaced out, his head up in the clouds, his mind already on the following day's race – Colotti loved racing. My first race with Fagor went off much better than I expected – even though I didn't finish. It wasn't my fault: a bolt in my handlebars came loose near the finish and I was forced to stop. The second race was more disappointing. I relaxed too much near the end of it, and got left behind when a cross-wind split the bunch to bits.

After the second race, the team split into two. Half would spend the month racing in the south of France, the others would return to their homes for a week and then fly to Venezuela and Miami for a stage race, the Tour of the Americas. Stephen was crossing the Atlantic, and as I was now part of his baggage I too was selected to travel. Before leaving I had a week back in Grenoble. David phoned me from the *Tribune* and asked me how the opening races had gone. He suggested that I do a weekly diary for the paper over the whole season. I hesitated. If I had won the two opening races of the year, there is no doubt in my mind that I would have turned him down. But I had made more sacrifices at Christmas than in any other year, I had trained harder than in any other winter, I had even taken a vitamin injection in the run-up to the race. And for what? I had abandoned the two opening races of the season. The writing was on the wall for me. As a pro cyclist I was Mr Bloody Average. Also-rans were nothing in this game, they are nothing in this world. You don't see too many sporting greats in dole queues, but they are often full of queuing also-rans. Writing a weekly column might open a few doors in journalism. It might keep me from the dole queue. I agreed.

19 JOURNALIST

It didn't take me long to start questioning my commitment to writing a weekly column for the *Tribune*. The first 'diary' was a piece of cake, 500 words on the opening races in the South of France, which I sent back by reading it over the phone. It was more difficult in Venezuela. I had never been to South America and had, on just two occasions, been to countries where bidets and telephones were not ordinary instruments of daily life. Venezuela was ghastly. The capital, Caracas, exuded wealth, but ten miles into the suburbs I witnessed the most incredible poverty. The residential areas were acres of tin-roofed and, in some cases walled, sheds that a 'civilised' western man would not use for a lavatory. I saw young kids without clothing, just a piece of sack-cloth covering their privates. It made me wonder about the morality of being paid to race a bicycle, while people lived in squalor.

Riding a bike wasn't easy here. The streets were covered in oil, making them dirty and incredibly slippy in the wet. Petrol was cheaper than water, and it was more economical to let a leaking tank drip than to have it repaired. Election posters littered walls and shop windows. The candidates' names pushed their credibility to the limit. How can people seriously vote for a man called 'El Tigre'? There were dead dogs everywhere, and the vile smell of rotting carcass choked the lungs and made me want to puke. The dreadful scenes moved me, and I wanted to write about them. Writing about it wasn't a problem, but trying to send it home was a nightmare. Our hotel had no direct lines, so phoning it back was out of the question. Our team interpreter informed me there was a fax machine in the press room. I knew nothing about fax machines and was unsure that a handwritten document could be sent. But it was worth a try, so I gave him a copy and he sent it off.

The first stage of the race was a long road stage from Valencia to Caracas. The second was a criterium up and down one of the principal boulevards of the capital and the third a circuit race in Maracay. The first two days went well: I was riding, dare I say it, average. The third stage was to have been a circuit race, but as we lined up waiting for the off I noticed a group of protesters blocking the road ahead. It was totally chaotic and as the protest developed, the live version of the U2 song, 'Bullet the Blue Sky' kept ringing in my head. The song is about the anarchy in another south American country, El Salvador, but on that day in Maracay it could so easily have been about Venezuela. In my article for the *Tribune* I described the day, mixing in it words from the song.

Professional cycling races have, in recent times, become an easy target for the demonstrator looking for publicity for his cause. Paris–Nice, the Tour de France, the Giro d'Italia, all have suffered at the protests of striking miners, of about to be laid off ship builders, of struggling farmers.

The demonstrations are an accepted nuisance that an unlucky race organiser must face. He will listen, sympathise with their problems and do almost anything to get them off the road.

When a bunch of students blocked the road three hundred metres from the start line at Maracay on the third day of the 'Tour de los Americas', nobody noticed. But then the fire started.

> 'From the fire flies
> a red orange glow
> See the face of fear
> running scared in the
> valley below'

The long finishing straight was adjoined by a huge field full of high grasses and scorched weeds. These weeds were only too accommodating as the students lit their matches and a huge fire rapidly spread.

A fire engine arrived. The firemen started hosing down the flames and soon had the initial section under control. But when it came to reversing to follow the direction of the fire, the 30 year old truck broke down and we were treated to the ridiculous sight of the truck being pushed down the road by the embarrassed firemen and a handful of spectators.

'Race director Germain Blanco decided that the time had come to do a deal. The students were protesting about the death of a young Caracas student at the hands of the local police the day before. Signor Blanco assured them that their protest had been noted, then asked them to clear the road. The students thought about it. They decided to kidnap him.

We had been standing on the start line for 15 minutes. No one knew what was going on. The fire engine breaking down gave us all a great laugh, but there was no sign of a replacement and we watched as the huge orange flames grew closer and listened as the students' protests grew louder. And for the first time I started to feel uncomfortable.

Stephen (Roche) was standing talking to Fabio Parra when one of the bikini-clad promotion girls walked by. He took out his feeding bottles and playfully squirted some water at her. He missed.

There was a young police officer standing facing the crowd three feet in front of them. The cold water hit him on the back of the neck. The water hit a panic button in his brain that made him draw the four foot long butcher's knife he was wearing and turn to face his aggressor.

Stephen saw the anger in the man's face and the sword in his hand. His mouth dropped. Parra, a Spanish-speaking Colombian, quickly gave an explanation to the confused cop. The bomb was defused but the tension remained.

> 'See them burning crosses
> see the flames grow higher 'n higher
> Bullet the blue sky
> Bullet the blue sky'

Most of the riders then abandoned the start line. Some climbed on to the roofs of their team cars to try and get a better view. The second fire engine still hadn't arrived as the flames blazed, rapidly approaching the large metal fence that separated the field from the road – and us.

And then the rats started running.

Out under the fence they ran, big ones, small ones, dirty ones. Their ship, a weedy field, was sinking and as is their great tradition they were deserting. Not all of them made it to safety. Some were crushed by cars, others had their heads stood on by amused spectators – hard men, these Venezuelans.

And then the rocks started flying.

The students pelted the line of riot police facing them with anything they could get their hands on. This was the final straw. The organisers, still minus their race director, cancelled the stage.

We were ordered on our bikes and it was decided that we ride the 50 kilometres back to the hotel. So we left that place and the angry young men. They had won. But as I rode out of the town I wondered at the price they would have to pay.

The peloton were in a jovial mood as we rode back to the hotel: 'It was good of those students to give us the day off.'

One guy even suggested putting them on the flight to Miami so they could do the same there.

All through the protest the jokes and wisecracks were flying. No one seemed to give a damn that the students were risking their lives 300 metres in front of them. This attitude disturbs me, for I too am guilty.

And there was of course the ride back to the hotel. How many noticed the barefooted sackcloth-knickered kids that lined the road? How many give a damn? Do I? I don't know. All this disturbs me. I don't feel comfortable here, and all of a sudden bike racing seems so trivial, so wasteful. I will be happy to leave.

Tomorrow we fly to Miami for two more races. Ah, Miami. Former Olympic champion Alexi Grewal calls it the sin capital of the world. It's full of rich people and lovely women and sandy beaches. I can't wait.

> 'I can run
> I can run
> into the arms. . . .
> of America'

I liked the piece. It gave me a huge buzz of satisfaction. Of having hit the button, done it right. It was definitely better than average and this is what pleased me most. Perhaps I had a future in journalism.

Miami was clean and sunny and lovely. There was a different smell here. Money – it reeked with wealth. I hated it. It came too quickly after Venezuela, and the culture shock was too brutal for my conscience to bear. It's a sick world.

I returned to Europe in good physical condition but was still left off the team for Paris–Nice. I didn't mind too much, and tried to train as hard as I could at home during the week-long race. My next race was to have been the French classic Mauleon–Moulin (a GP des Chaudières) but on the day before I was due to leave I received a most disturbing phone call. It was the team doctor, Monsieur Navarro. During Paris–Nice I had flown to Toulouse Hospital to do some medical tests for the team. Dr Navarro was ringing me with the results. They had found an abnormality in my heartbeat and prohibited me from racing at Mauleon.

'It might be nothing at all or it might mean you have to give up cycling.'

I was shocked and quite frightened. Three days later I returned to Toulouse for more tests. A tape recorder that monitored heartbeats was strapped to my chest for 24 hours, and the results were fed into a computer and analysed by the doctors. The result – nothing. They had made a mistake, there was nothing wrong with me. I was delighted: for more than a week I had been fully convinced I was going to snuff it prematurely. But then I became angry. I had not touched the bike for nine days, had not raced for three weeks and was not due to race for another two. I was back to square one. The sacrifices I had made all winter, the benefits I had acquired from racing hard in Venezuela, were now all for nothing. And all because some stupid doctor couldn't read a computer correctly. I could have cried. I did.

I don't know how I kept my sanity as I struggled to regain good physical shape. My weekly articles for the *Tribune* certainly helped. So too did the encouragement of a phone call from Stephen. But the most helpful of all was my directeur sportif Patrick Valke. Fagor, like most teams, had two directeurs sportifs: Pierre Bazzo, an ex-pro, was the principal directeur, while Patrick Valke was the assistant. Patrick and Stephen go back a long way. For seven years Patrick was his mechanic, but during the Giro of 1987 the roles changed. The wars with Visentini split the Carrera team into two camps. Stephen had just two men in his, Eddy Schepers and Patrick Valke. Eddy helped him on the road, but Patrick took over as directeur sportif of the two-man team and they won. When Fagor came looking for his signature later that year, one of the stipulations of the contract was that Patrick be made directeur sportif.

Patrick's greatest fault in his new job was his lack of diplomacy. With Patrick, a spade was always a spade. But some of the management at Fagor didn't take kindly to being addressed as spades, and half-way through the year he was sacked. The man he had replaced, Pierre Bazzo, was brought back and the Roche–Valke tandem spent the last four months of the year trying to find a way out of their marriage with the Basque electrical appliance firm. Contracts are signed to be honoured. Stephen needed a team, and Fagor were unable to find a leader of Roche's calibre and both parties decided to bury the hatchet and try again in 1989. Patrick was reinstated as directeur, but this time as assistant to Bazzo. This created one major problem – they hated each other. Splitting the team into two at the start of the year was a blessing in disguise. Bazzo and Valke never saw each other, and for a while the union seemed to work.

I started the year under Bazzo with an open mind. I had heard stories of his bungling, but I wasn't prejudiced against him, it was always my policy to give everyone a fair chance. It didn't last. After the 'heart' incident, I badly needed racing, but Bazzo didn't want to know. I formed the impression that he would have left me at home until the end of the season; that he didn't rate me and wasn't prepared to give me a fair trial. One of the team mechanics told me he used to insult me, and others on the team, behind our backs. True or not, the revelation turned me completely against him. After that, I never phoned him for information, and our conversations never extended beyond 'hello' and 'goodbye', and even that was an effort.

Thank God I had Patrick. He arranged for me to race in Belgium and was very encouraging. My form was terribly slow in coming at first, but the racing got me going and gradually I started feeling better. The four days of Dunkirk was my first real stage race of the year. Stephen won a stage and finished third overall, and his form was so good he decided to have a go at the Tour of Italy. I had never ridden a 'Giro' before and asked Patrick for a place in the team. Italy would be make or break, succeed or bust. A good performance would put me in the Tour team where, perhaps, my career might at last take off. A bad ride would mean the end. I wanted to push myself to the limits one more time to see if I could do it. On Friday May 19 we flew to Palermo, Sicily.

20 GIRO D'ITALIA

DAY 1: CATANIA

The Tour of Italy, second biggest stage race in the world. Three weeks of racing, 3,709 kilometres of cycling. I was nervous before the start. This is not just another bike race: it's history, legendary. And I'm here, doing it, participating in history. Starting out from Toarmina this morning, I felt like I was heading out on a great adventure. God knows what lies ahead. God knows how far I will go.

The first stage, a short one of 123 kilometres, was like all opening stages of big tours. Everyone was highly strung, and there were a lot of crashes. Everyone wanted to get to the front, to stay out of trouble, but also for another reason. The first stage is the only stage when any rider in the peloton can lead the Giro D'Italia. I was conscious of this as I took my place at the front. It's another tale for my grandchildren: 'the day Grandad led the Tour of Italy'. As a first stage it wasn't too bad, except for the finishing circuits which were very fast. Some stupid Italian 'gregario' (an Italian domestique) ran into me with three laps to go, and we both nearly fell. The bastard had the cheek to accuse me of swaying into him. He was short, dark, very ugly, and as I insisted on insulting him back we nearly came to blows. Typical Italian – they're gods in their own back garden.

A journalist came up to me after the finish. My face was blackened from street dust, and sweaty. My lungs were still heaving from the effort of the final sprint. And he looked at me and said, cool as a breeze: 'Oh, I suppose today was only a gallop?'

And I looked at him and thought seriously about telling him to fuck off. But I remembered what Roche had said and decided to be diplomatic: 'Yes I suppose it was, really.'

DAY 2: MOUNT ETNA

Today the stage finished on the slopes of the famous volcano. It used to terrify me as a child, this fiery mountain. I imagined it erupting and the lava rolling across the seas to the doorstep of Kilmore Avenue. It was another short stage, just 132 kilometres, but it was hard, with the climb to Etna at the finish. I didn't drink enough during the stage and was dehydrated on the climb – which was a pity, as I was going quite well. I lost three minutes to stage winner Acacio da Silva and finished on my hands and knees, absolutely cooked. There were others much worse than me: Greg LeMond was miles back and going really badly. Before getting into the team car after the finish, I picked up a piece of volcanic rock as a souvenir. I will take it home to Kilmore Avenue and the childhood fantasy will come true.

DAY 3: MESSINA

Team time trail day, a bit of a disaster for me. Didn't recover from the efforts of yesterday and spent most of the time sitting at the back. The lads rode quite well and we finished tenth. We showered and changed at a hotel beside the finish line which also housed the press room. The atmosphere of typewriters clacking and journalists scratching their heads intrigued me. Will I be one of them next year? As soon as we had changed, we left by car ferry for mainland Italy. I had expected an improvement, but if anything it's poorer and even more dirty.

DAY 4: COSENZA

A great day, fifteenth on the stage, I'm really delighted with myself. It was up and down, up and down, all day, – a really hard stage. I love it when it's like that. I was particularly strong near the finish, and able to close a lot of gaps for Stephen. I should have done better, really. I came out of the final hairpin in race leader da Silva's slipstream and he had two riders leading him out for the sprint. God, I couldn't believe it, I thought all my Christmases had come at once, an armchair ride to the line – this is it, I'm going to win. But then, 300 metres out, this six-foot Italian bastard from the Jolly team elbowed his way in on top of me and pushed me off Da Silva's back wheel. I should have pushed him back, but we were doing 60 kilometres an hour and I hadn't got the bottle at that speed. As soon as I lost the wheel I got boxed in and started slipping back to fifteenth on the line. The Italian with the big elbows crashed as we crossed it, and ripped all the skin off his arse. Serves him right.

157

DAY 5: POTENZA

My flirting with journalism is getting out of hand. I am not sure I have ever been this tired after a stage, and I can't even rest, as I'm typing out the final pages of this week's diary to fax it home tomorrow. But I'm totally knackered and it's a real strain. My eyes keep blurring and I have never made as many mistakes with the typing. We were up at six, for the longest stage of the race, 275 kilometres. But the race organiser, Vincente Torriani, got his sums wrong and the correct stage distance was 290 kilometres. After the stage we had an hour's drive to the hotel where there was no hot water for showering. I think I can be excused for feeling a little hard done by tonight. We suffer like dogs, are treated like dogs – and all for few quid and some glory. Am I mad? I am continuing to ride well, and I hope it lasts. Morale in the team is great with Patrick as directeur sportif. I get on really well with him, although he can be a ruthless bastard at times.

DAY 6: CAMPOBASSO

Some dirty, low-down, greasy Italian swine attacked from the gun today. The first 5 kilometres were up a mountain and the attack split the field to bits. Before I knew what was happening, the three cups of Colombian coffee, swallowed just before the off, were coming back up my throat. My muscles, sore and stiff from yesterday's marathon, took their time before responding and the climb was sheer hell. It was the ultimate in bad taste. This race is beginning to stink. Where was the Giro of legend, where riders laughed and joked for five hours and raced for two?

Managed to get my fax away. Gave it to English journalist John Wilcockson who will send it tonight from the press room. It's a big weight off my shoulders, which is a bit ridiculous. I mean, I shouldn't be bothered with the hassle, and yet I am. It would kill me if I didn't get it away, and I am beginning to wonder if this has become a new motivation for finishing the race. I mean, if I'm not racing, then I can't write, and it's got to the stage now where I actually love writing.

I didn't ride as well today and cracked a bit towards the end on a long cross-wind section which split the peloton. I'm not really surprised, as the last two days were so demanding. I've been having regular vitamin injections from Silvano. One, sometimes two, a night. My arse is beginning to feel like a dartboard and I'm not happy about it. It bugs me to have to stick needles in myself every night just to survive.

DAY 7: ROME

It's a pathetic sport. Here we are, in probably the most beautiful city in the world, and we don't have time to look around it. The stage finished outside the Colosseum, but we were sprinting so hard that I never got the chance to look left. On the way to the hotel we drove past the Vatican, but there wasn't even time to visit the square. The hotel was another disappointment. It was more like a factory than a hotel: too many teams there, not to mention the coach loads of tourists. We waited over an hour before they served us dinner, and when they did it wasn't worth waiting for. Tomorrow's a big day, the first mountain stage of the race.

DAY 8: GRAN SASSO D'ITALIA

Today we finished at the top of Gran Sasso d'Italia, Giant Stone of Italy. It was another fast start, but I was going really well and never felt under pressure. There was some fierce attacking on a long drag after 65 kilometres and the bunch split into bits. For once, Stephen was badly placed, but I bridged all the gaps with him in my slipstream and got the same pleasure from it as if I had won the stage. I never left his side until the final climb to the summit, where I lost the front group 3 kilometres from the top. It was a great day for the team, with our Dane, John Carlsen, winning the stage. Tonight, we had champagne and extra dessert as a reward, and spirits are high. The team is pulling well together under Patrick and uniting behind Stephen, who is still very much going for the win. I have been sharing a room with him since the start and I love it. Living with a champion gives me such great motivation: talking about his worries, dreaming his dreams, reliving the race as if *I* were in front.

DAY 9: GUBBIO

Grovelling to Gubbio. It's what I did today, grovelled. It was a bad day, a really bad day. I must have pushed too hard into my reserves yesterday for I hadn't an ounce of strength today. I cracked on the first climb after just 80 kilometres and spent the day in a big 'gruppetto' chasing to beat the time limit. The climb was terrible, so unbelievably hot I thought my head was going to blow open. The tar was running down the road like water in places: the tyres stuck to it, and I had the impression I was riding through a bog. The heat cracked me, and for the first time in the race I considered abandoning. That I didn't is no comfort to me tonight. The line between hanging in there and getting off can sometimes be so thin. It scares me. I want so desperately to

159

finish this race, but heat and gradient can melt the strongest of resolves. Today I was close to the edge.

We had a long drive to the hotel when it was over. I was in a car with Forest and Biondi. They had both ridden well and were chirping away like two little sparrows. They both knew I had ridden badly, and this no doubt added to their joy. In their shoes, I would undoubtedly act in the same way, so I don't hold it against them. It's just so absurd – grown men acting like children, delighted to have scored a few points against a rival. But as I say, I would have been the same.

DAY 10: RICCIONE TIME TRIAL

What a lovely place. Our hotel is 50 metres from the most beautiful beach I have ever seen in my life (my current situation is no doubt distorting its true valuation), but we can't use it. Still, the view from our terrace is just wonderful. Bare breasts and G-strings – the sexual frustration is unbearable. The mechanics have a great time: as soon as their work is done, it's off on the town for the night. And then, each morning at breakfast, they take such delight in reliving their lustful exploits. In the hotel opposite us, two elderly women are sunbathing naked on the terrace of their room. I was too embarrassed to look, but Patrick called the whole crew into the room and they gawped in disbelief before shouting obscenities. All of this took place after the time trial, of course.

It was a hard test, 36 kilometres of rolling coastal road, but I enjoyed it. I rode it at 80 per cent and caught a Russian from the Alfa Lum team, which had been off three minutes in front of me. Never thought I'd see the day when I'd be catching Russians in time trials. I used the free time in the afternoon to do some washing and to type some of Sunday's article.

Stephen has moved up to second overall behind Dutchman Eric Breukink. He is pleased with his performance but is getting a lot of pain from his back and tonight his doctor flew down by private plane from Germany to examine him. The doctor had just returned from Wimbledon where he was treating another of his patients, Boris Becker. Roche does not do things by halves. Tonight was special. When we switched off the lights, we talked for over an hour about how he could win the race. That's something new for me – to be working out how to win a Giro – it's very exciting and motivating. He proved today he can win the race. I must be at his side at all times until the finish. I want to be his lieutenant.

DAY 11: MANTOVA

The good weather deserted Riccione sometime during the night and when we awoke this morning, it was to blackened skies and pouring rain. We were soaked to the skin before we even left the outskirts of the town and the 240 kilometres were ridden under a constant deluge. My mood was at one with the skies. I hate racing in the rain, it makes life so uncomfortable. Spray from the wheels injects every kind of filth into your eyes and the cold wetness penetrates every pore in your skin. At Wimbledon, as soon as it rains they pull back the covers and everyone retires for tea. But the poor cyclist has always been the peasant of the sporting world: shove a fiver in his back pocket and he will do anything you ask him to.

I fell off today which is unusual – I don't often crash. It happened 30 kilometres from the finish, the speed was up and the lads were jostling for a good position. One guy touched a wheel, so those behind tried to brake but the brake pads don't work as efficiently in the wet and thirty of us ran up the guy's arse. I wasn't hurt, just a few cuts and bruises. I suppose it was just one of those days.

DAY 12: MIRA

There was another crash today, much more serious than yesterday's. It happened 100 metres from the line at over 60 kilometres an hour and at least six riders went down. I'm not a bit surprised, as they are crazy bastards here. Pulling and pushing, elbowing and shoving: my experiences at Cosenza had taught me that sprinting it out against the Italians was only for the very brave or the stupid. It was pretty horrific, and the Dane Rolf Sorensen came off worse. As I passed him, he lay against the barriers, blood gushing from his head. It took the quick intervention of a race official to stop him choking on his tongue, and he was immediately rushed to hospital. Seeing him lying there makes you wonder about the risks we take. I asked Stephen about it and he agrees, so it's not just me. But then you forget it, you have to. 'C'est la vie.'

Tomorrow we enter the Dolomites, where the race will be decided. It's another summit finish, to the three summits of Laverado – which is said to be incredibly steep.

DAY 13: TRE CIME DI LAVERADO

The rain started about half-way through the 207 kilometres stage, turning heavier as we neared the final mountain. The Laverado was as steep as its reputation, and we all suffered terribly. Near the top the

161

rain turned to sleet, then snow, and we were frozen getting off our bikes. I was ushered into the kitchen of a hotel opposite the finishing line and was given a basin of hot water and some hot tea. I had almost finished washing myself down when Greg LeMond walked in. I passed him at the bottom of the climb and he was riding really badly. He was shivering, and didn't bother to remove his shoes or socks before placing both feet in the basin of water. His words echoed the thoughts of many.

'God, that was awful.'

Stephen lost time to Breukink and is a bit disappointed tonight. He is talking about going out tomorrow and throwing down the gauntlet. An all-out attack that will win or lose him the race. Tomorrow is the race's big mountain rendezvous. It is only 130 kilometres, but we must climb five mountains.

DAY 14: CORVARA

When I think of the hundreds of thousands of kilometres I have ridden since my Da, Christy, gave me my first racing bicycle, the 130 between Misurina and Corvara are those I will remember longest. I remember every single kilometre, every single metre. It was an incredible day.

It was overcast but dry on the morning of the stage, but we all knew the rain was coming. I asked Silvano for a cafffeine suppository, just as an insurance in case of emergency. As we lined up, the first drops of rain started falling. Most of the lads immediately turned around and rushed back to their team cars for extra clothing. I pulled on a pair of woollen leg-warmers but couldn't find my gloves; I had left them at the hotel. Before leaving the car, I took the tin foil from the caffeine suppository, and shoved it up. There were just five minutes to the start and I hoped it might take effect immediately. I needed a lift, boy did I need a lift.

SUNDAY TRIBUNE, JUNE 11, '89

How do I explain today? A day quite unlike any other that I have known in the 16 years I have been racing. Looking back it all seems so unreal. The 130 kilometres stage from Misurina to Corvara was one of the shortest of the race, but with five mountains to be climbed it promised to be one of the hardest. It was.

As we approach the Marmolada, the third and hardest of the

162

climbs, I am part of a forty-man group already ten minutes behind the leading riders. It has rained since the start. I look towards the summit but it was hidden. Hidden in a mass of angry jet black clouds.

A huge crack of thunder warns us of the dangers to come, but on we climb. The cold rain turning to sleet and then three kilometres from the summit to snow. Hundreds of spectators leave the warmth of their cars to encourage us.

Two thousand metres above sea level I stop to take out the plastic jacket from my pocket. A group of *tifosi* (fans) surround me, one sheltering me from the falling snowflakes with his umbrella. Another offers me a sheet of newspaper that I place under my jersey. And then, I set off, their cheers warming me as I go to face my Calvary.

You see climbing a mountain in snow is not really a problem. With your heart tapping at 175 beats a minute the body generates enough heat to fend off the worst of weather. The trouble starts when you go down the other side.

There is no physical effort involved here, just the mental concentration of braking and turning. The heart rate drops and the body no longer produces heat and within minutes you are not sweating but shivering.

The snow was falling now at such a rate that it started to clog up the teeth of the back wheel, making the chain jump. It was difficult to see and our group had now disintegrated as we descended one by one, every man for himself.

My body got colder and colder, the leg muscles hardening and the arms now vibrating. I had no gloves. They were the last thing I had packed in my suitcase before leaving for the race, but I had forgotten them at the hotel. My fingers started freezing to the handlebars and I was finding it more and more difficult to brake.

I passed my young French team mate Francis Moreau. He was doubled over at the side of the road trying to warm his hands. He looked at me as I passed and his eyes told me he had had enough.

This frightened me. I screamed at the top of my voice in an effort to motivate myself but it was getting harder and harder to brake and I pulled to a halt at the side of the road.

I shook my arms and fingers, blowing my icy breath on them for warmth. The cold had gone into my bladder, giving me the urge to urinate. I was almost surprised at the steam rising from the yellow liquid flowing from my body. I placed my fingers in the hot springs and warmed them.

I still don't understand why I did not follow Moreau into the warmth of the team car. The conditions were inhuman. No directeur sportif in the world could criticise one of his riders abandoning on such a dreadful day.

But Roche was up ahead. What if he took the race lead? But no, it was not that, either. I suppose in a way it became a challenge, a survival of the fittest that appealed to the cannibal instincts in me. Absurd isn't it?

I was so happy to reach the bottom. The remaining two climbs of the day were not too hard and it was a relief to start climbing again to generate some heat. My mouth still quivered and I whined like a dog in pain until half-way up the climb, when I started getting warmer. The team car pulled alongside me. The mechanic taped two cloth feeding bags on my hands and this helped greatly on the last two descents of the day.

I crossed the finish line 33 minutes after stage winner Flavio Giupponi. We drove to the hotel and once again there was no hot water. Well, I mean, after a day like that how could anyone expect hot water? I did not care. I just covered my filthy legs with a track suit bottom and climbed into bed. I turned to Stephen and said, 'Don't bother waking me for dinner, just wake me in the morning and put me on my bike.'

Tonight I am happy. Ten riders abandoned the stage. Twenty others were outside the time limit but were excused because of deplorable weather conditions. I survived. The cannibal.

DAY 15: TRENTO

A split stage. The breakfast menu was a climb of Val Gardena pass, a long descent and some flat roads to Trento. It was snowing hard on Val Gardena and the sufferings of yesterday were repeated, but it wasn't quite as bad – we were prepared this time. I started the stage with so much clothing I looked like the Michelin man – but it still wasn't enough, I was still frozen on the descent. I didn't bother with caffeine today. Yesterday, my heart felt like it was going to jump out of my chest on the first climb, but after that, the effects wore off and my stomach was sick.

They should not have made us ride over Val Gardena. It would have been easy to divert us around the mountain, but yesterday's foul conditions have brought great publicity to the race and no changes were made. It's ironic really: Val Gardena is better known as a world cup downhill ski resort, but in weather like this the downhill would have been cancelled. We descended to Trento, the snow turning to sleet and then to rain. It wasn't a good day to be a pro cyclist.

The weather changed, and it was warm and sunny for the afternoon's circuit race around the town. I was knackered, riding down to the start but an Irish voice in the crowd drew my attention. It was my wife's cousin. She is working in Milan, but it was Sunday, so she got the train across to see the race. I told her of the snow and of the dreadful conditions we had endured that morning but it didn't register with her. All she could see was the bright colours of the jerseys and the glitter of the shiny wheel spokes.

'It must be very exciting being part of it all,' she said.

'No', I replied, 'not a bit.'

I don't think she believed me.

DAY 16: TRENTO

'Oh happy day, yeah baby, Oh happy day.' I think I must have sung the words of that song all morning. Or rather, all morning after we had heard the news. We had awoken to another fierce downpour. It was supposed to have been another mountain stage, taking in the notorious Gavia climb. The mood was very sombre at breakfast time. No one in the hotel wanted to ride bikes that day. We all knew what was waiting for us. I knew there was no way I could survive another day of snow and shivering. All I knew was that I would ride as far as possible within reason. We changed into our racing kit and gathered in the soigneurs' room to have embrocation and protection creams applied to legs and body. Patrick had been called to a manager's meeting and returned just as we were leaving the room. We looked to him, hoping but not expecting, and there was total silence as he spoke.

'Messieurs, due to a landslide on the Gavia pass, I have the pleasure of informing you that the stage has been cancelled. Today is a rest day, you can return to bed.'

There was a wild, roaring, cheer. Serious, moody faces suddenly cracked open with huge smiles. Chaubet, Forest and Biondi started jumping up and down, dancing with joy, and within minutes jokes and wisecracks were flying. I was absolutely delighted. We showered off the embrocation and spent the morning under the warm bedclothes, while outside, sheets of cold rain dashed against the windows.

DAY 17: COMO

A 10-kilometre mountain time trail. The rest yesterday did me a lot of good, and I rode strongly in the test without killing myself. I finished 44th, which is as good as I have ever ridden in a test as a pro. I finished one place in front of World Champion Maurizio Fondriest – another story for the rocking chair.

DAY 18: TORTONA

A relatively easy day except for the last 50 kilometres, which were very hard. I am still riding well, which is surprising for the last week of the race. Just two more hard mountain stages to go, and then the final day's time trial. I must hang in there. I must not crack.

DAY 19: LA SPEZIA

We lost Chaubet today. He was dropped after the first climb and abandoned shortly after. It is maddening to suffer what he has suffered, to get so close and not make it. If tomorrow was an easy stage I'm sure he would have kept going, but it will be very hard. I too felt the strain today; my good form of the last two days deserted me, and I struggled near the end of the stage. I feel very tired tonight, but there is just tomorrow to get through and then I'm home.

DAY 20: PRATO

I made it but it was close. I got the hunger knock after the first climb and had it not been for two System U riders, Thierry Marie and my old RMO team mate Jean Louis Peillon, who gave me some food, I don't know what I'd have done. Tonight I am content. There is just one more stage, a 50-kilometre time trial to go. For the first time in three weeks, I know I will finish.

DAY 21: FLORENCE

I had thought about that moment every day for twenty-one days: the moment, 300 metres before the line, when you look up and see the final finishing banner, 'Arrivo'. I knew what I was going to do, had it all planned out. On crossing the line I took both hands off the bars and blew two kisses at the banner and then waved a clenched fist in triumph. The adventure was over, and I had survived. My inner satisfaction was enormous. The nightmare of abandoning the Tour in 1987 was now buried and I could hold my head high. I was, once again, a Giant of the Road.

21 CARNON PLAGE

A beach. A warm, sunny beach looking out on a blue Mediterranean sea. Wind, a cooling, glorious puff blowing in off the waves. Sand – hot, golden sand, scorching the naked feet. Pretty girls browning beautiful curves; athletic boys flexing impressive muscles.

Far from the maddening tifosi. A million miles from piddling on my fingers, from sticking needles in my bum, from being deafened by car klaxons and sweating, lies Carnon Plage. A 20 – kilometre drive from Montpellier, it was just the place for a pro cyclist who had just ridden a hard Giro D'Italia. One week after returning from the Giro, Ann and I spent four of the most relaxing days of our lives in that place. We breakfasted late most mornings, drinking coffee with croissants on the sunny terrace of the apartment. After breakfast I would take the bike and ride two hours along the coastline, taking advantage of my wife's absence to drool over the vast assortment of bare nipples off the road. I returned for a shower and a light lunch, and then it was down to the beach for the afternoon. It felt great to sit there and do nothing. I would sleep and read and stare and think.

I thought quite a lot.

In the evenings we dined out, strolled around the port admiring the sailing craft and sipped beers on the terrace of a cafe. For the first time in my career I could honestly say that everything was rosy. It had been a good Giro. Stephen had finished ninth, Carlsen had won a stage, Fagor were best team and I had finished 88th out of 200 starters. My future was secure. I was assured of employment for as long as Stephen could remain competitive. And I had been told I was riding the Tour. Yes, everything really was rosy. But on our third evening at the bar, I decided I didn't want it any more. I decided to retire at the end of the season.

From the first day I threw my leg over a bike I have always tried to be honest with myself, a quality I inherited from my father. It was true I had ridden a good solid Giro, but in my own eyes I had failed. I was incapable of staying with Roche in the mountains, and wasn't strong enough to drive for him on the flat. The days when I was capable of good things were always followed by bad ones. I was sure of a job with Stephen, but did I really merit it? If we were not friends, would he still want me in his team? No, he would not.

I wasn't good enough: the Giro had spelled it out for me. I had given the race my best shot, had looked after myself with vitamin and mineral supplements from the start to finish. And for what? To be average! There was no way I was prepared to stick needles in my arse for the rest of my career just to survive, to be average. Not now that there was a way out – journalism.

The Tour of Italy pieces had produced a great reaction back in Ireland. The sports editor of the *Tribune*, Stephen Ryan, told me I could start with them whenever I wanted to. But the most satisfying thing was that my journalistic options were not confined to the *Tribune*. A rival paper was also interested in acquiring my services. I was thrilled. The future didn't look quite so daunting. So, in a quiet seafront bar, and after three days of examining the options, I decided 'no more.' I would ride the Tour and finish out the season with Fagor, and then hang up my wheels.

A week before the start of 'Le Grand Boucle', Patrick organised that we ride two kermesse races in Belgium. I hadn't planned to tell them yet of my decision to retire at the end of the year, but I ended up telling them anyway. They had been negotiating with Fagor for a new contract for months, and things were not working out. The deal was supposed to have been signed at the start of the Giro, then at the end of the Giro and then at the start of the Tour. But each time Fagor found a new excuse for delaying the signing of the contract. We all knew what they were playing at. They wanted to see how Stephen performed in the Tour before signing him up for another year. On the weekend of the Belgian kermesses Patrick had received news of a possible move for Stephen and seven of his team mates to the Colombian team, Postobon. Patrick told me of the deal, and assured me that I was one of the seven Stephen would take with him. I was delighted that Stephen still wanted me in his team but felt compelled to tell them of my decision. Their initial reaction was to advise me against doing anything hasty, but as soon as I explained about my opportunity to go into journalism, both agreed I would be foolish to turn it down. After I had told them, I felt a huge weight come off my shoulders. I was no longer part of Stephen's plans for next year. I had taken the dive and there was no turning back.

The races in Belgium were a disaster. My legs were still heavy from the sun on Carnon Plage and my mind was totally switched off. I returned to Grenoble and did some hard rides in the mountains to prepare myself for the Tour. One of these brought me to the slopes of the Galibier. It was a real trip down memory lane, for I had not cycled its gradient since my abandoning the Tour two years earlier. Riding it alone was a strange sensation, a bit like walking into an empty football stadium. I rode up the mountain locked in a trance, reliving the pedal strokes of my last visit. I saw my name on the road. It was written in fading white paint alongside the names of Roche and Earley. And as I examined other faded names I was reminded of a graveyard, the faded letters sticking out like tombstones. Would I notice my name in three weeks' time? Would I make it this far?

22 THE LAST CRUSADE

DAY 1: LUXEMBOURG
It feels good to be back on the race. The Tour is changing, becoming more modern. When I first rode in 1986, it was still the era of Monsieur Levitan's reign as race director. The public address system churned out never-ending quantities of accordion music giving the event a uniquely French flavour. That's all gone now: the race has been modernised, it's all Bon Jovi and Jean Michel Jarre now. Paul McCartney is the flavour of the month. They played 'My Brave Face' at least ten times this morning. I hate that song.

It's going to be a very difficult three weeks, and I'm not just talking about the race. We have not started yet but already, the ambience is at rock bottom. There are many reasons. Fagor still have not agreed Stephen's contract stipulations for next year. They were nearing verbal agreement and were originally going to sign a month ago, but it's still at status quo. None of the other riders have signed, either, and some are starting to get anxious about next year.

The second problem is the appointment of Pierre Bazzo as number 1 directeur sportif for the race. One of Stephen's demands for signing for another year was that Patrick be given control of the team for the Tour. Fagor initially agreed, but backed down three days before the race. Patrick is here, but must play second fiddle to Bazzo – and it's killing him. It's killing me too: I don't respect nor have any confidence in Bazzo as directeur sportif, and he knows it.

Patrick is taking it badly. He was not allowed to follow Stephen in this morning's prologue time trial and it's the first time in nine years he hasn't followed his friend in a time trial. We watched it together in my room, and he was so upset that tears started rolling down his face. Stephen didn't ride a good prologue. The mechanics gave him a front wheel with a bald tyre and a slow puncture, and forgot to bring his aerodynamic hat to the start – he was furious. When he returned to the hotel, he had a fierce row with Bazzo that nearly ended in blows. I have never seen him so mad.

My own prologue was pretty dismal. I was never going well and a dose of Tour nerves before the start didn't help either. The big news of the day was Pedro Delgado missing his start time by two minutes and forty seconds. I rang home tonight and talked to my brother Christopher. He wasn't very complimentary about my prologue performance: 'Delgado nearly beat you.' The sarcastic little swine.

DAY 2: LUXEMBOURG
Fame at last. Today was a split stage – 130-kilometre road stage in the morning, team time trial in the afternoon. After the time trial, I was invited to appear on French television station Antenne 2's chat show, broadcast daily at the finish of each stage. The show usually concentrates on the stars, but this year they have introduced a daily slot where they interview the lesser lights on the race. My conversion to journalism was my 'raison d'être', and I used the time allotted to me to talk about my former team mate André, and tried to blow the myth that it was a glamorous life. I was just warming up when they cut me short. Bible-thumping is not in mode with these people. The attitude here is: 'Don't rock the boat, for God's sake don't rock the boat. Talk about the Fignons and the LeMonds with awe and wonder, and say no more. It's what the people expect to hear.'

I rang Ann tonight. She didn't see me on TV – typical. Television apart, it was not a good day. I am riding very poorly. Maybe I took too much time off after the Giro, I don't know. I do know that I'm struggling at the moment. I rode badly in the morning's stage, so badly that I had to take a caffeine tablet for the team trial in the afternoon. We did 20 kilometres of a warm-up before it started, and I tried to shove it up as I was going along. But it was awkward, because Bazzo was in the car behind and I didn't want him to notice. He'd have a field day if he saw me with my finger up my arse, and I wasn't leaving myself open to his jibes. I stopped and pretended I was having a piss, and did it at the side of the road. It felt bloody degrading. I knew it wasn't going to make much of a difference but it was just a little insurance. It was doping, no mistake about it, but it was only pigeon shit to what some of the others were doing. It bothered me, but this was my last Tour and I didn't want to go out of it after just two days.

I rode better than in the team trials in the Giro, but I still wasn't great. I don't feel very proud of myself tonight.

DAY 3: SPA FRANCORCHAMPS

The first long stage, 240 kilometres. We had a really hard head-wind most of the day, which slowed us down a lot. It was a blessing in disguise, as I again rode badly. Stephen is having problems too: all this haggling and fighting is upsetting him. Team morale continues to slump. Bazzo addresses me now as 'le journaliste' which really infuriates me, for he uses a mocking tone when he says it. Some of the riders call me 'le journaliste' too, but from them it's almost a compliment. My conversation with Bazzo is limited to 'Bonjour' and 'Bonsoir', but I'm not sure I can even keep this up. We had no disc wheels for yesterday's team time trial. They were supposed to have been delivered at Fagor headquarters the week before the Tour but they have 'gone missing'. The team's supply of jerseys and shorts has gone missing too. The team is falling to bits.

Tomorrow we ride over the cobbles to Wasquehal, entering France for the first time. I hate cobbles.

DAY 4: WASQUEHAL

Today was awful. Tonight, my body is just so sore from those horrible stones. Bouncing along them, my balls up around my ears, sore hands, sore feet and the words of that wretched song turning in my head, driving me insane.

> 'now that I'm alone again
> living on my own again
> where I can't hide
> my brave face
> my brave my brave
> my brave face
> my brave my brave
> my brave face'

Oh, how I loathe that song!

The stage finished two hundred yards from where we lived as amateurs, at Wasquehal. When I think about it I realise that I've come a long way – and I'm still not happy.

DAY 5: TRANSFER

The morning was a right cock-up. The organisers had chartered a plane to fly us to Dinard, but there was a problem with it and we had to wait most of the morning until a replacement was found. We did two hours this evening to loosen out the legs a bit and I was able to wash and do a bit of work on my article.

Tonight I hit the jackpot. Phillipe Brunel from *L'Equipe* phoned to ask me if he could come for an interview. He arrived just as we were finishing dinner, and the other lads couldn't believe he had come to talk to me. The French lads would give both balls for an interview with *L'Equipe* – it's their bible. I could sense their frustration as I left the table to talk to him.

I was quite impressed with Brunel. He was intelligent, and obviously loves his job. We talked about my origins and my relationship with Stephen and Sean. I edited my comments on Kelly and Roche to a strict minimum and tried again to strike a blow for Chappuis. We talked late into the evening. He told me of his love for journalism and I enthused. My ranting over Chappuis had impressed him. He said I wasn't ruthless enough to be a pro cyclist. I took it as a compliment.

DAY 6: RENNES
Time trial day – the first of the race. Patrick insisted on following Stephen for the time trial, and Bazzo backed down and followed one of the others. Greg LeMond won, and I can't quite believe it. Three weeks ago I was dropping him on climbs of the Giro. I am happy for him. He has had a hard time of it since he won the Tour in 1986, but today bounced back in style – the real mark of a champion.

I enjoyed the solitude of racing on my own. The last few days have been terrible for crashes, and it was great to give the nerves a day off. That damned song continues to irritate me. They played it before the start, and my brain got hooked on it – playing it and replaying it during every kilometre of the time trial. Painful.

DAY 7: POITIERS
Shit – the word that best describes the stage. I was on and off the back like a yo-yo all day. Crashes, punctures – today I had it all. I spent the last 50 kilometres of the stage grovelling like an animal in the gutter. It's dangerous in the gutter, riding so close to the edge. I hit a ridge with 20 kilometres to go, and my front wheel turned sideways on it and started slicing. I got such a fright that I let out a roar of frustration – the others thought I was mad. Clavet came down in one of the many crashes and broke a bone in his hand. His days in the race are numbered. *L'Equipe* still haven't published the interview! What are

173

they waiting for? The way things are going I might not be around much longer.

DAY 8: BORDEAUX

Today, the story appeared – it looked quite well. There was a small photo of me sitting at my typewriter with my Fagor jersey and half a page of script. A lot of what I had said had been cut, but the good bits were still in. One of the most respected riders in the peloton, the System U rider Dominique Garde, told me he thought it was good. This pleased me. I feel a bit like the Lech Walesa of the peloton. A rebel with a cause.

It was the only bright note of the day. It rained heavily for most of the 260 kilometres and I was in a foul humour at the finish. A minute after I had crossed the line, Jim McArdle of the *Irish Times* approached me. The *Tribune* had asked him to contact me – they were waiting urgently for my copy to arrive. I couldn't understand why they hadn't got it. Before the stage I had paid a hotel receptionist £25 pounds to fax off the six pages of typescript. Had the bastard pulled a fast one? Obviously. I was furious. The sprint that I made to the hotel would probably have won me the stage. I jumped off the bike, and ran into reception. Had they a fax machine? Yes, my luck was in. I galloped up to my room and retrieved the original pages, which I had luckily stored in my suitcase. Another dash back to reception and into the fax machine. Pheeeew. . . !

My urgency to send away my piece made one thing suddenly clear to me. Unknown to myself, I had changed from a 'cyclist journalist' to a 'journalist cyclist'.

DAY 9: PAU

Found my legs for the first time this week. I was going well when things got hot at the end and even managed an attack. To my great delight, Martin won the stage. He jumped clear of three others a kilometre from the finish and won on his own. I knew he was going to win. I said it to Kelly about an hour from the finish, just got this gut feeling he was going to do it. As we arrived in Pau, I strained my ears to the commentary of race speaker Daniel Mangeas. When I heard him shout M–A–R–T–I–N E–A–R–L–E–Y, I waved a triumphant fist in the air. It couldn't happen to a nicer bloke, a more decent fellow, and I am thrilled for him, but: 'Why must there always be a "but" whenever I talk of Martin?'

I suppose it's because we were such keen rivals as amateurs. I suppose, deep down, I always felt I was better than him. Not any more. He had done something I know I can never do. I am not jealous of him. I really am pleased he won today, but I'm so envious. Years ago, when we were two schoolboys cycling around Howth Head, we'd dream of one day winning stages of the Tour. Today, he made the dream a reality. He guaranteed his place in the history books of this great race. He became a true Giant of the Road.

DAY 10: CAUTERETS
Everything was fine. I was going OK and really looking forward to the first day in the mountains. We had ridden about 20 kilometres and were approaching the first Col, Marie Blanque, when his hand went up. I immediately dashed to his side. As soon as Stephen's hand goes up I always dash to his side – I almost enjoy it when he punctures, for it gives me the chance to do something for him. There is no greater thrill than having him in your slipstream, weaving in and out the team cars after he has punctured. But this time it wasn't a puncture. It was his knee, the weak knee that he damaged in a six-day race in Paris in the winter of 1984. Suddenly it was giving him fierce pain, and we called the race doctor. The spray can was produced but we all knew that the solution was not to be found in an aerosol. He was cooked, it was over, the 'bête noire' had struck again.

I stayed with him on Marie Blanque along with Eddy, his faithful lieutenant. He was in terrible pain, and riding on one leg. We were quickly distanced by the leaders, but left a lot of struggling bodies behind us – men with two good knees. I stayed at his right shoulder, Eddy on his left. I never once put my bike in front of his, riding all of the time a half-length behind – I didn't want to insult his dignity any further. Photographers and television crews surrounded us, like vultures waiting to be called to dinner. They all wanted to capture the moment. The moment when the great champion puts his foot to the ground and abandons the race. But he wasn't going to give it to them. Roche's golden rule was that he never abandoned. He was riding to Cauterets.

I felt so proud riding at his side. This was what I had always wanted – to be at his side in the mountains. What a pity it had to be under these unpleasant circumstances. I advised him not to kill himself for I could see he was in great pain. Tears welled up in his eyes as we crossed the top and I felt terribly sorry for him. If he had abandoned at the top I am sure I would have abandoned too, but he kept going. He rode better on the second Col, Aubisque and I dropped back three quarters of the way up the climb. Eddy remained at his side – it wasn't the first time in my life that I wished I was him.

Tonight they were all banging on his door, looking for a story. But the door remained closed. There was just Patrick and Stephen and me to talk out his future. I have never seen him so low. He won't be starting tomorrow. Patrick has advised him to fly to Munich for treatment. I don't know how I'll get through the race without him. I don't have a great rapport with the other fellows on the team. I have noticed the way some of them are 'sneaking back to bed' with Bazzo, now that Stephen is having problems. I suppose they are worried for their futures; but even so, it never ceases to amaze me how low some will stoop to stay in a job. Stephen still hasn't signed his new contract with Fagor, and tonight Patrick saw two of the management in discussion with race leader Greg LeMond. The scum. Roche is not even out of the hotel and they are talking to other leaders.

DAY 11: SUPERBAGNÈRES
Patrick knew what was going through my head. He saw me being passed by group after group on the first climb of the day, the giant Tourmalet, and knew I was just giving up. He drove alongside me and tried to persuade me to keep going. I looked at him and thought about it. Roche's last words to me were instructions to ride all the way to Paris. Patrick said I would be letting him down if I climbed off. This hit the right note, and I sprinted after the group ahead. I was playing with fire. Physically I was going quite well, but my indecision about whether or not I was continuing in the race had cost me a lot of time. As we approached Superbagnères and its summit finish, we all knew it would be touch and go for the time limit. There were about 30 of us at the bottom but only 12 made it inside the limit. I made it by three minutes. Tonight I thanked Patrick for helping me on the Tourmalet. I am happy to be still in the race.

DAY 12: TOULOUSE
Bazzo called a team meeting this morning at the hotel, 'To generate some team spirit'. Patrick was not invited. He told us that Fagor would definitely be sponsoring a team in 1990 and that the contracts would be signed as soon as a leader for the team was found.

I am normally passive at team meetings and it takes a lot to get me riled, but this was too much – I cracked.

'Why was this meeting not held before the start of the race, two weeks ago, because it's a bit fucking late to be talking about team spirit now? And what's wrong with Roche as a leader? For two months now Fagor have been messing us about. The contracts were supposed to have been signed at the start of the Giro.'

Bazzo didn't appreciate my comments, and immediately started criticising Stephen. Only two other riders spoke up in Stephen's defence: Eddy and Laurent Biondi. This disgusted me.

Downstairs another war was taking place. Patrick was having a go at Julien Navarro, our team doctor. The previous evening Navarro had been interviewed on French television and spoke with great authority on the state of Stephen's knee. He claimed that modern medicine had reached its proper limits with Roche's knee. It was an amazing declaration from a doctor who had never treated the patient. Patrick was furious. He advised Navarro to keep his mouth closed regarding something he knew nothing about. Patrick has a volatile temper and has broken fingers throwing punches in Stephen's defence. That he restrained from stretching the doctor was a small miracle.

I repeat that all of this took place *before* the stage. Part 2 took place after the 150-kilometre ride to Blagnac–Toulouse. This time Patrick called the meeting. Bazzo was invited, but didn't turn up – which was probably just as well, as it would definitely have finished in violence. As it was, it was hot enough.

Patrick wanted to flush the rats out of the cupboard. He wanted the riders to commit themselves either to Stephen, or to Fagor, for next season. It was a bit unfair to ask riders to choose when he had nothing concrete to offer, but this was the whole attraction of it for Patrick – a test of loyalty. Biondi committed himself and chose Stephen. But Lavenu and Chaubet resented being cross-examined, so there was a row and a shouting match. The argument did not concern me – I was giving up at the end of the year. I said nothing. I watched and listened but couldn't really decide who was right and who was wrong. A month earlier the same bunch of lads had been totally committed as a group. In three week we had been reduced to this, disharmony and bitterness. Such a pity.

Patrick was told tonight by management to pack his bags and go home. It seems that Navarro put a gun to their heads and gave them the ultimatum, 'Valke or I'. Patrick will fly home to Lille tomorrow morning.

DAY 13: MONTPELLIER
I had no idea, riding into Toulouse before the start, that this would be

my last day on the race. I was a million miles from thinking it would be the last race I would ever ride. The bickering and fighting had disgusted and disheartened me but I had put it out of my head – there were other reasons for carrying on. If I abandoned the race it would mean the end of my race diary column for the *Tribune*. I was getting such great pleasure from writing it that it made the suffering worthwhile. I wanted another Tour medal. The 1986 medal meant more to me than anything I had ever won.

None of this even entered my head when I ran into trouble shortly after the start. I abandoned the race after 55 kilometres.

I don't regret it, it was almost a pleasure to leave the race. My grief on climbing into the broom wagon was nothing compared with what I had experienced in 1987.

> where I can't hide
> my brave face
> my brave my brave
> my brave face

The intention was still to finish my career at the Nissan Classic in Ireland in October, but I soon realised that I would never race again. As a cyclist, I was broken – no spirit. Thinking about racing made me ill and after a week's reflection I decided enough was enough. I was not going to race again. There would be no dramatic final day, no tearful wave of adieu to my 'adoring fans'. Tearful adieus were reserved for heroes, and I was no hero. I was a domestique, an also-ran. Also-rans did not have tearful adieus. They raced as pros in anonymity. They quit in anonymity. And I was one of them. Adieu.

23 SPITTING IN THE SOUP

The law of silence: it exists not only in the Mafia but in the peloton. Those who break the law, who talk to the press about the dope problems in the sport are despised. They are branded as having 'craché dans la soupe', they have 'spat in the soup'. In writing this book I have broken the law of silence. I have spat in the soup, and a lot of people will resent me for it. It wasn't easy, and on numerous occasions in my three months of writing, I wondered if I was doing the right thing. The last attack of conscience was on December 28, just before writing this chapter. I was banging away at my machine when the phone rang. It was Ma.

'Quick, Paul, switch on your TV. Channel 4 are showing a review of the Tour, and they've just shown the bit where you abandon.'

I followed her orders and tuned in just in time to hear Phil Ligget choking with excitement as Greg LeMond snatched the Tour from Laurent Fignon's grasp. It was riveting stuff, and my enthusiasm for a race that had five months earlier caused me so much pain surprised me. I was still in love with the sport. But was this really the same sport? I could see nothing bad on the TV screen. Was I justified in writing about my experiences? Would my shocking tales not spoil it for the young and innocent? I was troubled for the remainder of the day.

Then I started thinking about it. Before all this, I too was young and innocent. I looked into the sweaty faces of the stars through the TV screen and photographs and saw only glory. And now what do I see? I see dilated pupils and unnatural spots. I study not what they eat but what they swallow. Where once I applauded muscle, I now question its fabrication.

What has happened in between?

Inspired by the glory, enthralled by their courage, I set out on my

179

dream to join them. It was a hard struggle, one I gave all of my youth to, but I made it. I became a glorious, sweaty face. Unfortunately the promised land was not what I had dreamed it would be. It strangely resembled the world I was trying to escape. The jungle. It was hard, desperately hard. It was also dirty and corrupt. I wanted to leave, but realised that leaving was almost as hard as getting there. I had donated my youth to the acquisition of cycling excellence. But what use was cycling excellence in the real world? No, there was no turning back. So I went into the jungle and started to swing. To survive, I was forced, against my will, to take drugs. It happened three times. I was never caught. If I had been caught I would have been branded, as all drug takers are branded – a cheat. Isn't that ridiculous? A cheat, 'an unfair player'. I was never a cheat. I WAS A VICTIM. A victim of a corrupt system, a system that actually *promotes* drug taking in the sport.

In 1983, in an effort to modernise the sport, the professional world cycling body, F.I.C.P., established two new ranking tables. The first was for the riders as individuals. It was run along the same lines as the A.T.P. ratings for tennis. Every event was awarded a set number of points to be given to first, second, third etc. – the number of points varying with the size of the event. The second ranking table was for teams. Too many teams wanted to ride the big events, and the massive bunches were making racing much too dangerous. Under the new system the points of the five best riders of each team were added, giving the teams total. The top twenty teams had automatic entry for all the classics and major tours. It was a good idea that had damaging repercussions. Sponsors of the weaker teams were not prepared to pay out money to play in the 'second division'. Some pulled out, and their teams folded. Others merged, and suddenly a lot of professionals were without a job. The domestiques were in big trouble. There were no world ranking points to be gained for helping someone else, and directeurs sportifs were obliged to hire riders with points in order to survive. Riders became more selfish and it didn't take them long to cash in on the new system. The more points you had the more noughts you could put on the end of your salary. Points meant pounds.

The relevance of all this to the system *promoting* drug-taking becomes clear on reading the list of races where points are awarded. Throughout various chapters in the book I have talked about certain French classics that never have controls, the notorious Grand Prix des Chaudières. Take just one of these, Mauleon–Moulin, as an example.

To the uninformed it's a small race, worth a few paragraphs in *L'Equipe* and a nice trophy to the winner. Wrong: it's worth much more – world ranking points. A win in Mauleon is worth the same points as fifth in Paris–Roubaix, the queen of classics. And so, the night before Mauleon, when the directeur sportif starts the pre-race meeting by stressing the points to be gained, and in the same breath reminds you that there are never any controls here, what do you do? Do you laugh with the rest, or do you cry? How can you win? And all of these races, the 'GP de Chaudières', carry points. Ridiculous 'n'est-ce pas?'

In chapter 10, I talked about my experiences in my first Tour, 1986. On the last day, we all knew that there would be no random testing, just the race winner and stage winner, etc. Whenever there is no random testing, people will always find a reason to charge up. Several of my team mates didn't hesitate. It was a way of ensuring they would ride well on the Champs Elysées and would be mentioned on TV. Publicity automatically increases your market value. Nothing much, mind: the sport shop owner in your local village sees you breaking clear on the Champs Elysées and asks you around for some promotion. Or the criterium manager notices, and offers you a few contracts. But it all adds up. It's all cash in the bank.

In chapter 12 I described riding on an RMO team in the Midi Libre stage race. One of our riders, Patrick Esnault, was race leader at the start of the last day, a split stage. Because it was a split stage there was no random testing after the morning stage. And because the afternoon stage was the last stage it meant there was no random testing in the afternoon either. This gave us the green light to charge up on both stages to defend our team mate's lead. And provided we did not win the stage we would get away scot-free (not winning really is child's play, believe me). Esnault duly won, and his loyal team mates were rewarded with a big lump of prize money and a nice bonus from the sponsor. Money.

In 1989, my season opened with two races in the South of France but I then flew off to a race in Venezuela. My good friend, Jean Claude Colotti, spent the best part of six weeks racing on the Côte d'Azur with his team, RMO. He rode the usual season's openers: Bessèges, the Tour of the Mediterranean, the Grand Prix of Cannes, the Tour of Haut Var. All prestigious races, all carrying world ranking points. NOT ONE CONTROL. In March he lined up for Paris–Nice and Criterium International, ten days of stage racing. There were controls on just three of those days.

In May I rode in the 'Trophée des Grimpeurs'. It's a circuit race held at Chanteloup les Vignes, north-west of Paris near Pontoise. The 'grimpeurs' is a 'chaudières' race that has always received good coverage on French television. This year the organisers had trouble finding a sponsor, but with the help of French Prime Minister, Michel Rocard, who lives in the region, the necessary finance was raised – on one condition: Stephen Roche, another 'local boy' *had* to ride. Stephen agreed, but imposed his own condition – he insisted on dope control after the race. The organiser agreed.

On the night before the race, Patrick Valke conducted his team meeting around the dinner table. He emphasised that there would be dope control after the race, and warned us not to take any chances. On the morning of the event, Patrick attended a meeting for the directeurs sportifs. After the meeting the race organiser discreetly pulled him aside. She had a slight problem – no doctor to conduct the test. The French Federation designate certain doctors to conduct controls in the different regions. Patrick was told that the official regional doctor could not attend because it was his child's Communion day. Please don't laugh.

Patrick returned from the meeting and told us there would be no control. Perhaps he should have said nothing, but in a way it was his duty. Most of the other teams would know there was no control. Some of the riders would charge up and our lads would be at a disadvantage. It was Patrick's duty to tell us, even though it disgusted him to have to do so. This is what we are up against: we play with the rules we have been given to play with.

We are not to blame.

Perhaps that's not totally correct. One of the most frustrating parts of it all is the reluctance of the riders to change things. Too many are unwilling to breech the law of silence. The big men never talk and to be honest I don't really blame them – what have they to gain? They too were once young and innocent. Why should they jeopardise their hard-earned respect? If they took illegal substances it was only because everyone else was doing it. It's not their fault. If races were tightly controlled they would still come out on top. Why *should* they talk? So that some smutty columnist can label them as 'cheats'? No, we must not wait for confessions from the champions before taking action. They won't be painted as devils. I respect this. But I don't respect them when they start passing the buck, pointing the finger, promoting themselves as angels – for this is often the case.

On November 21 the French television channel TF1 broadcast a

182

special emission on the problems of drugs in sport. There was a large panel of invited French sportsmen present, including one professional cyclist, Marc Madiot. Madiot, a former winner of Paris–Roubaix, is one of the stars of French cycling. He knows what goes on, he has seen what I have seen. By agreeing to appear he knew exactly what he was getting himself into. He knew he would be questioned.

The panel were shown pre-recorded declarations from sportsmen and women whose lives were almost destroyed by drugs abuse. Didier Garcia was one of those interviewed. In 1985 Didier turned professional with the old System-U team and raced with them for two years. He was just 19 years old when he was thrown into Mauleon–Moulin and other 'chaudières' races. They were unbelievably fast, and he couldn't understand this at first. It didn't take him long, and he was faced with the choice of doing as everyone else was doing or being fired at the end of the year. He started taking amphetamines for the 'chaudières' races, but also started on a course of corticoids. Each cure lasted ten days, and he would do four cures a year. In the winter he rode six-day races. It was worse on the track. He needed amphetamines every night to race, and Valium to sleep once the races were over. Yes, it was much worse on the track. He once saw a rider go completely berserk at three o'clock in the morning. He smashed his room to pieces, broke the toilet bowl and was unapproachable for fifteen minutes. The drugs started to affect Didier also. His personality changed, his friends deserted him. In 1987 his employer, Kas, did not renew his contract. He was out of a job. It was hard at first and he went into depression. For three months he continued using amphetamines for kicks, but with help from his girlfriend he gradually returned to a sane lifestyle. He now earns £700 a month working in a hospital. It's three times less than he was earning on a bike – but he's happy.

When the interview ended the spotlight turned to the invited panel for their reaction. Marc Madiot was asked to comment. He looked straight at the camera.

'Well, this is a typical comment from a guy who was never any good.'

I was furious. I could identify with everything Garcia had said and agreed with him. It was the ideal occasion for Madiot to stand up and explain the problems we endure when organisers refuse to enforce dope controls, and what it can lead to. But what did we get?

'Typical comment from a guy who was never any good.'

Thank you Saint Marc, protector of the professional peloton. I won't bother phoning to ask his impressions of my book. I know exactly what he will say about it: 'Typical comment from a guy who was never any good'.

A lot of my former colleagues won't be pleased at what I have written. In particular I refer to two French team mates I raced with at Fagor. They are two smashing guys, but they do have peculiar views on the drugs issue. They believe in the law of silence. Whenever a big fish was caught in the drugs net they would always say: 'Encore un sale coup pour le vélo' ('Another dirty blow for cycling'). They love cycling, never see anything bad in the game. It's their life, their passion. Both use amphetamines liberally whenever the occasion demands it – part of the job. One of them told me an interesting story about last winter's Paris Six. The story gives an insight into how he views the drugs question.

On the third night, a medical team from the French Ministry of Sport arrived at the track. They had a ministerial order to perform controls on the top ten riders. It was supposed to have been a surprise swoop – but there was a leak. All of the riders knew – all of those tested were clean. Now if I had been riding, I would have been delighted with a control that kept everyone clean – but my team mate objected to it.

'Is it any wonder the crowds don't come to the six days any more? I mean, we have just come from a hard season on the road, all of us totally knackered. The people expect to see a performance, a show. How can we be expected to put on a show with just Vittel in our bottles?'

Hard as I try, I just can't come to terms with his argument. I know what he is saying but I simply can't find any justification in it. Perhaps I don't love the game as he does.

There are others who believe that the fairest way is to abolish dope controls completely. 'Let guys take what they want to take, and if they want to kill themselves then so be it – we're all grown men.'

TIME OUT: JANUARY 3, 16.14
This chapter really is heavy going, can't quite take all this analysis. I'm typing it out in David's office in the wilds of Kinnegad in County Westmeath. It's a nice office, he must have a hundred sports books. They tempt me each time I lift my head from the page. Just picked one up, it's called *Running in the Distance*, written by an athlete, Jack Buckner. Interesting fellow, a lot more famous than me – in 1986 he

was European 5,000 metres champion. I'm glancing through its pages, a diary of a year in athletics – Olympic year. 'Hmmm now that's interesting. We all know what happened at Seoul, don't we? Ben got caught. Jack should have something to say about that but the Johnson affair only gets half a page.' He writes . . .

Johnson's positive test once again throws the spotlight back on the problem of drugs in sport. No doubt there will be endless discussion and suggestions on what action should be taken. What I find most frustrating is how every athlete is smeared by the drugs story. There will be widespread pontificating on the immorality of modern sport, yet I and thousands of other Olympic athletes would hardly know the difference between an anabolic steroid and a packet of Smarties. I find it most irritating that the drugs story, which for me is the least interesting and relevant aspect of these Games, will dominate the Olympics.

The problem is that for years too many people have considered the drugs issue the least interesting and relevant aspect of the Games and of other major events. When these people awaken to the realities of modern sport, i.e. that it stinks and needs help, then perhaps some progress can be made.

Now, where was I?

Ah, yes, the solution. Who is to blame for the madness? Where is the antidote for this cancer incessantly devouring what was once pure and noble? Well, in order to combat the cancer we must admit that it exists. The professional cycling body won't admit their sport is dying of cancer. They will admit to a sore toe but not a cancer. Their defence of the system never changes.

'No other sport controls their members with the regularity with which cyclists are controlled.'

So what? If this book is saying anything, it is saying that these controls are not enough. Passing the buck is not a solution. Sooner or later the can of worms must be opened and the full magnitude of the abuse exposed. The governing body must be prepared to wash its dirty knickers in public if the sport is to hang on to some decency. When every professional race has comprehensive dope controls; when random controls are carried out anywhere and at any time; when penalties for offenders are stiffened to provide a reasonable deterrent – then, and only then, can we pass the buck.

But at the moment we are a million years from change. The men in power want a solution all right, but a painless one. One that won't damage the sport in the eyes of the public – and the TV companies. There are few morals in business, and cycling has become one – a business. The TV companies have stepped in, cheque book in hand, followed closely by the marketing men and their lucrative sponsorship deals. It's all about money now. Make it on the small screen and you make it big, and the sport of cycling now holds a coveted place. There are no morals left in professional sport, and amateur sport ceased to exist a long time ago. Money, money, money: TV sport is big business. There are a lot of race organisers lining their pockets and the last thing they want is a dope scandal. It's bad publicity, it tarnishes the glitter – and with bad publicity the sponsors start running.

The grapevine is a dreadfully frustrating source of knowledge. Facts are often distorted, but there is no smoke without fire. I've heard stories of corruption that would make you ill. Of race organisers giving the green light to champions to take anything they want. Of urine samples that never reach laboratories. The temptation by those on the make is to cover up and not own up. But by not owning up we will continue to suck in the innocents and spit out the victims.

Thank God we don't see any of this on TV. Thank God we don't hear about the nastiness, the dealing, the dirt. The champions deserve our applause. They merit our encouragement. They are not to blame. They need our help. Should I remain silent? No, I must not. It's what *they* want – those who profit from the law of silence. They would prefer that we sit back in awe, admiring but not questioning. Well, I'm questioning. It's such a beautiful sport . . .

Would I encourage my child in the pursuit of sporting excellence? No. I don't think I would.

24 ANDRÉ

Rumilly, Sunday, October 29. A crisp October afternoon. At three, the sharp sunlight has only just lifted the last whiteness of the morning's heavy frost. Soon, light will fade and the whiteness return. The apartment block is difficult to find. I had been here once before, late at night. We had taken his car to go to a cyclo-cross but I hadn't paid much attention to where he lived. Today, I don't recognise anything. Thought it was posher than this, though. It's a bit rougher-looking in the daylight. Dozens of Arab kids playing in the car parks, sons and daughters of Algerian emigrants. There's a lot of racial prejudice in this country – you can't help getting drawn into it. You sense it from the kids' stares. Perhaps they sense it from mine. No, these are not apartments, more like flats. André's was definitely an apartment. After a long search we find one that fits that description. It has four floors, seven dwellings to a floor. Twenty-seven of the doors have plaque's with the occupant's name, then just one door with no plaque. We ring. It opens. André Chappuis is standing at the other side. He smiles his lovely, innocent smile and we shake hands.

He is 34 now, and starting to look a bit rough. The wispy blond hair is tossed, but he never combs it. He is going a bit light on the crown. We used to slag him about it. There is a cheese ad. on TV, with monks gathered at a dinner table, singing in praise of the cheese, their bald patches glowing. We used to sing it for André – he never liked it.

He needs new shoes – he is wearing a pair of those given to us by RMO two years ago. The jeans are almost as worn, but the leather jacket is nice – his sister gave it to him. I haven't seen him since we were both given our marching orders from Vallet, twelve months earlier. I had panicked, worried about my future, but was saved by the offer from Stephen. I rode the Tour de France, stopped, and am now a journalist. God, it seems more than a year. André didn't panic, he knew it was coming: 'Que sera, sera'. He was an unemployed cyclist. He still is.

His winter was spent in Africa. He was one of six unemployed pros invited to tour the African continent for a series of criteriums against amateurs. Rumilly wasn't offering much. Why not? He laughs about it now. The amateurs, mostly inexperienced blacks, were not much opposition. Bike skills do not come naturally to them, and he loved watching the crashes on corners. Ghana, Togo, Senegal, Benin, Nigeria, there was no end to the countries to be visited. The travelling was tiring, but the wily old pros would reach for their medicine bags and a tiny syringe. The secrets of the old job were an instant cure. There was no money to be made, but all expenses were taken care of. When the series ended, five of the wild geese returned to France, but André stayed on. He got friendly with the organiser, himself an ex-pro, and was asked to help organise the next series. He returned to France in the summer to recruit new men for the next campaign, but never appeared at a pro race. There was no point: only the desperate go to Africa, those just laid off and disillusioned. He had their phone numbers.

The flat is almost empty. He has decided there is not much point in paying rent for it when he is never there and is moving out. The phone has been disconnected, the furniture sold and all that's left is a couch and a cabinet containing relics of old glory, cups and medals. He has moved his personal belongings to his parents derelict house just up the road – not that he owns much. He sold his bikes and racing equipment and only kept an old frame and a few bits and pieces for Africa.

He doesn't have to go back. The headquarters of Tefal, the non-stick kitchen appliance company are in Rumilly. If he wants, he can start work and earn £500 a month on the conveyor belt. But he doesn't want to. He's not ready for the factory floor yet. He's not ready for anything at the moment. He stopped being a professional cyclist a year ago, but he hasn't come to terms with it. It's hard for him in Rumilly. Everyone knows him. Along with the rugby team he was once the town's most famous asset. That was in the early 1980s, when he was winning stages in races like Criterium International. Now, after seven years of professionalism, of the Tour de France, of life at the top, he's an ex, a has-been. He has no house, owns no land and isn't married. He hasn't even a car. He loves cars, loves driving. He has gone through nineteen cars since he left school, all good cars, powerful: Porsche, Alfa Romeo and his favourite BMW. The last

BMW he had was a 528. He bought it in Marseilles and we think it was stolen because one day, when he went to have an engine job done, the garage told him it wasn't a 528 engine: it was a 535. Anyone else would have been disgusted, but André was thrilled – more power.

It was when he wrote off the BMW that I started to realise he was cracking. It was the night before the Grand Prix of Wallonie in 1988 – our last year together. He started drinking at the dinner table – whiskies, just kept knocking them back. The lads were knocking great fun out of him, but I tried to make him stop. I knew that inside something was eating him. After dinner, they decided to drive into town to stare at the prostitutes in the shop windows. André took the BMW, with Esnault in the front seat, Rault and Pineau in the back. There was a dual carriageway in front of the hotel, with a traffic light on the junction. The light was red. André didn't stop. He put his foot to the floor and the car screeched across the four lanes, but luckily nothing was coming. The other lads couldn't believe he would do such an irresponsible thing, and screamed at him to stop. He did, but the decision wasn't his – the gates of a level crossing were down a kilometre up the road. The two lads in the back didn't hesitate to jump out but Esnault, content to play the hard man, stayed. The gates were raised, and André put his foot down, but instead of going into town he decided to head out into the countryside. The car was moving much too fast on the small tracks and he ran off the road on a tight right-hander. The BMW mounted a pile of stacked tree trunks and stopped. Esnault was thrown forward and hit his head on the windscreen, but wasn't seriously hurt. André looked at the undercarriage and realised the car was gone. His first reaction was to set fire to it. If he claimed the car was stolen and burnt out, his insurance would cover him. But Rault and Pineau arrived on the scene, in a different car, and persuaded him to come back to the hotel. Next morning, the Belgian police arrived and started to ask questions. André owned up to having had an accident. The car was towed to a garage, good for only spare parts. Everyone had a great laugh. André laughed too; but inside, I knew, he was screaming.

He's at rock bottom now – broke. But he won't admit it. I suppose that's why he takes refuge in Africa. In a way it's like the old days – he can travel, race. But more than anything else, he can hold on to the dream just that little bit longer. Africa won't last forever, and he knows it, but the future has never concerned him. Africa is an escape. The day he walks on to the factory floor the dream will end.

It's a terrible pity he never married. A good woman might have given him a sense of responsibility, kept him on the rails. He was terribly fond of a lovely girl who lived just down the road, but he could never make the first move. And yet, it was rumoured that he had affairs with two married women in the town,.

We left the sad reality of the empty apartment and drove to Annecy. There was just time for a stroll around the lake before nightfall. He told humorous stories of his travels in Africa and we laughed about the good times we had spent together at RMO. We had a couple of beers and later dined in a restaurant. We – Ann was with us (she was very fond of him) – had invited André, but near the end of the meal he asked the waiter for the bill. Typical of André, always first to put his hand in his pocket, give you his last penny. I insisted on paying. He agreed but said he'd pay next time.

He came to stay with us for a weekend shortly after. I was covering a rugby match, so Ann collected him from the railway station. He gave her flowers and a chocolate cake. It was a nice weekend, but I noticed his frequent uneasiness. As if his skin wasn't fitting him properly. He seemed happiest when we went to the village bar. He liked the ambience – playing the 'tierce' (betting on horses), talking to the village bums, drinking a few beers and smoking a few smokes. He smokes quite a lot now, Marlboro – 'they sponsored the races in Africa'. In the mornings he'd get up early and slip out to the bar for a read of the paper and some coffee. He'd return to the house with some fresh baguettes and we'd have breakfast together. One thing was troubling me: a former team mate of ours had told me that André was still dabbling with amphetamines for kicks. On the day he was due to return home I invited him out for a beer and asked him about it. He smiled, and denied he was still using it. He said he had dumped his stock and was clean. I wasn't totally convinced. I told him about my plans on writing a book and of its content. I told him I was going to 'cracher dans la soupe'. He laughed and said I was right, but I knew there was no way he would ever do it himself. To him, it would be like ratting on your mates – and André would never rat on his mates. The fact that they didn't give a shit about him made no difference. I asked him about his experiences.

'In my first two years with (Jean) de Gribaldy at Sem I never touched the stuff, perhaps once in my second year at a criterium. Then I signed a contract with Systeme-U. This was the old Systeme-U team. I met up with a lot of "chaudières" there and picked up some bad habits. Once, twice, three times, the more I charged, the harder it became to stop. Every time I used it I noted it in my diary and each year I found I was using it more and more. In my final year at RMO I used it fifty or sixty times, hardly rode a race a l'eau ("on water" – clean).'

André never tested positive in his career. Not once. He rarely took a chance when there was control. The shame was in being caught. It tells a thing or two about the number of controls in France each year.

He was supposed to come for another weekend before leaving for the winter in Africa, but he never did. The phone never rang. Perhaps my probing on the drugs issue had made him uncomfortable. I don't really know. I have not seen nor heard from him since.

One of my biggest criticisms of *L'Equipe* and of the French cycling press in general is that they never talk to people like André. The lack of sufficient controls in France is common knowledge, but rarely highlighted. The papers and magazines know about the problems, but choose instead to fill their column inches with portraits of the stars – of present 'greats', Fignon, LeMond, Kelly, Roche; of 'greats' from the past, Hinault, Merckx, Anquetil. Of greats. When Philippe Brunel from *L'Equipe* came to interview me during last year's tour I told him about Chappuis.

'Go and talk to him, he will give you a great piece.'

He agreed, but the interview was never done. It is as if the André Chappuis's of the world do not exist; and yet under the carpet there are crowds of them. They have great stories to tell but no one will ever hear them.

I don't know if I will ever meet André again. When I'm in France I'll go looking for him, but I'm not sure he will be there. In Ireland, my door will always be open to him – but I know he won't come knocking. In my four years in the peloton, of the hundreds of professional cyclists I've had the pleasure and often displeasure of meeting, he stands alone in my esteem. He was the most likable and most decent of them all.

INDEX